This second volume of

SPECIAL WONDER

contains such SF classics as

- *Jack Vance*'s exploration of the perils of verdimancy, "Green Magic" . . .
- *Howard Schoenfeld*'s multi-dimensional farce/tragedy/drama, "Built up Logically" . . .
- *Chad Oliver*'s sardonic look at the past as remembered and as it was, "Pilgrimage" . . .

and ten other memorable stories of fantasy, science, of the future, the past, and of never-never.

The Anthony Boucher Memorial Anthologies

SPECIAL WONDER (2 volumes)
CRIMES AND MISFORTUNES (2 volumes)

in Beagle Books editions

Volume 2
of

SPECIAL WONDER

The Anthony Boucher
Memorial Anthology of
Fantasy and Science Fiction

Edited by
J. Francis McComas

BEAGLE BOOKS • NEW YORK
An Intext Publisher

Library of Congress Catalog Card Number: 76-102342

This edition published by arrangement with Random House, Inc.

First printing: February 1971

Printed in the United States of America

BEAGLE BOOKS, INC.
101 Fifth Avenue, New York, NY 10003

ACKNOWLEDGMENTS

RANSOM, by Horace B. Fyfe. Copyright 1952 by Fantasy House, Inc. Reprinted by permission of the author and *The Magazine of Fantasy and Science Fiction.*

THE MUDDLE OF THE WOAD, by Randall Garrett. Copyright © 1965 by Conde Nast Publications. First published in *Analog.* Reprinted by permission of the author and his agents, Scott Meredith Literary Agency, Inc., 580 Fifth Avenue, New York, N.Y. 10036.

YOU'RE ANOTHER, by Damon Knight. Copyright © 1955 by Fantasy House, Inc. Reprinted by permission of the author and *The Magazine of Fantasy and Science Fiction.*

OLD MAN HENDERSON, by Kris Neville. Copyright 1951 by Fantasy House, Inc. Reprinted by permission of the author and *The Magazine of Fantasy and Science Fiction.*

HE KILT IT WITH A STICK, by William F. Nolan. Copyright © 1967 by Mercury Press, Inc. Reprinted by permission of the author and *The Magazine of Fantasy and Science Fiction.*

THE CANVAS BAG, from *The Counterfeit Man,* by Alan E. Nourse. Copyright 1952, 1953, 1954, © 1955, 1956, 1963 by Alan E. Nourse. First published in *The Magazine of Fantasy and Science Fiction.* Reprinted by permission of David McKay Company, Inc.

PILGRIMAGE, by Chad Oliver. Copyright © 1957 by Fantasy House, Inc. Reprinted by permission of the author and *The Magazine of Fantasy and Science Fiction.*

GUN FOR HIRE, by Mack Reynolds. Copyright © 1960 by Conde Nast Publications. First published in *Analog.* Reprinted by permission of the author.

BRIGHTNESS FALLS FROM THE AIR, by Margaret St. Clair. Copyright 1951 by Fantasy House, Inc. Reprinted by permission of the author and *The Magazine of Fantasy and Science Fiction.*

BUILT UP LOGICALLY, by Howard Schoenfeld. Copyright 1951 by Fantasy House, Inc. First published as "Built Down Logically" in *The Magazine of Fantasy and Science Fiction.* Reprinted by permission of the author.

WARM MAN, by Robert Silverberg. Copyright © 1957 by Fantasy House, Inc. Reprinted by permission of the author and *The Magazine of Fantasy and Science Fiction.*

GREEN MAGIC, by Jack Vance. Copyright © 1963 by Mercury Press, Inc. Reprinted by permission of the author and *The Magazine of Fantasy and Science Fiction.*

DENY THE SLAKE, by Richard Wilson. Copyright © 1957 by Royal Publications, Inc. First published in *Infinity Science Fiction.* Reprinted by permission of the author and Royal Publications, Inc.

This book is lovingly dedicated
to the memory of Anthony Boucher
1911–1968

Born William A. P. White in California, where he was educated (B.A. from the University of Southern California and M.A. from the University of California) and lived all of his life. Author of seven novels (five as Anthony Boucher, two as H. H. Holmes) and innumerable novelettes, shorts, short-shorts, vignettes, fact crime articles, translations in French, Spanish, Portuguese, hundreds of radio shows (largely Sherlock Holmes). Editor of magazines and anthologies. Famous mystery reviewer (as Anthony Boucher) of the *San Francisco Chronicle, Ellery Queen's Mystery Magazine, New York Times Book Review;* and science fiction reviewer (as H. H. Holmes) of the *San Francisco Chronicle, Chicago Sun-Times, New York Herald Tribune Book Review.* One of the founding directors of Mystery Writers of America, a permanent lifetime director of the organization, national president in 1951, and recipient of their Edgar award for best criticism on many occasions. Frequently recognized as America's foremost authority on the mystery story. Major non-professional interests were historical vocal records, football, basketball, rugby, Elizabethan drama, food, Gibsons, imported dark beer.

"Can such things be,
And overcome us like a summer's cloud,
Without our special wonder?"

Macbeth, Act III, Scene iv

CONTENTS

SPECIAL WONDER
VOL. II

Horace B. Fyfe

RANSOM

My loss is in having known Tony Boucher only through correspondence, but that, too, was a pleasure.

If a story of mine was good, his generous admiration left a glow; if rotten, his plain talk encouraged rather than bruised; if in between, his time was sacrificed to suggest improvements—all with intelligence and imagination, for in his own writing he was gifted. Withal, he and Mick consistently edited an interesting, respected magazine.

All this you will hear from many others, for these are qualities that define a great editor—besides which he seems still to have a remarkable number of friends.

It was the day after Theot-Tu tried to kidnap me that I first saw the Earth beings who landed in my fields. At that time, I did not know they called themselves of Earth and came from the stars—in fact, their ship was not even to be seen from the castle because of the giant ferns to the south.

Theot-Tu had time in the dungeon to learn who was a fool. My rear guard had caught him fleeing the unsuccessful ambush.

"Very well, Kahkaw! he gasped. "Two of my best rowships and fifty slaves to work them."

I motioned the attendants of the place to put aside the hot chains and pincers. Theot-Tu was not the warrior he used to be, giving up the ships before I had so much as plucked a single feather from his head. I was rather disappointed.

Just then, a slave was hustled in by a pair of warriors. From the way the wing-muscles anchored to his breastbone quivered, I could see he was bursting with news. The philosophers claim the bone-ridges on our backs were free wings long, long ago and that our prehistoric ancestors could fly. This fellow seemed as if he might, at any moment. I pointed a claw at Theot-Tu.

"Take him out the rear gate and give him a *zinph* to ride back to his castle," I ordered. "I do not mean to doubt your given word, Theot-Tu, but I shall keep your warriors to work for me until the row-ships arrive."

He flung me an insulted glare at that, but prudently swallowed his protests.

Upstairs, the slave blurted out his story.

". . . and when I approached, two more came out of the ship, making seven. They brought a small machine. Believe me, Lord Kahkaw! With the machine, before I knew, they spoke to me, though they talked a wondrous strange gabble among themselves. Believe me!"

"Enough!" I commanded, turning to the warriors. "This I would see. Bring *zinphs* to the courtyard and find if any of my offspring are about, to accompany me!"

They located Turrrt and Hoo-Wup, the others being out hunting. Hoo-Wup, I noticed, was growing to be a handsome fellow with bulging muscles beneath his tanned skin. His crest feathers had a fine, blue-green sheen. But I had trained Turrrt myself, and knew him more reliable with lance or blowgun.

We rode out with ten warriors, the slave running before to show the way. It was not far. We crossed the river by the stone bridge, then bore seaward for the trail through the ferns. When we came out into the light again, there it was.

I looked at the panting slave, who had flung himself down to rest, but decided he had meant well enough. I, however, could see that it was not exactly a ship, though it lay high on the dunes along the beach.

At my wave, the warriors spread out and we rode forward. Before we reached this big thing of shining metal, a gate opened in its flank and some Earth beings came out. Immediately, I knew they were not of this world, unless they were evil spirits.

One of the warriors raised his blowgun, but I motioned him back. It is always good to learn a new thing. It might add to ones wealth or help in holding castle and lands.

It was as the slave had said. One of them brought out a machine in a small box, and then they could talk back to me.

"How do you do that?" I asked, seeking to put them at ease by pretending they knew more than I.

"We analyzed the speech of your companion this morning," one answered. "The machine translates as we speak into it."

He was a husky fellow, but his skin was pale and his face strange. He had no crest at all, just a sort of brownish down covering a big round head; and the soft-looking lump shaped almost like a beak was really not his mouth at all.

I glared into his bluish eyes—which both faced squarely forward—but decided he had meant no insult.

"He is not Kahkaw's companion," I said. "He is my slave."

Alien as he was, he had the wit to apologize. His name was Bill-something-or-other, and the others had similar funny sounds for names. They told me about their flight from their star to our world, and in such detail that I was of half a mind to believe them.

As they talked, I examined them. They were built somewhat like us—shorter and flatter in the body but longer in the legs. Their claws were soft and I do not think they *ever* had wings or feathers. Two were about as tall as I, one quite small, and the other four were in between.

The little one, which I took to be half-grown, had very long, thick, black down hanging down the neck to the shoulders. The ones of medium size had short thatches of different colors—brown, yellowish, and even red—and were sturdier, like warriors. The two big ones hung to the rear and never changed expression. They seemed to wear metal suits and masks.

"And why have you come here?' I asked Bill, when he had told his tale.

"We are exploring for other worlds with intelligent life."

"For what purpose?" I asked, lest they be spies.

"To exchange wisdom, and perhaps to trade goods."

"What?" I demanded. "Surely you are not mere merchants!"

He hesitated, then said they were not. It sounded like half a truth, but it was not worth a challenge yet.

In the end, I gave permission for them to remain on my land for a time, and to show me their ship the next day—it would be good excuse for a little ride.

Turrrt led up my *zinph*, but before I could mount, something caught my eye. The Earth beings had another small machine, which looked like a long tube sitting on three sticks.

"What is that for?" I asked.

They tried to tell me it was to look at stars so they could explain to others exactly where they were—obviously some kind of sorcery. The brown-topped one, Bill, showed me how to look through it.

By my last egg!

It happened to be pointing along the shore, and a spot half a day's ride away popped into view as though under my castle walls.

They said it was done with curved pieces of glass. Whatever worked it, it was just the thing for my watch tower. With a machine like this, it would be a lucky band who rode across my domain without yielding a juicy ransom. I saw myself becoming the richest lord in the countryside.

But no matter how extravagantly I admired the thing, the boors pretended not to understand, and declined to give it to me.

"Lord!" hissed Hoo-Wup, ashamed. "Must we watch Kahkaw lay himself open to the mockery of these slaves?"

"No!" I answered grimly, turning away to my *zinph*. "If

they don't understand that 'a present handsome is advanced ransom,' they will learn it soon!"

I even said farewell, but my temper stirred as we rode off. At the edge of the ferns, I bade the slave lurk and watch.

Early the next morning, the strategy was rewarded. A runner brought word that two of the aliens were walking on the beach. I summoned Turrrt, Hoo-Wup, and the warriors.

It was so easy it was hardly fun.

We swooped out of the ferns as they plodded back from the river toward their ship. One of the metal-suited ones led the way, carrying many small boxes, and the half-grown one followed. I pointed to the second figure. Turrrt and Hoo-Wup closed in amid a cloud of sand flung up by the claws of their *zinphs*.

A moment later, we were back in the dark of the ferns. The prisoner's companion did not even try to follow but continued on his way after one glance back to us.

We did not have long to wait. Before the midday meal, two of them showed up at the castle gate. The warriors brought in the brown-topped Bill I had talked with and one of the frozen-faced fellows. That one had the small talking-machine under one shiny, blue-back arm.

I wasted no time in tale-telling. With the warriors behind, we went right down to the dungeon where the little one was chained to the wall.

"Why did you do this?" cried Bill. "What do you want? Whatever you like—just name it. If I can manage at all, you shall have it!"

"You should have spoken this way yesterday," I reproved him, "instead of being so rude."

There was a great deal of babble over so simple a matter, what with the one in the cell crying out to the ones not yet in, and so on; but when I mentioned the seeing-machine, they agreed promptly.

I assured them I would not for the world doubt their word, but Bill insisted on remaining while they sent the shiny one off to get the present. Even when I had all the chains and instruments removed from sight, that pair persisted in acting extremely nervous. I had them brought up to the great hall, where they huddled together in a disgusting, weak fashion.

When the seeing-machine was brought, I freed them promptly, as befitted my honor as lord of the district. Then we took the machine up to the watch tower. May I lay a square egg! It was marvelous!

I had a watch kept on the ship the next day. They went about their foolish business of looking at the plants of the fields and the wiggling things along the beach.

It was then that it occurred to me I had been too modest in my requests. The seeing-machine was all very well, but what if I could make them carry me and my warriors through the air in their ship!

Some might laugh at that idea, but I am known as a lord with rare imagination. I pictured Theot-Tu's wide eyes when our band dropped straight down into his courtyard to earn another pair of row-ships.

Accordingly, I sent Turrrt and Hoo-Wup forth to catch another one. Knowing the obvious deep bonds between these Earth beings, I anticipated no complications.

Shortly before dark, they brought in the one with the red head. He had performed very defiantly, obliging them to lay a lance-butt across his crest. We waited for one to come with the talking-machine. Sure enough, the yellow-crested one arrived with the darkness.

"*Now* what do you want?" he asked in a manner I deemed insolent.

For the moment, I overlooked that. I informed him of my desire. To my indignation, the pair of them flatly refused!

"You may not understand what will happen," I warned them.

"We can't help what you do," said the red one. "The others would never think of giving up the ship, nor would we ask them!"

The argument lasted a long time. Of course, I might have brought it to an end by other means, but I rather liked the stupid fellows. They acted more like warriors than the first pair. They also sounded as if they were telling the truth about planning to fly off the next night and the others' being willing to abandon them.

"But the last time," I objected, "I got prompt results."

"Oh," said the red-thatched one, "that was only because Ellen is Bill's wife. He couldn't leave *her*. But they can run the ship without us."

"What is a wife?" I asked, waving back Turrrt, who thought they were mocking.

"What's a wife? What do we have to do—tell you the facts of life?"

"You are in a poor place to joke," I told him sternly. "And I'll have you know I have as many offspring as the next."

"Well, then, you know what a wife is," he persisted. "How did you get your children and who brought them up?"

"You stupid *zinph!* They cracked out of their shells by themselves!" I roared. "And *I* brought them up! *Who else?"*

The next thing I knew, he was trying to tell me that on their world, it took more than one individual to make a living egg. I admit I did not swallow all of it, but clearly there was need of beating them at their own game of wits. Besides, I remembered that there *did* seem to be several kinds of them.

Turrrt wanted to flung them into the fire, and Hoo-Wup ranted about hot chains; but I overruled them both. The story must be an allegory—plain if it could be solved—and they *had,* after all, borne themselves boldly as warriors should.

I let them go, taking them on *zinphs* across the river to the beach, and accepting no other present than a little machine they had for making light in the dark without burning anything.

"You are losing your wits," grumbled Turrrt on the ride back. "I shall soon be lord of the castle if you keep on."

"Patience!" I answered. "I want them to think I have given up the idea, but I am still plotting a way!"

I thought long about how they obtained their offspring, till it began to seem there might be something to it. I remembered that we have little animals in the jungles and some swimming-things in the sea whose eggs have never been seen

—yet which multiply in vaster numbers than seems possible. And too, these Earth beings did look varied.

I had had two varieties in my dungeon, but only the first time had I held all of any one kind. . . .

That must be the answer, I decided.

Shortly after dawn the next day, we rode out again. I was sure that I would out-trick them this time.

The little one called Ellen was not seen; but we lurked in the ferns until we caught together the other two I wanted. The red-headed one was with them, ordering them about with burdens, but my warriors drove him off.

"Do not hurt him!' I called. "I may need him in the ship."

Then we started to load the prisoners on the backs of the led *zinphs.* There was a great bustle, but my fellows were terribly slow about it. At last, five warriors heaved one of the aliens across the pack-pad and tied him down. He just kept moving his legs as if he still walked.

"How many arms have you broken?" I snapped to Hoo-Wup, as his gang struggled to lift the other one. "Do you want to be here still, knee-deep, when they come from the ship with weapons?"

"He's heavy!" Hoo-Wup gasped. "It's easy to perch up there and sneer down your beak at us. It isn't *your* wing-muscles he's pulling loose!"

My molting azure crest!

I swarmed down from my *zinph* to show him, but I might have saved my dignity. Hoo-Wup was right; the fellow was heavy as stone. It took six of us.

At last, we rode off—and just in time. Even as we slipped into the ferns, some of the Earth beings ran out the gate in the flank of their ship and made loud *bangs* at us. Some things *zzzzmmmmmed* through the ferns all around. Then an object at least the size of my head screamed past to one side, trailing a wake of fire behind it.

"Never mind," I said. "This time I have them between my claws."

We made it to the castle all right. Behind the stone walls, I awaited their next emissary with confidence.

"There are three kinds of them," I explained to Turrrt. "You remember how soft they were when we had the little Ellen? Now I have all of *this* kind. They will never leave without them!"

"I hope so," he answered dubiously.

"They themselves revealed the reason. It is simple. They must desire offspring as much as we."

I was so sure of this that when the watcher came down to report the Earth ship gone, I thought to cast him into a cell. But it was true! I was in time to see for myself the long trail of flame high in the night sky.

The warriors looked at the two frozen-faced metal wearers when I came in, for they know my temper, but I thought it might be a trick. I decided to wait for the ship to come back.

I am known as a patient lord, when I want to get my way, but they never did come back. Nor could I get anything out of the prisoners. They sat where they were tossed in a corner and ignored us. We had no talking-machine, and so could not understand the clicking and buzzing under their suits.

During that winter, even that stopped; and after a while their iron suits and masks rusted. I think they must have died inside even before Turrrt broke the white-hot pincers on them.

"You and your ideas about their needing many to make one egg!" he shouted in a rage. "The only egg *these* could ever lay would be as hard as your head!"

I am beginning to think he was right.

Randall Garrett

THE MUDDLE OF THE WOAD

I have yet to meet a man who could honestly claim that he shared all *of Tony's interests with him; the Compleat Anthony Boucher had more breadth and depth than any other man I have known. I, for example, have a musical ear roughly forged from low-grade tin, while his was exquisitely wrought of purest silver; so, except for Gilbert & Sullivan, we could not share music together. I do not play poker, and Tony was a genius at it. I could easily list a dozen more such examples. But we did share an honest appreciation of women, a liking for good booze, and a love of fantasy, science fiction and the formal detective story.*

Tony very much liked and enjoyed Lord Darcy's adventures in the alternate-history world of the Anglo-French Empire, where magic works according to strict laws, and he was kind enough to say so in several reviews. One of his favorites was "Muddle of the Woad"; he insisted that it should be anthologized and was thinking of doing it himself.

Well, here it is, Tony. I hope you enjoy it as much on re-reading as you did the first time.

BOTH PAIN AND PRIDE were sending their counterbalancing energies through the nervous system of Walter Gotobed, Master Joiner for His Grace, the Duke of Kent, as he opened the door of his workshop. The pain, like the pride, was mental in origin; in spite of his seventy-odd years, Master Walter was still blessed with strength in his wiry body and steadiness in his careful hands. With his spectacles perched properly on his large, thin, bony nose, he could still draw an accurate plan for anything from a closet to a cigar box. Come next Trinity Sunday, the twenty-fourth of May, the Year of Our Lord 1964, Master Walter would be celebrating his fortieth anniversary of his appointment as Master Joiner to the Duke. He was now on his second Duke, the Old Duke having died in 1927, and would serve a third before long. The Dukes of Kent were long-lived, but a man who works with fine woods, absorbing the strength and the agelessness of the great trees from which they come, lives longer still.

The workshop was full of woody smells—the spiciness of cedar, the richness of oak, the warm tang of plain pine, the fruity sweetness of apple—and the early morning sunlight coming in through the windows cast gleaming highlights on the cabinets and desks and chairs and tables that filled the shop in various stages of progress. This was Master Walter's world, the atmosphere in which he worked and lived.

Behind Master Walter came three more men: Journeyman Henry Lavender and the two apprentices, Tom Wilderspin and Harry Venable. They followed the Master in, and the four of them walked purposefully towards a magnificent creation in polished walnut that reposed on a bench in one corner. Two paces from it, Master Walter stopped.

"How does it look, Henry?" Master Walter asked without turning his head.

Journeyman Henry, not yet thirty, but already having about him the tone of a woodcraftsman, nodded with satisfaction and said: "Very beautiful, Master Walter, very beautiful." It was honest appreciation, not flattery, that spoke.

"I think Her Grace the Duchess will be pleased, eh?" the old man said.

"More than pleased, Master. Mm-m-m. There's a bit of dust on it, even since last night. You, Tom! Get a clean rag with a little lemon oil on it and give it another polish." As Tom the 'prentice scampered off in obedience, Henry Lavender continued: "His Grace the Duke will appreciate your work, Master; it's one of the finest things you've turned out for him."

"Aye. And that's something you must remember, Henry—and something you two lads must get through your heads. It's not fancy carving that makes the beauty of wood; it's the wood itself. Carving's all right in its place, mind you; I've nothing against carving if it's properly done. But the beauty's in the wood. Something plain like this, without fanciness, without ornament, shows that wood, *as wood,* is a creation of God that can't be improved upon. All you can ever hope to do is bring out the beauty that God Himself put there. Here, give me that rag, young Tom; I'll put the final polish on this myself." As he moved the oily rag, with its faint lemon scent, over the broad, flat surface, Master Walter went on: "Careful craftsmanship is what does it, lads. Careful craftsmanship. Each piece joined solidly to the next, glued tightly, screws in firmly, with no gaps or spaces—that's what makes *good* work. Matching the grain, carefully choosing your pieces, planing and sanding to a perfect surface, applying your finish, wax or varnish or shellac, to a fine smoothness—that's what makes it *fine* work. And design—ah, *design—that* makes it *art!*

"All right, now, you, Tom, take the front end. Harry, you take the other. We've a stairway to climb, but you're both strong lads and it's not too heavy. Besides, a joiner and cabinet maker must have strong muscles to do his work and the exercise will be good for the both of you."

Obediently, the 'prentices grasped the ends they had been assigned and lifted. They had carried it before and knew to a pound how much it weighed. They heaved upwards.

And the beautifully polished walnut scarcely moved.

"Here! What's the matter?" said Master Walter. "You almost dropped it!"

"It's *heavy,* Master," said Tom. "There's something in it."

"Something in it? How could there be?" Master Walter

reached out, lifted the lid. And almost dropped it again. "Good God!"

Then there was a stunned silence as the four men looked at the thing that lay within.

"A dead man," said Journeyman Henry after a moment.

That was obvious. The corpse was certainly a corpse. The eyelids were sunken and the skin waxy. The man was thoroughly, completely dead.

To make the horror even worse, the nude body—from crown of head to tip of toe—was a deep, almost indigo, blue.

Master Walter found his breath again. His feelings of surprise and horror had vanished beneath a wave of indignation. "But he don't belong here! He'd got no right! No right at all!"

"Daresay it ain't his fault, Master Walter," Journeyman Henry ventured. "He didn't get there by himself."

"No," said Master Walter, gaining control of himself. "No, of course not. But what a *peculiar* place to find a corpse!"

In spite of his own feelings, it was all Apprentice Tom could do to suppress a snigger.

What better place to find a corpse than in a coffin?

Even the most dedicated of men enjoys a holiday now and then, and Lord Darcy, Chief Criminal Investigator for His Royal Highness, Prince Richard, Duke of Normandy, was no exception. He not only enjoyed his work, but preferred it above all others. His keen mind found satisfaction in solving the kind of problems that, by the very nature of the work, were continually being brought to his attention. But he also knew that a one-track brain became stale very shortly—and besides he enjoyed letting his mind drift for a while.

Then, too, there was the pleasure of coming home to England. France was fine. It was an important part of the Empire, and working for His Highness was pleasurable. But England was his home, and getting back to England once a year was . . . well, a relief. In spite of the fact that England and France had been one country for eight hundred years, the differences were still enough to make an Englishman feel faintly foreign in France. And, he supposed, vice versa.

Lord Darcy stood at one side of the ballroom and surveyed the crowd. The orchestra was pausing between numbers, and the floor was full of people talking, waiting for the next dance. He took a drink from the whisky-and-water that he had been nursing along. This sort of thing, he congratulated himself, palled within two weeks, while his real work took fifty weeks to become irritating. Still, each was a relief from the other.

Baron Dartmoor was a decent sort, an excellent chess player, and a good man with a story now and then. Lady Dartmoor had a knack of picking the right people to come to a dinner or a ball. But one couldn't stay forever at Dartmoor House, and London society wasn't everything it was assumed to be by those who didn't live there.

Lord Darcy found himself thinking that it would be good to get back to Rouen on the twenty-second of May.

"Lord Darcy, do pardon me, but something has come up."

Darcy turned at the sound of the woman's voice and smiled. "Oh?"

"Will you come with me?"

"Certainly, my lady."

He followed her, but there was a nervousness in her manner, a tautness in her behavior, that told him there was something out of the ordinary here.

At the door to the library, she paused. "My lord, there is a . . . a gentleman who wishes to speak to you. In the library."

"A gentleman? Who is he, my lady?"

"I—" Lady Dartmoor drew herself up and took a breath. "I am not at liberty to say, my lord. He will introduce himself."

"I see." Lord Darcy unobtrusively put his hands behind his back and with his right hand drew a small pistol from the holster concealed by the tails of his green dress coat. This didn't exactly have the smell of a trap, but there was no reason to be careless.

Lady Dartmoor opened the door. "Lord Darcy, S . . . sir."

"Show him in, my lady," said a voice from within.

Lord Darcy went in, his pistol still concealed behind his back and beneath his coattails. Behind him, he heard the door close.

The man was standing with his back to the door, looking out the window at the lighted streets of London. "Lord Darcy," he said without turning, "if you are the man I have been brought to believe you are, you are dangerously close to committing the capital crime of High Treason."

But Lord Darcy, after one look at that back, had re-holstered his pistol and dropped to one knee. "As Your Majesty knows, I would rather die than commit treason against Your Majesty."

The man turned, and for the first time in his life Lord Darcy found himself face to face with His Imperial Majesty, John IV, King and Emperor of England, France, Scotland, Ireland, New England, New France, Defender of the Faith, et cetera.

He looked a great deal like his younger brother, Richard of Normandy—tall, blond, and handsome, like all the Plantagenets. But he was ten years older than Duke Richard, and the difference showed. The King was thirty, only a few years younger than Lord Darcy, but the lines in his face made him look older.

"Rise, my lord," said His Majesty. He smiled. "You *did* have a gun in your hand, didn't you?"

"I did, Your Majesty," Lord Darcy said, rising smoothly. "My apologies, Sire."

"Not at all. Only what I should have expected of a man of your capabilities. Please be seated. We will not be interrupted; my lady of Dartmoor will see to that. Thank you. We have a problem, Lord Darcy."

Darcy seated himself and the King took a chair facing him. "For the time being, my lord," said the King, "we shall forget rank. Don't interrupt me until I have given you all the data I have. Then you may ask questions as you will."

"Yes, Sire."

"Very well. I have a job for you, my lord. I know you are on holiday, and it pains me to interrupt your leisure—but this needs looking into. You are aware of the activities of the so-called Holy Society of Ancient Albion."

It was a statement, not a question. Lord Darcy and every other Officer of the King's Justice knew of the Society of Albion. They were more than just a secret society; they were a pagan sect which repudiated the Christian Church. They were reputed to dabble in Black Magic, they practiced a form of nature-worship, and they claimed direct organizational descent from the pre-Roman Druids. The Society, after a period of toleration during the last century, had been outlawed. Some said that it had remained in hiding during all the centuries since the triumph of Christianity and had only revealed itself during the easy-going Nineteenth Century, others said that its claim of antiquity was false, that it had been organized during the 1820s by the eccentric, perhaps slightly mad, Sir Edward Finnely. Probably both versions were partly true.

They had been outlawed because of their outspoken advocation of human sacrifice. Rejecting the Church's teaching that the Sacrifice of the Cross obviated for all time any further sacrifice of human life, the Society insisted that in times of trouble the King himself should die for the sake of his people. The evidence that William II, son of the Conqueror, had been killed "by an arrow offshot" by one of his own men for just that purpose added weight to the story of the antiquity of the Society. William Rufus, it was believed, had been a pagan himself, and had gone willingly to his death—but it was not likely that any modern Anglo-French monarch would do so.

Originally, it had been one of the tenets of their belief that the sacrificial victim must die willingly, even gladly; mere assassination would be pointless and utterly lacking in efficacy. But the increasing tension between the Empire and the Kingdom of Poland had wrought a change. This was a time of troubles, said the Society, and the King must die, will he or no. Evidence showed that such sentiments had been instilled in the membership of the Society by agents of King Casimir IX himself.

"I doubt," said King John, "that the Society poses any real threat to the Imperial Government. There simply aren't that many fanatics in England. But a King is as vulnerable to a lone assassin—especially a fanatic—as any one else. I do not consider myself indispensable to the Empire; if my death would benefit the people, I would go to the block today. As it is, however, I rather feel that I should like to go on living for a time.

"My own agents, I must tell you, have infiltrated the Society successfully. Thus far, they have reported that there is no hint of any really organized attempt to do away with me. But now something new has come up.

"This morning, shortly before seven o'clock, His Grace the Duke of Kent passed away. It was not unexpected. He was only sixty-two, but his health had been failing for some time and he has been failing rapidly for the past three weeks. The best Healers were called in, but the Reverend Fathers said that when a man has resigned himself to dying there is nothing the Church can do.

"At exactly seven o'clock, the Duke's Master Joiner went into his shop to get the coffin that had been prepared for His Grace. He found it already occupied—by the body of Lord Camberton. Chief Investigator for the Duchy of Kent.

"He had been stabbed—*and his body was dyed blue!*"

Lord Darcy's eyes narrowed.

"It is not known," the King continued, "how long Lord Camberton has been dead. It is possible that a preservative spell was cast over the body. He was last seen in Kent three weeks ago, when he left for a holiday in Scotland. We don't know yet if he ever arrived, though I should get a report by teleson very shortly. Those are the facts as I know them. Are there any questions, Lord Darcy?"

"None, Sire." There was no point in asking the King questions which could be better answered in Canterbury.

"My brother Richard," said the King, "has a high regard for your abilities and has communicated to me in detail regarding you. I have full respect for his judgment, which was fully borne out by your handling of the 'Atlantic Curse' case last January. My personal agents, working for months, had got nowhere; you penetrated to the heart of the matter in two days. Therefore, I am appointing you as Special Investigator for the High Court of Chivalry." He handed Lord Darcy a document which he had produced from an inside coat pocket. "I came here incognito," he went on, "because I do not want it known that I am taking a personal interest in this case. As far as the public is to know, this was a decision by the Lord Chancellor—quite routine. I want you to go to Canterbury and find out who killed Lord Camberton and *why*. I have no data. I want you get me the data I need.

"I am honored, Sire," said Lord Darcy, pocketing the commission. "Your wish is my command."

"Excellent. A train leaves for Canterbury in an hour and"—His Majesty glanced at his wrist watch—"seven minutes. Can you make it?"

"Certainly, Sire."

"Fine. I have made arrangements for you to stay at the Archbishop's Palace—that will be easier, I think, and more politic than putting you in with the Ducal family. His Grace the Archbishop knows that I am interested in this case; so does Sir Thomas Leseaux. No one else does."

Lord Darcy raised an eyebrow. "Sir Thomas Leseaux, Sire? The theoretical thaumaturgist?"

The King's smile was that of a man who has perpetrated a successful surprise. "The same, my lord. A member of the Society of Albion—and my agent."

"Perfect, Sire," said Lord Darcy with a smile of appreciation. "One would hardly suspect a scientist of his standing of being either."

"I agree. Are their any further questions, my lord?"

"No. But I have a request, Sire. Sir Thomas, I understand, is not a practicing sorcerer—"

"Correct," said the King. "A theoretician only. He is perfecting something he calls the Theory of Subjective Congruency—whatever that may mean. He works entirely with the symbology of subjective algebra and leaves others to test his theories in practice."

Lord Darcy nodded. "Exactly, Sire. He could hardly be called an expert in forensic sorcery. I should like the aid of Master Sean O Lochlainn; we work well together, he and I. He is in Rouen at the moment. May I send word for him to come to Canterbury?"

His Majesty's smile grew broader. "I am happy to say that I have anticipated your request. I have already sent a teleson message to Dover. A trusted agent has already left on a special boat to Calais. He will teleson to Rouen and the boat will be held for Master Sean at Calais to return to Dover. From Dover, he can take the train to Canterbury. The weather is good; he should arrive sometime tomorrow."

"Sire," said Lord Darcy, "as long as the Imperial Crown decorates a head like yours, the Empire cannot fail."

"Neatly worded, my lord. We thank you." His Majesty rose from his chair and Lord Darcy did likewise. His reversion to the royal first person plural indicated that they were no longer speaking as man to man, but as Sovereign to subject. "We give you carte blanche, my lord, but there must be no further contact with Us unless absolutely necessary. When you are finished, We want a complete and detailed report—for Our eyes only. Arrangements for anything you need will be made through His Grace the Archbishop."

"Very well, Your Majesty."

"You have Our leave to go, Lord Darcy."

"By Your Majesty's leave." Lord Darcy dropped to one knee. By the time he had risen, the King had turned his back and was once more staring out the window—making it unnecessary for Lord Darcy to back out of the room.

Lord Darcy turned and walked to the door. As his hand touched the door handle, the King's voice came again.

"One thing, Darcy."

Lord Darcy turned to look, but the King still had his back to him.

"Sire?"

"Watch yourself. I don't want you killed. I need men like you."

"Yes, Sire."

"Good luck, Darcy."

"Thank you, Sire."

Lord Darcy opened the door and went out, leaving the King alone with his thoughts.

Lord Darcy vaguely heard a bell. *Bon-n-n-ng. Bon-n-n-ng. Bon-n-n-ng.* Then a pause. During the pause, he drifted off again into sleep, but it was only a matter of seconds before the bell rang three more times. Lord Darcy came slightly more awake this time, but the second pause was almost enough to allow him to return to comfortable oblivion. At the third repetition of the three strokes, he recognized that the Angelus was ringing. It was six in the morning, and that meant that he had had exactly five hours sleep. During the final ringing of the nine strokes, he muttered the prayers rapidly, crossed himself, and closed his eyes again, resolving to go back to sleep until nine.

And, of course, couldn't sleep.

One eventually gets used to anything, he thought, feeling sleepily grumpy, *even great, clangy bells.* But the huge bronze monster in the bell tower of the cathedral church of Canterbury was not more than a hundred yards away in a direct line, and its sound made the very walls vibrate.

He pulled his head out of the pillows again, propped himself up to a sitting position, and looked around at the unfamiliar but pleasant bedroom which had been assigned him by His Grace the Archbishop. Then he looked out the window. At least the weather looked as if it would be fine.

He threw back the bedclothes, swung his legs over the

edge of the bed, put his feet into his slippers, and then pulled the bell cord. He was just tying the cord of his crimson silk dressing gown—the one with the gold dragons embroidered on it—when the young monk opened the door. "Yes, my lord?"

"Just a pot of caffe and a little cream to match, Brother."

"Yes, my lord," the novice said.

By the time Lord Darcy had showered and shaved, the caffe was already waiting for him, and the young man in the Benedictine habit was standing by. "Anything else, my lord?"

"No, Brother; that will be all. Thank you."

"A pleasure, my lord." The novice went promptly.

That was one thing about the Benedictine novitiate, Lord Darcy reflected; it taught a young man from the lower classes how to behave like a gentleman and it taught humility to those who were gently born. There was no way of knowing whether the young man who had just come in was the son of a small farmer or a cadet of a noble family. If he hadn't been able to learn, he wouldn't have come even this far.

Lord Darcy sat down, sipped at the caffe, and thought. He had little enough information as yet. His Grace the Archbishop, a tall, widely built, elderly man with an impressive mane of white hair and a kindly expression on his rather florid face, had had no more information than Lord Darcy had already received from the King. Via teleson, Lord Darcy had contacted Sir Angus MacReady, Chief Investigator for His Lordship the Marquis of Edinburgh. Lord Camberton had come to Scotland, all right; but it had not been for a holiday. He had not told Sir Angus what he was doing, but he had been engaged in investigative work of some kind. Sir Angus had promised to determine what that work had been. "Aye, m' laird," he'd said, "I'll do the job masel'. I'll no say a word tae anybody, and I'll report tae ye direct."

Whether Lord Camberton's investigations in Scotland had anything to do with the reason for his being killed was an open question. The Holy Society of Ancient Albion had very little following in Scotland, and the murder had almost certainly not taken place there. Taking a human body from Edinburgh to Canterbury would be so difficult that there would have to be a tremendous advantage to having the body found in Canterbury that would outweigh the dangers of transportation. He would not ignore the possibility, Lord Darcy decided, but until evidence appeared that made it more probable, he would look for the death spot closer to Canterbury.

The local Armsmen had definitely established that Lord Camberton had not been killed in the place where he was found. The deep stab wound had, according to the chirurgeon, bled copiously when it had been inflicted, but there was no blood in the Duke's casket. Still, he would have to investigate the cabinetmaker's shop himself; the report of the Armsmen, relayed to him through My Lord Archbishop, was not enough.

There would be no point in viewing the body itself until Master Sean arrived; that blue dye job had a definitely thaumaturgical feel about it, Lord Darcy thought.

Meantime, he would stroll over to the ducal castle and ask a few qestions. But first, breakfast was definitely in order.

Master Walter Gotobed bowed and touched his forehead as the gentleman entered the door of his shop. "Yes, sir. What may I do for you, sir?"

"You are Walter Gotobed, Master Joiner?" asked Lord Darcy.

"At your service, sir," said the old man politely.

"I am Lord Darcy, Special Investigator for His Majesty's Court of Chivalry. I should like a few moments of your time, Master Walter."

"Ah, yes. Certainly, your lordship." The old man's eyes took on a pained expression. "About Lord Camberton, I've no doubt. Will you come this way, your Lordship? Yes. Poor Lord Camberton, murdered like that; an awful thing, your lordship. This is my office; we won't be disturbed here, your lordship. Would you care to take this chair, your lordship? Here, just a moment, your lordship, let me dust the sawdust off it. Sawdust *do* get everywhere, your lordship. Now, what was it your lordship wanted to know?"

"Lord Camberton's body was found here in your shop, I believe?" Lord Darcy asked.

"Ah, yes, your lordship, and a terrible thing it was, too, if I may say so. A terrible thing to have happen. Found him, so we did, in His Grace's coffin. The Healers had told me there wasn't much hope for His Grace, and Her Grace, the Duchess, asked me to make a specially nice one for His Grace, which of course I did, and yesterday morning when we came in, there he was, Lord Camberton, I mean, in the coffin where he didn't ought to be. All over blue he was, your lordship, all over blue. We didn't even recognize him because of that, not at first."

"Not an edifying sight, I dare say," Lord Darcy murmured. "Tell me what happened."

Master Walter did so, with exhausting particulars.

"You have no idea how he came here?" Lord Darcy asked when the recital was finished.

"None at all, your lordship; none at all. Chief Bertram asked us the same thing, your lordship, 'How did he get in here?' But none of us knew. The windows and the doors was all locked up tight and the back door barred. The only ones as has keys is me and my journeyman, Henry Lavender, and neither of us was here at all the night before. Chief Bertram thought maybe the 'prentices had put him in there as a practical joke—that was before Chief Bertram recognized who he was and thought they'd stole it from the Chirurgeon's College or something—but the boys swear they don't know nothing about it and I believe 'em, your lordship. They're good boys and they wouldn't pull anything like that on me. I said as much to Chief Bertram."

"I see," said Lord Darcy. "Just for the record, where were you and Journeyman Henry and the apprentices Sunday night?"

Master Walter jerked a thumb toward the ceiling. "Me and the boys were upstairs, your lordship. That's my home, and I have a room for my 'prentices. Goodwife Bailey comes in of a day to do the cleaning and fix the meals—my wife has been dead now these eighteen years, God rest her soul." He crossed himself unobtrusively.

"Then you can come in the shop from upstairs?"

Master Walter pointed toward the wall of his office. "That ladder goes up to my bedroom, your lordship; you can see the trapdoor. But it hasn't been used for nigh on ten years now. My legs aren't what they used to be, and I don't fancy a ladder any more. We all use the stairway on the outside of the building."

"Could someone have used the ladder without your knowing it, Master Walter?"

The old man shook his head firmly. "Not without my knowing of it, your lordship. If I was down here, I'd see 'em. If I was upstairs, I'd hear 'em; they'd have to move my bed from off the trapdoor. Besides, I'm a very light sleeper. A man don't sleep as well when he's past three-score and ten as he did when he were a young man, your lordship."

"And the bolts and bars were all in place when you came down yesterday morning?"

"Indeed they were, your lordship. All locked up tight."

"Journeyman Henry had the other key, you say. Where was he?"

"He were at home, your lordship. Henry's married, has a lovely wife—a Tolliver she were afore she married, one of Ben Tolliver's daughters. That's Master Ben, the baker. Henry and his wife live outside the gates, your lordship, and the guard would have seen him if he'd come in, which he and his wife say he didn't and I believe 'em. And Henry would have no cause to do such a thing no more than the boys would."

"Have you had protective spells put on your locks and bars?" Lord Darcy asked.

"Oh, yes, your lordship; indeed I have. Wouldn't be

without 'em, your lordship. The usual kind, your lordship; cost me a five-sovereign a year to have 'em kept up, but it's worth every bit."

"A licensed sorcerer, I trust? None of these hedge-magicians or witch-women?"

The old man looked shocked. "Oh, no, your lordship! Not I! I abides by the law, I do! Master Timothy has a license all right and proper, he do. Besides, the magic of them you mentioned is poor stuff at best. I don't believe none of the heresy about black magic being stronger nor white. That would be saying that the Devil were stronger nor God, and"—he crossed himself again—"I for one would never think such a thing."

"Of course not, Master Walter," Lord Darcy said soothingly. "You must understand that it is my duty to ask such questions. The place was all locked up tight, then?"

"Indeed, your lordship, indeed it was. Why, if it hadn't been that His Grace died in the night, Lord Camberton might have stayed there until this morning. But for that, we wouldn't have opened up the shop at all, it being a holiday and all."

"Holiday?" Lord Darcy looked at him questioningly. "What made the eighteenth of May a holiday?"

"Only in Canterbury, your lordship. Special day of thanksgiving it is. On that day in 1589—or '98, I misremember which—a band of assassins were smuggled into the castle by a traitor. Five of them there were. A plot to kill the Duke and his family, it were. But the plot were betrayed and the castle searched and all of 'em were found and taken before they could do anything. Hanged, they were, right out there in the courtyard." Master Walter pointed out the front of his shop. "Since then, on the anniversary, there's a day of thanksgiving for the saving of the Duke's life—though he died some years later, you understand. There's a special Mass said at the chapel and another at the Cathedral, and the guard is turned out and there's a ceremonial searching of the castle, with all the Duke's Own Guard in full dress and a parade and a trooping of the colors and five effigies hanged in the courtyard and fireworks in the evening. Very colorful it is, your lordship."

"I'm sure it is," said Lord Darcy. Master Walter's recitation had recalled the facts of history to mind. "Was it carried out as usual yesterday?"

"Well, no, your lordship, it wasn't. The captain of the Duke's Own didn't think it would be right, what with the family in mourning and all. And My Lord Archbishop agreed. 'Twouldn't be proper to give thanks for the saving of the life of a Duke that's four centuries, nearly, in his grave with His late Grace not even *in* his grave yet. The guard was turned out for five minutes of silence and a salute to His Grace instead."

"Of course. That would be the proper thing," Lord Darcy agreed. "You would not have come into the shop until this morning, then, if His Grace had not passed away. When did you lock the shop last before you unlocked it yesterday morning?"

"Saturday evening, your lordship. That is, *I* didn't lock it. Henry did. I was a little tired and I went upstairs early. Henry usually locks up at night."

"Was the coffin empty at that time?" Lord Darcy asked.

"Positively, your lordship. I took special pride in that coffin, if I may say so, your lordship. Special pride. I wanted to make sure there weren't no sawdust or such on the satin lining."

"I understand. And at what o'clock did you lock up Saturday evening?"

"You'd best ask Henry, your lordship. *Henn-nry!*"

The journeyman appeared promptly. After the introduction, Lord Darcy repeated his question.

"I locked up at half past eight, your lordship. It were still light out. I sent the 'prentices upstairs and locked up tight."

"And no one came in here at all on Sunday?" Lord Darcy looked in turn at both men.

"No, your lordship," said Master Walter.

"Not a soul, your lordship," said Henry Lavender.

"Not a soul, perhaps," Lord Darcy said dryly. "But a body did."

Lord Darcy was waiting on the station platform when the 11:22 pulled in from Dover, and when a tubby little Irishman wearing the livery of the Duke of Normandy and carrying a large, symbol-decorated carpetbag stepped out of one of the coaches and looked around, Lord Darcy hailed him:

"Master Sean! Over here!"

"Ah! There you are, my lord! Good to see you again, my lord. Had a good holiday, I trust? What there was of it, I mean."

"To be honest, I was beginning to become a bit bored, my good Sean. I think this little problem is just what we both need to shake the cobwebs out of our brains. Come along; I have a cab waiting for us."

Once inside the cab, Lord Darcy began speaking in a low voice calculated to just barely carry above the clatter of the horses' hoofs and the rattle of the wheels. Master Sean O Lochlainn listened carefully while Lord Darcy brought him up to date on the death of the Duke and the murder of Lord Camberton, omitting nothing except the fact that the assignment had come personally from the King himself.

"I checked the locks in the shop," he concluded. "The rear door has a simple slip bar that couldn't be opened from the outside except magically. The same with the windows. Only the front door has a key. I'll want you to check the spells; I have a feeling that those men are telling the truth about locking up, that none of them had anything to do with the murder."

"Did you get the name of the sorcerer who serviced the locks, my lord?"

"A Master Timothy Videau."

"Aye. I'll look him up in the directory." Master Sean looked thoughtful. "I don't suppose there's anything suspicious about the death of His Grace the Duke, eh, my lord?"

"I am chronically suspicious of all deaths intimately connected with a murder case, Master Sean. But first we will have a look at Lord Camberton's body. It's being held in the mortuary at the Armsmen's Headquarters."

"Would it be possible, my lord, to instruct the cab driver to stop at an apothecary's shop before we get to the mortuary? I should like to get something."

"Certainly." Lord Darcy gave instructions, and the cab pulled up before a small shop. Master Sean went in and came out a few moments later with a small jar. It appeared to be filled with dried leaves. The whole ones were shaped rather like an arrowhead.

"Druidic magic, eh, Master Sean?" Lord Darcy asked.

Master Sean looked startled for a moment, then grinned. "I ought to be used to you by now, my lord. How did you know?"

"A blue-dyed corpse brings to mind the ancient Briton's habit of dying himself blue when he went into battle. When you go into an apothecary's shop and purchase a jar full of the typically sagittate leaves of the woad plant, I can see that your mind is running along the same lines that mine had. You intend to use the leaves for a similarity analysis."

"Correct, my lord."

A few minutes later, the cab drew up to the front door of the Armsmen's Headquarters, and shortly afterwards Lord Darcy and Master Sean were in the morgue. An attendant stood by while the two men inspected the late Lord Camberton's earthly husk.

"He was found this way, my lord? Naked?" Master Sean asked.

"So I am told," Lord Darcy said.

Master Sean opened his symbol-covered carpetbag and began taking things out of it. He was absorbed in his task of selecting the proper material for his work when Bertram Lightly, Chief Master-at-Arms of the City of Canterbury, entered. He did not bother Master Sean; one does not trouble a sorcerer when he is working.

Chief Bertram was a round-faced, pink-skinned man with an expression that reminded one of an amiable frog. "I was told you were here, your lordship," he said softly. "I had to finish up some business in the office. Can I be of any assistance?"

"Not just at the moment, Chief Bertram, but I have no doubt that I shall need your assistance before this affair is over."

"Excuse me," said Master Sean without looking up from his work, "but did you have a chirurgeon look at the body, Chief Bertram?"

"Indeed we did, Master Sorcerer. Would you want to speak to him?"

"No. Not necessary at the moment. Just give me the gist of his findings."

"Well, Dr. Dell is of the opinion that his late lordship had been dead forty-eight to seventy-two hours—plus whatever time he was under a preservative spell, of course. Can't tell anything about that time lapse, naturally. Died of a stab wound in the back. A longish knife or a short thrust with a sword. Went in just below the left shoulder blade, between the ribs, and pierced the heart. Died within seconds."

"Did he say anything about bleeding?"

"Yes. He said there must have been quite a bit of blood from that stab. Quite a bit."

"Aye. So I should say. Look here, my lord."

Lord Darcy stepped closer.

"There was a preservative spell on the body, all right. It's gone now—worn off—but there's only traces of micro-organisms on the surface. Nothing alive within. But the body was washed after the blood had coagulated, and it was dyed after it was washed. The wound is clean, and the dye is *in* the wound, as you see. Now, we'll see if that blue stuff is actually woad."

"Woad?" said Chief Bertram.

"Aye, woad," said Master Sean. "The Law of Similarity allows one to determine such things. The dye on the man may be exactly similar to the dye in the leaf, d'ye see. If it is, we get a reaction. Actually, all these come under the broad Law of Metonymy—an effect is similar to its cause, a symbol is similar to the thing symbolized. And vice versa, of course." Then he muttered something unintelligible under his breath and rubbed his thumb along the leaf of woad. "We'll see," he said softly. "We'll see." He put the leaf on the blue skin of the dead man's abdomen, then lifted it off again almost immediately. The side of the leaf that had touched the skin was blue. On the abdomen of the corpse was a white area, totally devoid of blueness, exactly the size and shape of the leaf.

"Woad," said Master Sean with complacency. "Definitely woad."

Master Sean was packing his materials away in his carpet-bag. Half an hour had been sufficient to get all data he needed. He dusted off his hands. "Ready to go, my lord?"

Lord Darcy nodded, and the two of them headed toward the door of the mortuary. Standing near the door was a smallish man in his middle fifties. He had graying hair, a lean face, mild blue eyes and a curiously hawk-like nose. On the floor at his feet was a symbol-decorated carpet bag similar to Master Sean's own.

"Good day, colleague," he said in a high voice. "I am Master Timothy Videau." Then he gave a little bow. "Good day, your lordship. I hope you don't mind, but I was interested in watching your procedure. Forensic sorcery has always interested me, although it isn't my field."

"I am Sean O Lochlainn," said the tubby little Irishman. "This is my superior, Lord Darcy."

"Yes, yes. So Chief Bertram informed me. Isn't it terrible? Lord Camberton being murdered that way, I mean."

As he talked, he fell into step with the other two men and walked with them toward the street. "I suppose you do a lot of similarity analysis in your work, Master Sean? It is a technique with which I am not at all familiar. Protective spells, avoidance spells, repairs—that's my work. Household work. Not as exciting as your work, but I like it. Gives a man a sense of satisfaction and all that. But I like to know what my colleagues are doing."

"You came down here to watch Master Sean at work, then, Master Timothy?" Lord Darcy asked in a bland voice, betraying no trace of the thoughts in his mind.

"Oh, no, your lordship. I was asked down by Chief Bertram." He looked at Master Sean and chuckled. "You'll get a laugh out of this, Master Sean. He wanted to know what it would cost to buy a preservator big enough to serve the kitchen in the Armsmen's barracks!"

Master Sean laughed softly, then said: "I dare say that when you told him he decided to stick with a good, old-fashioned icehouse. You're the local agent, then?"

"Yes. But there's not much profit in it yet, I fear. "I've only sold one, and I'm not likely to sell any more. Much too expensive. I get a small commission, but the real money for me would be in the servicing. The spell has to be reinforced every six months or so."

Master Sean smiled ingratiatingly. "Sounds interesting. The spell must have an interesting structure."

Master Timothy returned the smile. "Yes, quite interesting. I'd like to discuss it with you . . ."

Master Sean's expression became more attentive.

". . . But unfortunately Master Simon has put the whole process under a seal of secrecy."

"I was afraid of that," Master Sean said with a sigh.

"Would I be intruding if I asked what you two are talking about?" Lord Darcy asked.

"Oh, I'm sorry, my lord," Master Sean said hurriedly. "Just shop talk. Master Simon of London has invented a new principle for protecting food from spoilage. Instead of casting a spell on each individual item—such as the big vintners do with wine casks and the like—he discovered a way to cast a spell on a specially-constructed chest so that anything put in it is safe from spoilage. The idea being that, instead of enchanting an *object*, a *space* is given the property necessary to do the same thing. But the process is still pretty expensive."

"I see," said Lord Darcy.

Master Sean caught the tone of his voice and said: "Well,

we mustn't talk shop, Master Timothy. Er . . . did your lordship want me to have a look at those locks? Might be a good idea, if Master Timothy is free for an hour."

"Locks?" said Master Timothy.

Master Sean explained about the locks on the cabinet-maker's shop.

"Why, certainly, Master Sean," said Master Timothy. "I'd be glad to be of any assistance I can."

"Excellent," said Lord Darcy. "Come to My Lord Archbishop's Palace as soon as you have the data. And thank you for your assistance, Master Timothy."

"It's a pleasure to be of service, your lordship," said the hawk-nosed little sorcerer.

In a quiet sitting room in the palace, His Grace the Archbishop introduced Lord Darcy to a tall, lean man with pale features and light brown hair brushed straight back from a broad, high forehead. He had gray-blue eyes and an engaging smile.

"Lord Darcy," said the Archbishop, "may I present Sir Thomas Leseaux."

"It is a pleasure to meet your lordship," said Sir Thomas with a smile.

"The pleasure is mine," said Lord Darcy. "I have read with great interest your popularization, 'Symbolism, Mathematics, and Magic.' I am afraid your more technical work is beyond me."

"You are most kind, my lord."

"Unless you need me," said the Archbishop, "I shall leave you two gentlemen alone. I have some pressing matters at hand."

"Certainly, Your Grace," said Lord Darcy.

When the door had closed behind His Grace, Lord Darcy waved Sir Thomas to a chair. "No one knows you're meeting me here, I trust?" he said.

"Not if I can help it, my lord," said Sir Thomas. There was a wry smile on his lips and one eyebrow lifted slightly. "Aside from the fact that I might get my throat cut, I would lose my effectiveness as a double agent if the Brotherhood found that I was having an appointment with a King's Officer. I used the tunnel that goes from the crypt in the Cathedral to the Palace cellars to get here."

"You might have been seen going into the church."

"That wouldn't bother them, my lord," Sir Thomas said with a negligent flip of one hand. "Since the Society was outlawed, we're expected to dissemble. No use calling attention to oneself by staying away from church, even if we don't believe in Christianity." His smile twisted again. "After all, why not? If a man can be expected to pretend to belief in pagan Druidism, to verbally denounce the Christian faith in grubby little meetings of fanatics, then why shouldn't those pagans pretend to the Christian faith for the same reason—to cover up their real activities. The only difference is in whether one is on one side of the law or the other."

"I should think," said Lord Darcy, "that the difference would be in whether one was for or against King and Country."

"No, no." Sir Thomas shook his head briskly. "That's where you err, my lord. The Holy Society of Ancient Albion is as strongly for King and Country as you or I."

Lord Darcy reached into his belt pouch, took out a porcelain pipe and a package of tobacco, and began to fill the bowl. "Elucidate, Sir Thomas. I am eager to hear details of the Society—both operational data and theory."

"Theory, then, my lord. The Society is comprised of those who believe that these islands have a Destiny—with an upper-case D—to bring peace and contentment to all mankind. In order to do this, we must return to the practices and beliefs of the original inhabitants of the islands—the Keltic peoples who had them by right at the time of the Caesarian invasion of 55 B.C."

"*Were* the Kelts the aborigines of these islands?" Lord Darcy asked.

"My lord, bear with me," Sir Thomas said carefully. "I am trying to give you what the Society officially believes.

In judging human behavior, one must go by what an individual *believes* is true—not by what is *actually* true."

Lord Darcy fired up his pipe and nodded. "I apologize. Continue."

"Thank you, my lord. These practices to which I refer are based upon a pantheistic theology. God is not just a Trinity, but an Infinity. The Christian outlook, they hold, is true but limited. God is One—true. He is more than Three in One, however; He is Infinity in One. They hold that the Christian belief in the Three Persons of God is as false—and as true—as the statement: 'There are three grains of sand on the beaches of England.'" He spread his hands. "The world is full of spirits—trees, rocks, animals, objects of all kinds—all full of . . . well, call it spirit for want of a better word. Further, each spirit is intelligent—often in ways that we can't fathom, but intelligent, nonetheless. Each is an individual, and may be anywhere on the spectrum from 'good' to 'evil.' Some are more powerful than others. Some, like dryads, are firmly linked to a specific piece of material, just as a man is linked to his body. Others are 'free spirits'—what we might call 'ghosts,' 'demons,' and 'angels.' Some—most, in fact—can be controlled; some directly, some indirectly, through other spirits. They can be appeased, bribed, and threatened.

"Now the ancient Britons knew all the secrets for appeasing these spirits—or bribing or controlling them—whatever you want. So, it appears, do the Brotherhood of Druids—the inner circle of the Society. At least, so they tell the lesser members. Most of them are of The Blood, as they call it—people from Scotland, Ireland, Wales, Brittany, the Orkneys, the Isle of Man, and so on. Pure Keltic—or so they claim. But those of Anglo-Saxon, Norman, or Frankish descent are allowed in occasionally. No others need apply.

"Don't get the idea they're not for Country, my lord. They are. We're meant to rule the world eventually. The King of the British Isles is destined to be ruler of an empire that will cover the globe. And the King himself? He's the protection, the hex shield, the counter-charm that keeps the hordes of 'bad spirits' from taking over and making life miserable for everybody. The King keeps the storms in place, prevents earthquakes, keeps pestilence and plague away, and, in general, protects his subjects from harm.

"For King and for Country, my lord—but not in exactly the way you or I think of it . . ."

"Interesting," Lord Darcy said thoughfully. "How do they explain away such things as the storms and frosts that *do* hit Britain?"

"Well, that's His Majesty's fault, you see," said Sir Thomas. "If the Sovereign does not comport himself properly, in other words, if he doesn't follow the Old Faith and do things by the Druidic rules, then the Evil Ones can get through the defenses."

"I see. And one of those rules is that His Majesty must allow his life to be taken any time the Brotherhool feels like it?"

"That's not quite fair, my lord," Sir Thomas said. "Not 'anytime they feel like it'—only when danger threatens. Or every seventh year, whichever comes first."

"What about other sacrifices?"

Sir Thomas frowned. "So far as I know, there have been no human deaths. But every one of their meetings involves the ritual killing of an animal of some kind. It depends upon the time of year and the purpose of the meeting, whether one animal or another is sacrificed."

"All of which is quite illegal," Lord Darcy said.

"Quite," Sir Thomas said. "My dossiers and reports are all on file with His Grace the Archbishop. As soon as we have all the evidence we need, we will be able to make a clean sweep and round up the whole lot of them. Their pernicious doctrines have gone far enough."

"You speak with some heat, Sir Thomas."

"I do. Superstition, my lord, is the cause of much of the mental confusion among the lower classes. They see what is done every day by sorcerers using scientific processes and are led to believe in every sort of foolishness because they confuse superstition with science. That's why we have hedge magicians, black wizards, witches' and warlocks' covens, and all the rest of that criminal fraternity. A person becomes ill, and instead of going to a proper Healer, he goes to a witch, who may cover a wound with moldy bread and make meaningless incantations or give a patient with heart trouble a tea brewed of foxglove or some such herb which has no symbolic relationship to his trouble at all. Oh, I tell you, my lord, this sort of thing must be stamped out!"

The theoretician had dropped his attitude of bored irony. He evidently felt quite strongly about the matter, Lord Darcy decided. Licensed Healers, of course, used various herbs and drugs on occasion, but always with scientific precision according to the Laws of Magic; for the most part, however, they relied on the Laying on of Hands, the symbol of their Healing Art. A man took his life in his hands whenever he trusted his health to anyone but a priestly Healer or took his pains and ills to anyone who operated outside the Church.

"I have no doubt of the necessity of clearing up the whole Society, Sir Thomas," said Lord Darcy, "but unless you intend to notify His Majesty the King that the time to strike is near, I fear I cannot wait for the gathering in of the net. I am looking specifically for the murderer of Lord Camberton."

Sir Thomas stood up and thrust his hands into his coat pockets while he stared moodily at a tapestry on the wall. "I've been wondering about that ever since I heard of Lord Camberton's death."

"About what?"

"About the woad dye—I presume it *was* woad, my lord?"

"It was."

"It points clearly toward the Society, then. Some of the Inner Circle have the Talent—poorly trained and misused, but a definite Talent. There is nothing more pitiful in this world, my lord, than to see the Talent misused. It is criminal!"

Lord Darcy nodded in agreement. He knew the reason for Sir Thomas' anger. The theoretician did not, himself, possess the Talent to any marked degree. He theorized; others did his laboratory work. He proposed experiments; others, trained sorcerers, carried them out. And yet Sir Thomas wished passionately that he could do his own experimenting. To see another misuse what he himself did not have, Lord Darcy thought, must be painful indeed to Sir Thomas Leseaux.

"The trouble is," Sir Thomas went on, "that I can give you no clue. I know of no plot to kill Lord Camberton. I know of no reason why the Society should want him dead. That does not mean, of course, that no such reason exists."

"He, was not, then, investigating any of the activities of the Society?"

"Not that I know of. Of course, he may have been investigating the private activities of someone connected with the Society."

Lord Darcy looked thoughtfully at the smoldering tobacco in the bowl of his pipe. "And that hypothetical someone used the resources of the Society to rid himself of whatever exposure Lord Camberton might have threatened?" he suggested.

"It's possible," Sir Thomas said. "But in that case the person would have to be rather high up in the Inner Circle. And even then I doubt that they would do murder for a private reason."

"It needn't have been a private reason. Suppose Camberton had found that someone in this city was a Polish agent, but did not know he was connected with the Society. Then what?"

"It's possible," Sir Thomas repeated. He turned away from his inspection of the tapestry and faced Lord Darcy. "If that were the case, then he and other Polish agents might do away with Lord Camberton. But that gets us no further along, my lord. After months of work, I still have no evidence that any one of the Inner Circle is, in fact, a Polish agent. Further, out of the seven members of the Inner Circle, there are still at least three I cannot identify at all."

"They remain hidden?"

"In a way. At the meetings, the members wear a white gown and hood, similar to a monastic habit, while the Inner

Circle wear green gowns and hoods that completely cover the head, with a pair of eyeholes cut in them. No one knows who they are, presumably. I have positively identified four of them and am fairly certain of a fifth."

"Then why did you say there were at least three you could not identify? Why the qualification?"

Sir Thomas smiled. "They are shrewd men, my lord. Seven of them always appear for the functions. But there are more than seven. Possibly as many as a dozen. At any given meeting, seven wear green and the remainder wear white. They switch around, so that those not of the Inner Circle are led to believe that Master So-and-So is not a member of the Circle because they have seen him at meetings wearing common white."

"I take it, then, that the complete membership never attends any given meeting," said Lord Darcy. "Otherwise the process of elimination would eventually give the whole trick away."

"Exactly, my lord. One is notified as to date, time, and place."

"Where do they usually take place?"

"In the woods, my lord. There are several groves nearby. Perfectly safe. There are guards posted round the meeting, ready to sound the alarm if Men-at-Arms should come. And no ordinary person would come anywhere near or say a word about it to the King's Officers; they're frightened to death of the Society."

"You say there are always seven. Why seven, I wonder?"

Sir Thomas gave a sardonic chuckle. "Superstition again, my lord. It is supposed to be a mystic number. Any apprentice sorcerer could tell them that only the number five has any universal symbolic significance."

"So I understand," said Lord Darcy. "Inanimate nature tends to avoid fiveness."

"Precisely, my lord. There are no five-sided crystals. Even the duo-decahedron, a regular solid with twelve pentagonal faces, does not occur naturally. I will not bore you with abstruse mathematics, but if my latest theorems hold true, the hypothetical 'basic building blocks' of the material universe—whatever they may be—cannot occur in aggregates of five. A universe made of such aggregates would go to pieces in a minute fraction of a second." He smiled. "Of course such 'building blocks,' if they exist, must remain forever hypothetical, since they would have to be so small that no one could see them under the most powerful microscope. As well try to see a mathematical point on a mathematical line. These are symbolic abstractions which are all very well to work with, but their material existence is highly doubtful."

"I understand. But then living things—?"

"Living things show fiveness. The starfish. Many flowers. The fingers and toes of the human extremities. Five is a very potent number to work with, my lord, as witness the use of the pentacle or pentagram in many branches of thaumaturgy. Six also has its uses; the word 'hex' comes from 'hexagon,' as in the Seal of Solomon. But that is because of the prevalence of the hexagon in nature, both animate and inanimate. Snowflakes, honeycombs, and so on. It hasn't the power of five, but it is useful. Seven, however, is almost worthless; its usefulness is so limited as to be nearly nil. Its use in the Book of the Apocalypse of St. John the Divine is a verbal symbology which—" He stopped abruptly with a wry smile. "Pardon me, my lord. I find that I tend to fall into a pedagogical pattern if I don't watch myself."

"Not at all. I am interested," Lord Darcy said. "The question I have in mind, however, is this: It is possible that Lord Camberton was the victim of some bizarre sacrificial rite?"

"I . . . don't . . . know." Sir Thomas spoke slowly, thoughtfully. He frowned for a moment in thought, then said: "It's possible, I suppose. But it would indicate that Lord Camberton himself was a member of the Inner Circle."

"How so?"

"He would have had to go *willingly* to his death. Otherwise the sacrifice would be worthless. Granted, there has been an attempt of late—fomented by Polish agents—to make an exception in the case of the King. But it hasn't taken hold very strongly. Most of these people, my lord, are misguided fanatics—but they are quite sincere. To change a tenet like that is not as easy as King Casimir IX seems to think. If His Slavonic Majesty were to be told that a marriage, in which the bride was forced to make her responses against her will at gun-point, was a true sacrament, he would be shocked that anyone could believe such a thing. And yet he seems to think that believers in Druidism can be manipulated into believing something non-Druidic very easily. His Slavonic Majesty is not a fool, but he has his blind spots."

"Is it possible, then," Lord Darcy asked, "that Camberton *was* one of the Inner Circle?"

"I really don't think he was, my lord, but it's certainly possible. Perhaps it would be of benefit to look over my written reports. My Lord Archbishop has copies of all of them."

"An excellent idea, Sir Thomas," said Lord Darcy, rising from his chair. "I want a list of known members and a list of those you suspect." He glanced at his watch. He had two and a half hours yet before his appointment with the family of the late Duke of Kent. That should be time enough.

"This way, your lordship. Their Graces and Sir Andrew will see you now," said the liveried footman. Lord Darcy was escorted down a long hallway toward the room where the family of the late Duke awaited him.

Lord Darcy had met the Duke, his wife, and his son socially. He had not met either the daughter, Lady Anne, or the Duchess' brother, Sir Andrew Campbell-MacDonald.

De Kent himself had been a kindly but austere, rather humorless man, strict in morals but neither harsh nor unforgiving. He had been respected and honored throughout the Empire and especially in his own duchy.

Margaret, Duchess of Kent, was some twenty years younger than her husband, having married the Duke in 1944, when she was twenty-one. She was the second child and only daughter of the late Sir Austin Campbell-MacDonald. Vivacious, witty, clever, intelligent, and still a very handsome woman, she had, for two decades, been a spark of action and life playing before the quieter, more subdued background of her husband. She liked gay parties, good wines, and good food. She enjoyed dancing and riding. She was a member of The Wardens, one of the few women members of that famous London gambling club.

Nonetheless, no breath of scandal had ever touched her. She had carefully avoided any situation that might cast any suspicion of immoral behavior or wrongdoing upon either herself or her family.

There had been two children born of the union: Lord Quentin, nineteen, was the son and heir. Lady Anne, sixteen, was still a schoolgirl, but, according to what Lord Darcy had heard, she was already a beautiful young lady. Both children showed the vivaciousness of their mother, but were quite well-behaved.

The Duchess of Kent's brother, Sir Andrew, was, by repute, an easy-going, charming, witty man who had spent nearly twenty-five years in New England, the northern continent of the New World, and now, nearing fifty, he had been back in England for some five years.

The Dowager Duchess was seated in a brocaded chair. She was a handsome woman with a figure that maturity had ripened but not over-padded and rich auburn hair that showed no touch of gray. The expression on her face showed that she had been under a strain, but her eyes were clear.

Her son, Lord Quentin, stood tall, straight and somber by her side. Heir Apparent to the Ducal Throne of Kent, he was already allowed to assume the courtesy titles of "Your Grace" and "My Lord Duke," although he could not assume control of the government unless and until his position was confirmed by the King.

Standing a short, respectful distance away was Sir Andrew Campbell-MacDonald.

Lord Darcy bowed. "Your Grace Sir Andrew, I am grieved that we should have to meet again under these circumstances. I was, as you know, long an admirer of His late Grace."

"You are most kind, my lord," said the Dowager Duchess.

"I am further grieved," Lord Darcy continued, "that I must come here in an official capacity as well as in a personal capacity to pay my respects to His late Grace."

Young Lord Quentin cleared his throat a little. "No apologies are necessary, my lord. We understand your duty."

"Thank you, Your Grace. I will begin, then, by asking when was the last time any of you saw Lord Camberton alive".

"About three weeks ago," said Lord Quentin. "The latter part of April. He went to Scotland for a holiday."

The Dowager Duchess nodded. "It was a Saturday. That would have been the twenty-fifth."

"That's right," the young Duke agreed. "The twenty-fifth of April. None of us has seen him since. Not alive, I mean. I identified the body positively for the Chief Master-at-Arms."

"I see. Does any of you know of any reason why anyone would want to do away with Lord Camberton?"

Lord Quentin blinked. Before he could say anything, his mother said: "Certainly not. Lord Camberton was a fine and wonderful man."

Lord Quentin's face cleared. "Of course he was. I know of no reason why anyone should want to take his life."

"If I may say so, my lords," said Sir Andrew, "Lord Camberton had, I believe, turned many a malefactor over to the mercies of the King's Justice. I have heard that he was threatened with violence on more than one such occasion, threatened by men who were sentenced to prison after their crimes were uncovered through his efforts. Is it not possible that such a person may have carried out his threat?"

"Eminently possible," Lord Darcy agreed. He had already spoken to Chief Bertram about investigations along those lines. It was routine in the investigation of the death of an Officer of the King's Justice. "That may very likely be the explanation. But I am, naturally, bound to explore every avenue of investigation."

"You are not suggesting, my lord," the Dowager Duchess said coldly, "that anyone of the House of Kent was involved in this dreadful crime?"

"I suggest nothing, Your Grace," Lord Darcy replied. "It is not my place to suggest; it is my duty to discover facts. When all the facts have been brought to light, there will be no need to make suggestions or innuendoes. The truth, whatever it may be, always points in the right direction."

"Of course," said the Duchess softly. "You must forgive me, my lord; I am overwrought."

"You must forgive my sister, my lord," Sir Andrew said smoothly, "her nerves are not of the best."

"I can speak for myself, Andrew," the Dowager Duchess said, closing her eyes for a moment. "But my brother is right, Lord Darcy," she added. "I have not been well of late."

"Pray forgive me, Your Grace," Lord Darcy said gently. "I have no desire to upset you at so trying a time. I think I have no further questions at the moment. Consider my official duties to be at an end for the time being. Is there any way in which I can serve you personally?"

She closed her eyes again. "Not at the moment, my lord, though it is most kind of you to offer. Quentin?"

"Nothing at the moment," Lord Quentin repeated. "If there is any way in which you can help, my lord, rest assured that I will inform you."

"Then, with Your Graces' permission, I shall take my leave. Again, my apologies."

As he walked down the corridor that led toward the great doorway, escorted by the seneschal, Lord Darcy was suddenly confronted by a young girl who stepped out of a nearby doorway. He recognized her immediately; the resemblance to her mother was strong.

"Lord Darcy?" she said in a clear young voice. "I am Lady Anne." She offered her hand.

Lord Darcy smiled just a little and bowed. The kissing of young ladies' hands was now considered a bit old-fashioned, but Lady Anne, at sixteen, evidently felt quite grown up and wanted to show it.

But when he took her hand, he knew that was not the reason. He touched his lips to the back of her hand. "I am honored, my lady," he said as he dexterously palmed the folded paper she had held.

"I am sorry I could not welcome you, my lord," she said calmly, "but I have not been well. I have a terrible headache."

"Perfectly all right, my lady. I trust you will soon be feeling better."

"Thank you, my lord. Until then—" And she walked on past him. Lord Darcy went on without turning, but he knew that one of the three he had left in the room behind him had opened the door and observed the exchange between himself and Lady Anne.

Not until he had left the main gates of the Ducal Palace did he look at the slip of paper.

It said:

"My lord, I must speak with you. Meet me at the Cathedral, near the Shrine of St. Thomas, at six. *Please!*"

It was signed "Anne of Kent."

At five thirty, Lord Darcy was sitting in his rooms in the Archiepiscopal Palace listening to Master Sean make his report.

"Master Timothy and I checked the locks and bars on the cabinetmaker's shop doors and windows, just as you instructed, my lord. Good spells they are, my lord; solid, competent work. Of course, I could have opened any one of 'em myself, but it would take a sorcerer who knew his stuff. No ordinary thief could have done it, nor an amateur sorcerer."

"What condition are they in, then?" Lord Darcy asked.

"As far as Master Timothy and myself could tell, not a one of 'em had been broken. O' course, that doesn't mean that they hadn't been tampered with. Just as a good locksmith can open a lock and relock it again without leaving any trace, so a good sorcerer could have opened those spells and re-set 'em without leaving a trace. But it would take a top-flight man, my lord."

"Indeed." Lord Darcy looked thoughtful. "Have you checked the Guild Register, Sean?"

Master Sean smiled. "First thing I did, my lord. According to the Register of the Sorcerer's Guild, there is only one man in Canterbury who has the necessary skill to do the job —aside from meself, that is."

"That exception is always granted, my good Sean," said Lord Darcy with a smile, "Only one? Then obviously—"

"Exactly, my lord. Master Timothy himself."

Lord Darcy nodded with satisfaction and tapped the dottle from his pipe. "Very good. I will see you later, Master Sean. I must do a little more investigating. We need more facts."

"Where are you going to look for them, my lord?"

"In church, Master Sean; in church."

As his lordship walked out, Master Sean gazed after him in perplexity. What had he meant by that?

"Maybe," Master Sean murmured to himself, half in jest, "he's going to pray that the Almighty will tell him who did it."

The Cathedral was almost empty. Two women were praying at the magnificently jeweled Shrine of St. Thomas Becket, and there were a few more people at other shrines. In spite of the late evening sun, the ancient church was dim within; the sun's rays came through the stained glass windows almost horizontally, illuminating the walls but leaving the floor in comparative darkness.

St. Thomas was still a popular saint. The issues for which he had fought and died eight centuries before were very dead issues indeed. Even the question of whether Henry II, the first Plantagenet King, had been intentionally involved in the death of Archbishop Thomas was now of interest only to historians and would probably never be settled. After his near-death from a crossbow bolt at the Siege of Chaluz, Richard the Lion Hearted had taken pains to exonerate his father, even though he had fought with old Henry till the day of his death. Young Arthur—the "Good King Arthur" who was so often confused in popular legend with Arthur of Camelot—had, as grandson of Henry II, probably done a bit of white-washing, too. It matters little now. Arthur's decendants, including the present John IV, held on to the Empire that Henry had founded.

Henry II had his place in history as Thomas had his in Heaven.

As he neared the shrine, Lord Darcy saw that one of the two kneeling women was Lady Anne. He stopped a few yards away and waited. When the girl rose from prayer, she looked around, saw Lord Darcy, and came directly toward him.

"Thank you for coming, my lord," she said in a low voice. "I'm sorry I had to meet you this way. The family thought it would be better for me not to talk to you because they think I'm being a silly hero-worshiping girl. But that's not so, really—though I *do* think you're just wonderful." She was looking up at him with wide eyes. "You see, my lord, I know all about you. Lady Yvonne is a schoolmate of mine. She says you're the best Investigator in the Empire."

"I try to be, my lady," Lord Darcy said. He had not spoken more than a score of words to Yvonne, daughter of the Marquis of Rouen, but evidently she had been smitten by a schoolgirl crush—and from the look in Lady Anne's eyes, the disease was contagious.

"I think the sooner you solve the murder of Lord Camberton, the better for everyone, don't you?" Lady Anne asked. "I prayed to St. Thomas to help you. He ought to know something about murders, oughtn't he?"

"I should think so, yes, my lady," Lord Darcy admitted. "Do you feel that I will need special intercession by St. Thomas to solve this problem?"

Lady Anne blinked, startled—then she saw the gleam of humor in the tall man's steel-gray eyes. She smiled back. "I don't think so, my lord, but one should never take things for granted. Besides, St. Thomas won't help you unless you really need it."

"I blush, my lady," Lord Darcy said without doing so. "I assure you there is no professional jealousy between St. Thomas and myself. Since I work in the interests of justice, Heavenly intervention often comes to my assistance, whether I ask for it or not."

Looking suddenly serious, she said: "Does Heaven never interfere with your work? In the interest of Divine Mercy, I mean?"

"Perhaps, sometimes," Lord Darcy admitted somberly. "But I should not call it 'interference'; I should call it, rather, an 'illumination of compassion'—if you follow me, my lady."

She nodded. "I think I do. Yes, I think I do. I'm glad to hear you say so, my lord."

The thought flashed through Lord Darcy's mind that Lady Anne suspected someone—someone she hoped would not be punished. But was that necessarily true? Might it not simply be compassion on her own part?

Wait and see, Lord Darcy cautioned himself. *Wait and see.*

"The reason I wanted to talk to you, my lord," Lady Anne said in a low voice, "is that I think I found a Clue."

Lord Darcy could almost hear the capital letter. "Indeed, my lady? Tell me about it."

"Well, *two* Clues, really," she said, dropping her voice still further to a conspiratorial whisper. "The first one is something I saw. I saw Lord Camberton on the night of the eleventh, last Monday, when he came back from Scotland."

"Come, this is most gratifying!" Lord Darcy's voice was a brisk whisper. "When and where, my lady?"

"At the castle, at home. It was very late—nearly midnight, for the bells struck shortly afterward. I couldn't sleep. Father was so ill, and I—" She stopped and swallowed, forcing back tears. "I was worried and couldn't sleep. I was looking out the window—my rooms are on the second floor—and I saw him come in the side entrance. There's a gas lamp there that burns all night. I saw his face clearly."

"Do you know what he did after he came in?"

"I don't know, my lord. I thought nothing of it. I stayed in my rooms and finally went to sleep."

"Did you ever see Lord Camberton alive again?"

"No, my lord. Nor dead either, if it comes to that. Was he *really* painted blue, my lord?"

"Yes, my lady, he was." He paused, then: "What was the other clue, my lady?"

"Well, I don't know if it means anything. I'll leave that for you to judge. Last Monday night, when Lord Camberton came home, he was carrying a green cloak folded across his arm. I noticed it particularly because he was wearing a dark blue cloak and I wondered why he needed two cloaks."

Lord Darcy's eyes narrowed just a trifle. "And—?"

"And yesterday . . . well, I wasn't feeling very well, you understand, my lord. My father and I were very close, my lord, and—" Again she stopped for a moment to fight back tears. "At any rate, I was just walking through the halls. I wanted to be alone for a while. I was in the West Wing. It's unused, except for guests, and there's no one there at the present time. I smelled smoke—a funny odor, not like wood or coal burning. I tracked the smell to one of the guests rooms. Someone had built a fire in the fireplace, and I thought that was odd, for yesterday was quite mild and sunny, like today. There was still smoke coming from the ashes, though they had been all stirred up. The smoke smelled like cloth burning, and I thought *that* was very odd, too, so I poked about a bit—and I found *this!*" With a flourish, she took something from the purse at her belt, holding it out to Lord Darcy between thumb and forefinger.

"I think, my lord, that one of the servants at the castle knows something about Lord Camberton's murder!"

She was holding a small piece of green cloth, burnt at the edges.

Master Sean O Lochlainn came into Lord Darcy's room bearing a large box under one arm and a beaming smile on his round Irish face. "I found some, my lord!" he said triumphantly. "One of the draper's shops had a barrel of it. Almost the same color, too."

"Will it work then?" Lord Darcy asked.

"Aye, my lord." He set the box on the nearby table. "It'll take a bit o' doing, but we'll get the results you want. By the by, my lord, I stopped by the hospital at the abbey and spoke to the Healer who performed the autopsy on His late Grace, the Duke. The good Father and the chirurgeon who assisted both agree: His Grace died of natural causes. No traces of poison."

"Excellent! A natural death fits my hypothesis much better than a subtle murder would have." He pointed at the box that Master Sean had put on the table. "Let's have a look at this floc."

Master Sean obediently opened the box. It was filled to the brim with several pounds of fine green fuzz. "That's floc, my lord. It's finely-chopped linen, such as that bit of cloth was made of. It's just lint, is all it is. But it's the only thing that'll serve our purpose." He looked around and spotted the piece of equipment he was looking for. "Ah! I see you got the tumbling barrel."

"Yes. My Lord Archbishop was good enough to have one of his coopers make it for us."

The device was a small barrel, with a volume of perhaps a dozen gallons, with a crank at one end, and mounted in a frame so that turning the crank would cause the barrel to rotate. The other end of the barrel was fitted with a tight lid.

Master Sean went over to the closet and took out his large, symbol-decorated carpet bag. He put it on the table and began taking various objects out of it. "Now, this is quite a long process, my lord. Not the simplest thing in the world by any means. Master Timothy Videau prides himself on being able to join a rip in a piece of cloth so that the seam can't be found, but that's a simple bit of magic compared to a job like this. There, all he has to do is make use of the Law of Relevance, and the two edges of a rip in cloth have such high relevance to each other that the job's a snap.

"But this floc, d'ye see, has no direct relevance to the bit o' cloth at all. For this, we have to use the Law of Synecdoche, which says that the part is equivalent to the whole—and contrariwise. Now, let's see. Is everything dry?"

As he spoke, he worked, getting out the instruments and materials he needed for the spells he was about to cast.

It was always a pleasure for Lord Darcy to watch Master Sean at work and listen to his detailed explanations of each step. He had heard much of it countless times before, but there was always something new to be learned each time, something to be stored away in the memory for future reference. Not, of course, that Lord Darcy could make direct use of it himself; he had neither the Talent nor the inclination. But in his line of work, every bit of pertinent knowledge was useful.

"Now, you've seen, my lord," Master Sean went on, "how a bit of amber will pick up little pieces of lint or paper if you rub it with a piece of wool first, or a glass rod will do the same if you rub it with silk. Well, this is much the same process, basically, but it requires patterning and concentration of the power, d'ye see. That's the difficult part. Now, I must have absolute silence for a bit, my lord."

It took the better part of an hour for Master Sean to get the entire experiment prepared to his satisfaction. He dusted the floc and the bit of scorched cloth with powders, muttered incantations, and made symbolic designs in the air with his wand. During it all, Lord Darcy sat in utter silence. It is dangerous to disturb a magician at work.

Finally, Master Sean dumped the box of floc into the barrel and put the bit of green cloth in with the fluffy lint. He clamped the cover on and made more symbolic tracings with his wand while he spoke in a low tone.

Then he said: "Now comes the tedious part, my lord. This is pretty fine floc, but that barrel will still have to be turned for an hour and a half at least. It's a matter of probability, my lord. The damaged edges of the cloth will try to find a bit of floc that is most nearly identical to the one that was there previously. Then that bit of floc finds another that was most like the next one and so on. Now, it's a rule that the finer things are divided, the more nearly identical they become. It is theorized that if a pure substance, such as salt, were to be reduced to its ultimate particles, they'd all be identical. In a gas—but that's neither here nor there. The point is that if I had used, say, pieces of half-inch green thread, I'd have to use tons of the stuff and the tumbling would take days. I won't bore you with the mathematics of the thing. Anyhow, this will take time, so—"

Lord Darcy smiled and raised a hand. "Patience, my dear Sean. I have anticipated you." He thought of how the King had done the same to him only the day before. He pulled a bell rope.

A knock came at the door and when Lord Darcy said "Come in" a young monk clad in novice's robes entered timidly.

"Brother Daniel, I think?" said his lordship.

"Y-yes, my lord."

"Brother Daniel, this is Master Sean. Master Sean, the Novice Master informs me that Brother Daniel is guilty of a minor infraction of the rules of his Order. His punishment is to be a couple of hours of monotonous work. Since you are a licensed sorcerer, and therefore privileged, it is lawful for a lay brother to accept punishment from you if he so wills it. What say you, Brother Daniel?"

"Whatever my lord says," the youth said humbly.

"Excellent. I leave Brother Daniel to your care, Master Sean. I shall return in two hours. Will that be plenty of time?"

"Plenty, my lord. Sit down on this tool, Brother. All you have to do is turn this crank—slowly, gently, but steadily. Like this. That's it. Fine. Now, no talking. I'll see you later, my lord."

When Lord Darcy returned, he was accompanied by Sir Thomas Leseaux. Brother Daniel was thanked and dismissed from his labors.

"Are you ready, Master Sean?" Lord Darcy asked.

"Ready, indeed, my lord. Let's have a look at it, shall we?"

Lord Darcy and Sir Thomas watched with interest as Master Sean opened the end of the barrel.

The tubby little sorcerer drew on a pair of thin leather gloves. "Can't get it damp, you see," he said as he put his hands into the end of the wooden cylinder, "nor let it touch metal. Falls apart if you do. Come out, now . . . easy . . . easy . . . ahhhhh!"

Even as he drew it out, tiny bits of floc floated away from

the delicate web of cloth he held. For what he held was no longer a mass of undifferentiated floc; it had acquired texture and form. It was a long robe of rather fuzzy green linen, with an attached hood. There were eyeholes in the front of the hood so that if it were brought down over the head the wearer could still see out.

Carefully, the round little Irish sorcerer put the reconstituted robe on the table. Lord Darcy and Sir Thomas looked at it without touching it.

"No question of it," Sir Thomas said after a moment. "The original piece came from one of the costumes worn by the Seven of the Society of Albion." Then he looked at the sorcerer. "A beautiful bit of work, Master Sorcerer. I don't believe I've ever seen a finer reconstruction. Most of them fall apart if one tries to lift them. How strong is it?"

"About that of a soft tissue paper, sir. Fortunately, the weather has been dry lately. In damp weather"—he smiled—"well, it's more like damp tissue paper."

"Elegantly put, Master Sean," said Sir Thomas with a smile.

"Thank you, Sir Thomas." Master Sean whipped out a tape measure and proceeded to go over the reconstituted garment carefully, jotting down the numbers in his notebook. When he was through, he looked at Lord Darcy. "That's about it, my lord. Will we be needing it any further?"

"I think not. In itself it does not constitute evidence; besides, it would dissolve long before we could take it to court."

"That's so, my lord." He picked up the flimsy garment by the left shoulder, where the original scrap of material was located, and lowered most of the hooded cloak into the box which had held the floc. Then, still holding to the original bit of cloth with gloved thumb and forefinger, he touched the main body of the cloak with a silver wand. With startling suddenness, the material slumped into a pile of formless lint again, leaving the original cloth scrap in Master Sean's fingers.

"I'll file this away, my lord," he said.

Three days later, on Friday the twenty-second, Lord Darcy found himself becoming impatient. He wrote more on the first draft of the report which would eventually be sent to His Majesty and reviewed what he had already written. He didn't like it. Nothing new had come up. No new clues, no new information of any kind. He was still waiting for a report from Sir Angus MacReady in Edinburgh, hoping that would clear matters up. So far, nothing.

His late Grace, the Duke of Kent had been buried on Thursday, with My Lord Archbishop officiating at the Requiem Mass. Half the nobility of the Empire had been there, as had His Majesty. And Lord Darcy had induced My Lord Archbishop to allow him to sit in choir in the sanctuary so that he could watch the faces of those who came. Those faces had told him almost nothing.

Sir Thomas Leseaux had information that showed that either Lord Camberton himself or Sir Andrew Campbell-MacDonald or both were very likely members of the Society of Albion. But that proved nothing; it was extremely possible that one or both might have been agents sent in by the Duke himself.

"The question, good Sean," he had said to the tubby little Irish sorcerer on Thursday afternoon, "remains as it was on Monday. Who killed Lord Camberton and why? We have a great deal of data, but they are, thus far, unexplained data. Why was Lord Camberton placed in the Duke's coffin? When was he killed? Where was he between the time he was killed and the time he was found?

"Why was Lord Camberton carrying a green costume? Was it the same one that was burnt on Monday? If so, why did whoever burnt it wait until Monday afternoon to destroy it? The green habit would have fit either Lord Camberton or Sir Andrew, both of whom are tall men. It certainly did not belong to any of the de Kents; the tallest is Lord Quentin, and he is a good six inches too short to have worn that outfit without tripping all over the hem.

"I am deeply suspicious, Sean; I don't like the way the evidence is pointing."

"I don't quite follow you, my lord," Master Sean had said.

"Attend. You have been out in the city; you have heard

what people are saying. You have seen the editorials in the *Canterbury Herald.* The people are convinced that Lord Camberton was murdered by the Society of Albion. The clue of the woad was not wasted upon Goodman Smith, the proverbial average man.

"And what is the result? The members of the Society are half scared to death. Most of them are pretty harmless people, in the long run; belonging to an illegal organization gives them the naughty feeling a little boy gets when he's stealing apples. But now the Christian community is up in arms against the pagans, demanding that something be done. Not just here, but all over England, Scotland, and Wales.

"Lord Camberton wasn't killed as a sacrifice, willing or otherwise. He'd have been disposed of elsewhere—buried in the woods, most likely.

"He was killed somewhere inside the curtain wall of Castle Canterbury, and it was murder—not sacrifice. Then why the woad?"

"As a preservative spell, my lord," Master Sean had said. "The ancient Britons knew enough about symbolism to realize that the arrowhead leaves of the woad plant could be used protectively. They wore woad into battle. What they didn't know, of course, was that the protective spells don't work that way. They—"

"Would you use woad for a protective spell, as a preservative to prevent decomposition of a body?" interrupted Lord Darcy.

"Why . . . no, my lord. There are much better spells, as you know. Any woad spell would take quite a long time, and the body has to be thoroughly covered. Besides, such spells aren't very efficient."

"Then why was it used?"

"Ah! I see your point, my lord!" Master Sean's broad Irish face had suddenly come all over smiles. "Of course! The body was *meant* to be found! The woad was used to throw the blame on the Holy Society of Ancient Albion and divert suspicion from somewhere else. Or, possibly, the entire purpose of the murder was to give the Society a bad time, eh?"

"Both hypotheses have their good points, Master Sean, but we still do not have enough data. We need *facts,* my good Sean. *Facts!*"

And now, nearly twenty-four hours had passed and no new facts had come to light. Lord Darcy dipped his pen in the ink bottle and wrote down that disheartening fact.

The door opened and Master Sean came in, followed almost immediately by a young novice bearing a tray which contained the light luncheon his lordship had asked for. Lord Darcy pushed his papers to one side to indicate where the tray should be placed. Master Sean held out an envelope in one hand. "Special delivery, my lord. From Sir Angus MacReady in Edinburgh."

Lord Darcy reached eagerly for the envelope.

What happened was no one's fault, really. Three people were crowded around the table, each trying to do something, and the young novice, in trying to maneuver the tray, had to move it aside when Master Sean handed over the envelope to Lord Darcy. The corner of the tray caught the neck of the ink bottle, and that theretofore upright little container promptly toppled over on its side and disgorged its contents all over the manuscript Lord Darcy had been working on.

There was a moment of stunned silence, broken by the profuse apologies of the novice. Lord Darcy inhaled slowly, then calmly told the lad that there was no damage done, that he was certainly not at fault, and that Lord Darcy was not the least bit angry. He was thanked for bringing up the tray and dismissed.

"And don't worry about the mess, Brother," Master Sean said. "I shall clean it up myself."

When the novice had left, Lord Darcy looked ruefully at the ink-stained sheets and then at the envelope he had taken from Master Sean's fingers. "My good Sean," he said quietly, "I am not, as you know, a nervous or excitable man. If, however, this envelope does not contain good news and useful information, I shall undoubtedly throw myself on the floor in a raving convulsion of pure fury and chew holes in the rug."

"I shouldn't blame you in the least, my lord," said Master Sean, who knew perfectly well that his lordship would do no such thing. "Go sit down in the easy-chair, my lord, while I do something about this minor catastrophe."

Lord Darcy sat in the big chair near the window. Master Sean brought over the tray and put it on the small table at his lordship's elbow. Lord Darcy munched a sandwich and drank a cup of caffe while he read the report from Edinburgh.

Lord Camberton's movements in Scotland, while not exactly done in a blaze of publicity, had not been gone about furtively by any means. He had gone to certain places and asked certain questions and looked at certain records. Sir Angus had followed that trail and learned what Lord Camberton had learned, although he confessed that he had no notion of what his late lordship had intended to do with that information or what hypothesis he may have been working on or whether the information he had obtained meant anything, even to Lord Camberton.

His lordship had visited, among other places, the Public Records Office and the Church Marriage Register. He had been checking on Margaret Campbell-MacDonald, the present Dowager Duchess of Kent.

In 1941, when she was only nineteen, she had married a man named Chester Lowell, a man of most unsavory antecedents. His father had been imprisoned for a time for embezzlement and had finally drowned under mysterious circumstances. Chester's younger brother, Ivan, had been arrested and tried twice on charges of practicing magic without a license, but had been released both times after a verdict of "Not Proven," and had finally gone up for six years for a confidence game which had involved illegal magic and had been released in 1959. Chester Lowell himself was a gambler of the worst sort, a man who cheated at cards and dice to keep his pockets lined.

After only three weeks of marriage, Margaret had left

Chester Lowell and returned home. Evidently the loss had meant little to Lowell; he did not bother to try to get her back. Six months later, he had fled to Spain under a cloud of suspicion; the authorities in Scotland believed that he had been connected with the disappearance of six thousand sovereigns from a banking house in Glasgow. The evidence against him, however, was not strong enough to extradite him from the protection of the King of Aragon. In 1942, the Aragonese authorities reported that the "Inglés," Chester Lowell, had been shot to death in Zaragoza after an argument over a card game. The Scottish authorities sent an investigator who knew Lowell to identify the body, and the case against him was marked "Closed."

So! thought Lord Darcy, *Margaret de Kent is twice a widow.*

There had been no children born of her brief union with Lowell. In 1944, after an eight months courtship, Margaret had become the Duchess of Kent. Sir Angus MacReady did not know whether the Duke had been aware then of the previous marriage, or, indeed, whether he had ever known.

Sir Andrew Campbell-MacDonald had also had his history investigated by Lord Camberton. There was certainly nothing shady in his past; he had had a good reputation in Scotland. In 1939, he had gone to New England and had served for a time in the Royal Legion. He had comported himself with honor in three battles against the red aborigines and had left the service with a captain's commission and an excellent record. In 1957, the small village in which he had been living was raided by the red barbarians and burnt to the ground after great carnage, and it had been believed for a time that Sir Andrew had been killed in the raid. He had returned to England in 1959, nearly penniless, his small fortune having vanished as a result of the destruction during the raid. He had been given a minor position and a pension by the Duke of Kent and had lived with his sister and brother-in-law for the past five years.

Lord Darcy put the letter aside and thoughtfully finished

his caffe. He did not look at all as though he were about to have a rug-chewing fit of fury.

"The only thing missing is the magician," he said to himself. "Where is the magician in this? Or, rather, *who* is he? The only sorcerer in plain sight is Master Timothy Videau, and he does not apparently have any close connection with Lord Camberton or the Ducal Palace. Sir Thomas suspects that Sir Andrew might be a member of the Society of Albion, but that does not necessarily mean he knows anything about sorcery."

Furthermore, Lord Darcy was quite certain that Sir Andrew, if he was a member of the Inner Circle, would not draw attention to the Society in such a blatant manner.

"Here is your report, my lord," said Master Sean.

Lord Darcy came out of his reverie to see Master Sean standing by his side with a sheaf of papers in his hand. His lordship had been vaguely aware that the tubby little Irish sorcerer had been at work at the other end of the room, and now it was obvious what he had been doing. Except for a very slight dampness, there was no trace of the ink that had been spilled across the pages, although the clear, neat curves of Lord Darcy's handwriting remained without change. It was, Lord Darcy knew, simply a matter of differentiation by intention. The handwriting had been put there with intention, with purpose, while the spilled ink had got here by accident; thus it was possible for a removal spell to differentiate between them.

"Thank you, my good Sean. As usual, your work is both quick and accurate."

"It would've taken longer if you'd been using these new indelible inks," Master Sean said deprecatively.

"Indeed?" Lord Darcy said absently as he looked over the papers in his hand.

"Aye, my lord. There's a spell cast on the ink itself to make it indelible. That makes it fine for documents and bank drafts and such things as you don't want changed, but it makes it hard as the very Devil to get off after it's been spilled. Master Timothy was telling me that it took him a good two hours to get the stain out of the carpet in the Ducal study a couple of weeks ago."

"No doubt," said Lord Darcy, still looking at his report. Then, suddenly, he seemed to freeze for a second. After a moment, he turned his head slowly and looked up at Master Sean. "Did Master Timothy mention exactly what day that was?"

"Why . . . no, my lord, he didn't."

Lord Darcy put his report aside and rose from his chair. "Come along, Master Sean. We have some important questions to ask Master Timothy Videau—very important."

"About ink, my lord?" Master Sean asked, puzzled.

"About ink, yes. And about something so expensive that he has sold only one of them in Canterbury." He took his blue cloak from the closet and draped it around his shoulders. "Come along, Master Sean."

"So," said Lord Darcy some three-quarters of an hour later, as he and Master Sean strolled through the great gate in the outer curtain wall of Castle Canterbury, "we find that the work was done on the afternoon of May 11th. Now we need one or two more tiny bits of evidence, and the lacunae in my hypothesis will be filled."

They headed straight for Master Walter Gotobed's shop. Master Walter, Journeyman Henry Lavender informed them, was not in at the moment. He and young Tom Wilderspin had taken the cart and mule to deliver a table to a gentleman in the city.

"That is perfectly all right, Goodman Henry," Lord Darcy said. "Perhaps you can help us. Do you have any zebrawood?"

"Zebrawood, my Lord? Why, I think we have a little. Don't get much call for it, my lord. It's very dear, my lord."

"Perhaps you would be so good as to find out how much you have on hand, Goodman Henry? I am particlarly eager to know."

"O' course, my lord. Certainly." The journeyman joiner went back to the huge room at the rear of the shop.

As soon as he had disappeared from sight, Lord Darcy sprang to the rear door of the shop. It had a simple drop bar as a lock; there was no way to open it from the outside. Lord Darcy looked at the sawdust, shavings, and wood chips at his feet. His eye spied the one he wanted. He picked up the wood chip and then lifted the bar of the door and wedged the chip in so that it held the bar up above the two brackets that it fitted in when the door was locked. Then he took a long piece of string from his pocket and looped it over the wood chip. He opened the door and went outside, trailing the two ends of the string under the door. Then he closed the door.

Inside, Master Sean watched closely. The string, pulled by Lord Darcy from outside, tightened. Suddenly the bit of wood was jerked out from between the bar and the door. Now unsupported, the bar fell with a dull thump. The door was locked.

Quickly, Master Sean lifted the bar again, and Lord Darcy re-entered. Neither man said a word, but there was a smile of satisfaction on both their faces.

Journeyman Henry came in a few minutes later; evidently he had not heard the muffled sound of the door bar falling. "We ain't got very much zebrawood, my lord," he said dolefully. "Just scrap. Two three-foot lengths of six-by-three-eights. Leftovers from a job Master Walter done some years ago. We'd have to order it from London or Liverpool, my lord." He put the two boards on a nearby workbench. Even in their unfinished state, the alternate dark and light bands of the wood gave it distinction.

"Oh, there's quite enough there," Lord Darcy said. "What I had in mind was a tobacco humidor. Something functional —plain but elegant. No carving; I want the beauty of the wood to show."

Henry Lavender's eyes lit up. "Quite so, my lord! To be sure, my lord! What particular design did my lord have in mind?"

"I shall leave that up to you and Master Walter. It should be of about two pounds capacity."

After a few minutes, they agreed upon a price and a delivery date. Then: "Oh, by the by, Goodman Henry . . . I believe you had a slip of the memory when I questioned you last Tuesday."

"My lord?" Journeyman Henry looked startled, puzzled, and just a little bit frightened.

"You told me that you locked up tight on Saturday night at half past eight. You neglected to tell me that you were not alone. I put it to you that a gentleman came in just before you locked up. That he asked you for something which you fetched for him. That he went out the front door with you and stood nearby while you locked that door. Is that not so, my good Henry?"

"It's true as Gospel, my lord," said the joiner in awe. "How on Earth did you know that, my lord?"

"Because that is the only way it could have happened."

"That's just how it did happen, my lord. It were Lord Quentin, my lord. That is, the new Duke; he were Lord Quentin then. He asked me for a bit of teak to use as a paperweight. He knew we had a polished piece and he offered to buy it, so I sold it to him. But I never thought nothing wrong of it, my lord!"

"You did nothing wrong, my good Henry—except to forget to tell me that the incident had happened. It is of no consequence, but you should have mentioned it earlier."

"I humbly beg your pardon, my lord. But I don't think nothing of it."

"Of course not. But in future, if you should be asked questions by a King's Officer, be sure to remember details. Next time, it might be more important."

"I'll remember, my lord."

"Very good. Good day to you, Goodman Henry. I shall look forward to seeing that humidor."

Outside the shop, the two men walked across the busy courtyard toward the great gate. Master Sean said: "What if he hadn't had any zebrawood, my lord? How would you have got him out of the shop?"

"I'd have asked for teak," Lord Darcy said dryly. "Now

we must make a teleson call to Scotland. I think that within twenty-four hours I shall be able to make my final report."

There were six people in the room. Margaret, Dowager Duchess of Kent, looked pale and drawn but still regal, still mistress of her own drawing room. Quentin, heir to the Duchy of Kent, stood with somber face near the fireplace, his eyes hooded and watchful. Sir Andrew Campbell-MacDonald stood solemnly by the window, his hands in the pockets of his dress jacket, his legs braced a little apart. Lady Anne sat in a small, straight-backed chair near Sir Andrew. Lord Darcy and Master Sean faced them.

"Again I apologize to Your Graces for intruding upon your bereavement in this manner," Lord Darcy said, "but there is a little matter of the King's Business to be cleared up. A little matter of willful murder. On the 11th of May last, Lord Camberton returned secretly from Scotland after finding some very interesting information—information that, viewed in the proper light, could lend itself very easily to blackmail. Lord Camberton was murdered because of what he had discovered. His body was then hidden away until last Saturday night or early Sunday morning, at which time it was put in the coffin designated for His late Grace, the Duke.

"The information was more than scandalous; if used in the right way, it could be disastrous to the Ducal Family. If someone had offered proof that the first husband of Her Grace the Duchess was still living, she would no longer have any claim to her title, but would still be Margaret Lowell of Edinburgh—and her children would be illegitimate and therefore unable to claim any share in the estates or government of the Duchy of Kent."

As he spoke, the Dowager Duchess walked over to a nearby chair and quietly sat down. Her face remained impassive.

Lord Quentin did not move.

Lady Anne looked as though someone had slapped her in the face.

Sir Andrew merely shifted a little on his feet.

"Before we go any further, I should like you to meet a colleague of mine. Show him in, Master Sean."

The tubby little Irish sorcerer opened the door, and a sharp-faced, sandy-haired man stepped in.

"Ladies and gentlemen," said Lord Darcy, "I should like you to meet Plainclothes Master-at-Arms Alexander Glencannon."

Master Glencannon bowed to the silent four. "Your Graces. Lady Anne. An honor, I assure ye." Then he lifted his eyes and looked straight at Sir Andrew. "Good morrow to ye, Goodman Lowell."

The man who had called himself Sir Andrew merely smiled. "Good morrow, Glencannon. So I'm trapped, am I?"

"If ye wish to put it that way, Lowell."

"Oh, I think not." With a sudden move, Lowell, the erstwhile "Sir Andrew" was behind Lady Anne's chair. One hand, still in his jacket pocket, was thrust against the girl's side. "I would hesitate to attempt to shoot it out with two of His Majesty's Officers, but if there is any trouble about this, the girl dies. You can only hang me once, you know." His voice had the coolness of a man who was used to handling desperate situations.

"Lady Anne," said Lord Darcy in a quiet voice, "do exactly as he says. *Exactly,* do you understand? So must the rest of us." Irritated as he was with himself for not anticipating what Lowell would do, he still had to think and think fast. He was not even certain that Lowell had a gun in that pocket, but he had to assume that a gun was there. He dared not do otherwise.

"Thank you, my lord," Lowell said with a twisted smile. "I trust no one will be so foolish as not to take his lordship's advice."

"What next, then?" Lord Darcy asked.

"Lady Anne and I are leaving. We are walking out the door, across the courtyard, and out the gate. Don't any of you leave here for twenty-four hours. I should be safe by then. If I am, Lady Anne will be allowed to return—unharmed. If there is any hue and cry . . . well, well, there won't be, will there?" His twisted smile widened. "Now clear away from that door. Come, Anne—let's go on a nice trip with your dear uncle."

Lady Anne rose from her chair and went out the door of the room with Lowell, who never took his eyes off the others. He closed the door. "I shouldn't like to hear that door opened before I leave," his voice said from the other side. Then footsteps echoed away down the corridor.

There was another door to the room. Lord Darcy headed for it.

"No! Let him go!"

"He'll kill Anne, you fool!"

Lord Quentin and the Duchess both spoke at once.

Lord Darcy ignored them. "Master Sean! Master Alexander! See that these people are kept quiet and that they do not leave the room until I return!" And then he was out the door.

Lord Darcy knew all the ins and outs of Castle Canterbury. He had made a practice of studying the plans to every one of the great castles of the Empire. He ran down a corridor and then went up a stone stairway, taking the steps two at a time. Up and up he went, flight after flight of stairs, heading for the battlements atop the great stone edifice.

On the roof, he paused for breath. He looked out over the battlement wall. Sixty feet below, he saw Lowell and Lady Anne, walking across the courtyard—slowly, so as to attract no attention from the crowds of people. They were scarcely a quarter of the way across.

Lord Darcy raced for the curtain wall.

Here, the wall was only six feet wide. He was protected from being seen from below by the crenelated walls on either side of the path atop the greater curtain wall. At a crouch, he ran for the tower that topped the great front gate. There was no one to stop him; no soldiers walked these battlements; the castle had not been attacked for centuries.

Inside the gate tower was the great portcullis, a vast mass of crossed iron bars that could be lowered rapidly in case of attack. It was locked into place now, besides being held up by the heavy counterweight in the deep well below the gate entrance.

Lord Darcy did not look over the wall to see where his quarry was now. He should be in front of them, and if he was, Lowell might—just might—glance up and see him. He couldn't take that chance.

He did not take the stairs. He went down the shaft that held the great chain that connected the portcullis to its counterweight, climbing down the chain hand over hand to the flagstone sixty feet beneath him.

There was no guardsman in the chamber below during the day, for which Lord Darcy was profoundly grateful. He had no time to answer questions or to try to keep an inquisitive soldier quiet.

There were several times when he feared that his life, not Lady Anne's, would be forfeit this day. The chain was kept well oiled and in readiness, even after centuries of peace, for such was the ancient law and custom. Even with his legs wrapped around the chain and his hands gripping tightly, he slipped several times, burning his palms and thighs and calves. The chain, with its huge, eight-inch links, was as rigid as an iron bar, held taut by the great pull of the massive counterweight below.

The chain disappeared through a foot-wide hole that led to the well beneath where the counterweight hung. Lord Darcy swung his feet wide and dropped lightly to the flagstoned floor.

Then, cautiously, he opened the heavy oak door just a crack.

Had Lowell and the girl already passed?

Of the two chains that held up the great portcullis, Lord Darcy had taken the one that would put him on the side of the gate to Lowell's left. The gun had been in Lowell's right hand, and—

They walked by the door, Lady Anne first, Lowell following slightly behind. Lord Darcy flung open the door and hurled himself across the intervening space.

His body slammed into Lowell's, hurling the man aside, pushing his gun off the girl's body, just before the gun went off with a roar.

The two men tumbled to the pavement and people scattered as they rolled over and over, fighting for possession of the firearm.

Guardsmen rushed out of their places, converging on the struggling figures.

They were too late. The gun went off a second time.

For a moment, both men lay still.

Then, slowly, Lord Darcy got to his feet, the gun in his hand.

Lowell was still conscious, but there was a widening stain of red on his left side. "I'll get you Darcy," he said in a hoarse whisper. "I'll get you if it's the last thing I do."

Lord Darcy ignored him and faced the guardsmen who had surrounded them. "I am Lord Darcy, Investigator on a Special Commission from His Majesty's Court of Chivalry," he told them. "This man is under arrest for willful murder. Take charge of him and get a Healer quickly."

The Dowager Duchess and Lord Quentin were still waiting when Lord Darcy brought Lady Anne back to the Palace.

The girl rushed into the Duchess' arms. "Oh, Mama! Mama! Lord Darcy saved my life! He's wonderful! You should have seen him!"

The Duchess looked at Lord Darcy. "I am grateful to you, my lord. You have saved my daughter's life. But you have ruined it. Ruined us all.

"No, let me speak," she said as Lord Darcy started to say something. "It has come out, now. I may as well explain.

"Yes, I thought my first husband was dead. You can imagine how I felt when he showed up again five years ago.

What could I do? I had no choice. He assumed the identity of my dead brother, Andrew. No one here had ever seen either of them, so that was easy. Not even my husband the Duke knew. I could not tell him.

"Chester did not ask much. He did not try to bleed me white as most blackmailers would have. He was content with the modest position and pension my husband granted him, and he behaved himself with decorum. He—" She stopped suddenly, looking at her son, who had become pale.

"I . . . I'm sorry, Quentin," she said softly. "Truly I am. I know how you feel, but—"

Lord Quentin cut his mother short. "Do you mean, Mother, that it was Uncle An . . . *that man* who was blackmailing you?"

"Why, yes."

"And Father didn't know? No one was blackmailing Father?"

"Of course not! How could they? Who—?"

"Perhaps," said Lord Darcy quietly, "you had best tell your mother what you thought had happened on the night of May 11th."

"I heard a quarrel," Lord Quentin said, apparently in a daze. "In Father's study. There was a scuffle, a fight. It was hard to hear through the door. I knocked, but everything had become quiet. I opened the door and went in. Father was lying on the floor, unconscious. Lord Camberton was on the floor nearby—dead—a letter opener from Father's desk in his heart."

"And you found a sheaf of papers disclosing the family skeleton in Lord Camberton's hand."

"Yes."

"Further, during the struggle, a bottle of indelible ink had fallen over, and Lord Camberton's body was splashed with it."

"Yes, yes. It was all over his face. But how did you know?"

"It is my business to know these things," Lord Darcy said. "Let me tell the rest of it. You assumed immediately that

Lord Camberton had been attempting to blackmail your father on the strength of the evidence he had found."

"Yes. I heard the word 'blackmail' through the door."

"So you assumed that your father had attacked Lord Camberton with the letter opener and then, because of his frail health, fallen in a swoon to the floor. You knew that you had to do something to save the family honor and save your father from the silken noose.

"You had to get rid of the body. But where? Then you remembered the preservator you had bought."

Lord Quentin nodded. "Yes. Father gave me the money. It was to have been a present for Mother. She sometimes likes a snack during the day, and we thought it would be convenient if she could have a preservator full of food in her rooms instead of having to call to the kitchen every time."

"Quite so," said Lord Darcy. "So you put Lord Camberton's body in it. Master Timothy Videau has explained to me that the spell cast upon the wooden chest keeps a preservative spell on whatever is kept within, so long as the door is closed. Lord Camberton was supposed to be in Scotland, so no one would miss him. Your father never completely recovered his senses after that night, so he said nothing.

"Actually, he probably never knew. I feel he probably collapsed when Lord Camberton, who had been sent to Scotland by your father for that purpose, confirmed the terrible blackmail secret. Lowell was there in the room, having been taken in to confront the Duke. When His Grace collapsed, Lord Camberton's attention was diverted for a moment. Lowell grabbed the letter opener and stabbed him. He knew the Duke would say nothing, but Lord Camberton's oath as a King's Officer would force him to arrest Lowell.

"Lowell, by the by, was a member of the Holy Society of Ancient Albion. Camberton had found that out, too. Lowell probably had lodgings somewhere in the city under another name, where he kept his paraphernalia. Camberton discovered it and brought along the green costume Lowell owned for proof. When Lowell talks, we will be able to find out where that secret lodging is.

"He left the room with the Duke and Lord Camberton still on the floor, taking the green robe with him. He may or may not have heard you knock, Lord Quentin. I doubt it, but it doesn't matter. How long did it take you to clean up the room, Your Grace?"

"I . . . I put Father to bed first. Then I cleaned the blood off the floor. I couldn't clean up the spilled ink, though. Then I took Lord Camberton to the cellar and put him in the preservator. We'd put it there to wait for Mother's birthday—which is next week. It was to be a surprise. It—" He stopped.

"How long were you actually in the room?" Lord Darcy repeated.

"Twenty minutes, perhaps."

"We don't know what Lowell was doing during those twenty minutes. He must have been surprised on returning to find the body gone and the room looking tidy."

"He was," said Lord Quentin. "I called Sir Bertram, our seneschal, and Father Joseph, the Healer, and we were all in Father's room when . . . *he* . . . came back. He looked surprised, all right. But I thought it was just shock at finding Father ill."

"Understandable," said Lord Darcy. "Meanwhile, you had to decide what to do with Lord Camberton's body. You couldn't leave it in that perservator forever."

"No. I thought I would get it outside, away from the castle. Let it be found a long ways away, so there would be no connection."

"But there was the matter of the blue inkstain," Lord Darcy said. "You couldn't remove it. You knew that you would have to get Master Timothy, the sorcerer, to remove the stain from the rug, but if the corpse were found later with a similar stain, Master Timothy might be suspicious. So you covered up. Literally. You painted the body with woad."

"Yes. I thought perhaps the blame would fall on the Society of Albion and divert attention from us."

"Indeed. And it very nearly succeeded. Between the use of the preservator and the use of woad, it looked very much like the work of a sorcerer.

"But then came last Monday. It is a holiday in Canterbury, to celebrate the saving of a Duke's life in the Sixteenth Century. A part of the celebration includes a ritual seaching of the castle. Lord Camberton's body would be found."

"I hadn't been able to find a way of getting it out," Lord Quentin said. "I'm not used to that sort of thing. I was becoming nervous about it, but I couldn't get it out of the courtyard without being seen."

"But you had to hide it that day. So you made sure the shop of Master Walter was unlocked on Saturday night and you put the body in the coffin, thinking it would stay there until after the ceremony, after which you could put it back in the preservator.

"Unfortunately—in several senses of the word—your father passed away early Monday morning. The body of Lord Camberton was found."

"Exactly, my lord."

"Lowell must have nearly gone into panic himself when he heard that the body had been found covered with woad. He knew it connected him—especially if anyone knew he was a member of the Society. So, that afternoon, he burnt his green robe in a fireplace, thinking to destroy any evidence that he was linked with the Society. He was not thorough enough."

The Duchess spoke again. "Well, you have found your murderer, my lord. And you have found what my son has done to try to save the honor of our family. But it was all unsuccessful in the end. Chester Lowell, my first husband, still lives. My children are illegitimate and we are penniless."

Master-at-Arms Alexander Glencannon coughed slightly. "Beggin' your pardon, Your Grace, but I'm happy to say you're wrong. I've known those thievin' Lowells for years. 'Twas I who went to Zaragoza back in '42 to identify Chester Lowell. I saw him masael', and 'twas him, richt enow. The resemblance is close, but this one happen tae be his younger brother, Ian Lowell, released from prison in 1959. He was nae a card-sharp, like his brother Chester, but he's a bad 'un, a' the same."

The Dowager Duchess could only gape.

"It was not difficult to do, Your Grace," said Lord Darcy. "Chester had undoubtedly told Ian all about his marriage to you—perhaps even the more intimate details. You had only known Chester a matter of two months. The younger brother looked much like him. How could you have been expected to tell the difference after nearly a quarter of a century? Especially since you did not even know of the existence of the younger Ian."

"Is it true? Can it be true?"

"It is true, Your Grace, in every particular," Lord Darcy said. "You have reason to be thankful to Him. There was no need for Ian Lowell to bleed you white, as you put it. To have done so might have made you desperate—for all he knew, desperate enough to kill him. He might have avoided that by taking money and staying out of your reach, but that was not what he wanted.

"He didn't want money, Your Grace. He wanted protection, a hiding place in such plain sight that no one would think of looking for him there. He wanted a front. He wanted camouflage.

"Actually, he is in a rather high position in the Holy Society of Ancient Albion—a rather lucrative position, since the leaders of the Society are not accountable to the membership for the way they spend the monies paid them by the members. In addition, I have reason to believe that he is in the pay of His Slavonic Majesty, Casimir of Poland—although, I suspect, under false pretenses, since he must know that it is not so easy to corrupt the beliefs of a religion as King Casimir seems to think it is. Nonetheless, Ian Lowell was not above taking Polish gold and sending highly colored reports back to His Slavonic Majesty.

"And who would suspect that Sir Andrew Campbell-MacDonald, a man whose record was that of an honorable soldier and an upright gentleman, of being a Polish spy and a leader of the subversive Holy Society of Albion?

"Someone finally did, of course. We may never know what led His Grace and Lord Camberton to suspect him, although perhaps we can get Ian Lowell to tell us. But their suspicion has at last brought about Lowell's downfall, though it cost both of them their lives."

There was a knock at the door. Lord Darcy opened it. Standing there was a priest in Benedictine habit. "Yes, Reverend Father?" Lord Darcy said.

"I am Father Joseph. You are Lord Darcy?"

"Yes, I am, Reverend Father."

"I am the Healer the guardsmen called in to take care of your prisoner. I regret to say I could do nothing, my lord. He passed away a few minutes ago from a gunshot wound."

Lord Darcy turned and looked at the Ducal Family. It was all over. The scandal need never come out, now. Why should it, since it had never really existed?

Sir Thomas Leseaux would soon finish his work. The Society of Albion would be rendered impotent as soon as its leaders were rounded up and confronted with the King's High Justice. All would be well.

"I should like to speak to the bereaved family," said Father Joseph.

"Not just now, Reverend Father," said the Dowager Duchess in a clear voice. "I would like to make my confession to you in a few minutes. Would you wait outside, please?"

The priest sensed that there was something odd in the air. "Certainly, my daughter. I will be waiting." He closed the door.

The Duchess, Lord Darcy knew, would tell all, but it would be safe under the seal of the confessional.

It was Lord Quentin who summed up their feelings.

"This," he said coldly, "will be a funeral I will really enjoy. We thank you, my lord."

"The pleasure was mine, Your Grace. Come, Master Sean; we have a Channel crossing awaiting us."

Damon Knight

YOU'RE ANOTHER

This story is an appropriate choice for the Boucher anthology because it is one which Tony not only bought but improved—he suggested an expansion of one scene that made it much funnier, and even wrote some of the lines for it. This sticks in my memory because it was the only time an editor ever volunteered to write part of my story without making me sore, and because it was the only time Tony did anything of that sort: mostly he was just very nice, and bought the story, and published it under a marvelous blurb. Nobody ever excelled him in the art of buttering-up an author. It was nice to have the checks other editors sent, but Tony always made you feel that he understood the story and relished it. I took it as a high compliment when he called me civilized in the introduction to In Search of Wonder; *I can't think of anyone to whom that adjective applied as it did to him.*

IT WAS a warm spring Saturday, and Johnny Bornish spent the morning in Central Park. He drew sailors lying on the grass with their girls; he drew old men in straw hats, and Good Humor men pushing their carts. He got two quick studies of children at the toy-boat pond, and would have had another, a beauty, except that somebody's dammed big Dalmatian, romping, blundered into him and made him sit down hard in the water.

A bright-eyed old gentleman solemnly helped him arise. Johnny thought it over, then wrung out his wet pants in the men's rest room, put them back on and spread himself like a starfish in the sun. He dried before his sketchbook did, so he took the bus back downtown, got off at 14th Street and went into Mayer's.

The only clerk in sight was showing an intricate folding easel to a tweedy woman who didn't seem to know which end was which. Johnny picked up the sketchbook he wanted from a pile on the table, and pottered around looking at clay figures, paper palettes and other traps for the amateur. He glimpsed some interesting textured papers displayed in the other aisle and tried to cross over to them, but misjudged his knobby-kneed turning circle, as usual, and brought down a cascade of little paint cans. Dancing for balance, somehow he managed to put one heel down at an unheard-of angle, buckle the lid of one of the cans and splash red enamel all over hell.

He paid for the paint, speechless, and got out. He had dropped the sketchbook somewhere, he discovered. Evidently God did not care for him to do any sketching today.

Also, he was leaving little red heel-prints across the pavement. He wiped off his shoe as well as he could with some newspaper from the trashbasket at the corner, and walked down to the Automat for coffee.

The cashier scooped in his dollar and spread two rows of magical dimes on the marble counter, all rattling at once like angry metal insects. They were alive in Johnny's palm; one of them got away, but he lunged for it and caught it before it hit the floor.

Flushed with victory, he worked his way through the crowd to the coffee dispenser, put a china cup under the spigot and dropped his dime in the slot. Coffee streamed out, filled his cup and went on flowing.

Johnny watched it for a minute. Coffee went on pouring over the lip and handle of the cup, too hot to touch, splashing through the grilled metal and gurgling away somewhere below.

A white-haired man shouldered him aside, took a cup from the rack and calmly filled it at the spigot. Somebody else followed his example, and in a moment there was a crowd.

After all, it was his dime. Johnny got another cup and waited his turn. An angry man in a white jacket disappeared violently into the crowd, and Johnny heard him shouting something. A moment later the crowd began to disperse.

The jet had stopped. The man in the white jacket picked up Johnny's original cup, emptied it, set it down on a bus-boy's cart, and went away.

Evidently God did not care for him to drink any coffee, either. Johnny whistled a few reflective bars of "Dixie" and left, keeping a wary eye out for trouble.

At the curb a big pushcart was standing in the sunshine, flaming with banana yellows, apple reds. Johnny stopped himself. "Oh, no," he said, and turned himself sternly around, and started carefully down the avenue, hands in pockets, elbows at his sides. On a day like what this one was shaping up to be, he shuddered to think what he could do with a pushcart full of fruit.

How about a painting of that? Semi-abstract—"Still Life in Motion." Flying tangerines, green bananas, dusty Concord grapes, stopped by the fast shutter of the artist's eye. By Cézanne, out of Henry Moore. By heaven, it wasn't bad.

He could see it, big and vulgar, about a 36 by 30—(stretchers: he'd have to stop at Mayer's again, or on second thought somewhere else, for stretchers) the colors grayed on a violet ground, but screaming at each other all the same like a gaggle of parakeets. Black outlines here and there, weaving a kind of cockeyed carpet pattern through it. No depth, no light-and-dark—flat easter-egg colors, glowing as enigmatically as a Parrish cut up into jigsaw pieces. Frame it in oyster-white moulding—wham! The Museum of Modern Art!

The bananas, he thought, would have to go around this

way, distorted, curved like boomerangs up in the foreground. Make the old ladies from Oshkosh duck. That saturated buttery yellow, transmuted to a poisonous green . . . He put out a forefinger absently to stroke one of the nearest, feeling how the chalky smoothness curved up and around into the dry hard stem.

"How many, Mac?"

For an instant Johnny thought he had circled the block, back to the same pushcart: then he saw that this one had only bananas on it. He was at the corner of 11th Street; he had walked three blocks, blind and deaf.

"No bananas," he said hurriedly, backing away. There was a shriek in his ear. He turned; it was a glitter-eyed tweedy woman, brandishing an enormous handbag.

"Can't you watch where you're—"

"Sorry, ma'am," he said, desperately trying to keep his balance. He toppled off the curb, grabbing at the pushcart. Something slithery went out from under his foot. He was falling, sliding like a bowling ball, feet first toward the one upright shaft that supported the end of the pushcart. . .

The first thing that he noticed, as he sat there up to his chest in bananas, with the swearing huckster holding the cart by main force, was that an alert, white-haired old gentleman was in the front rank of the crowd, looking at him.

The same one who—?

And come to think of it, that tweedy woman—

Ridiculous.

All the same, something began to twitch in his memory. Ten confused minutes later he was kneeling asthmatically on the floor in front of his closet, hauling out stacks of unframed paintings, shoeboxes full of letters and squeezed paint tubes, a Scout ax (for kindling), old sweaters and mildewed magazines, until he found a battered suitcase.

In the suitcase, under untidy piles of sketches and watercolors, was a small cardboard portfolio. In the portfolio were two newspaper clippings.

One was from the *Post,* dated three years back: it showed Johnny, poised on one heel in a violent adagio pose, being whirled around by the stream of water from a hydrant some Third Avenue urchins had just opened. The other was two years older, from the *Journal:* in this one Johnny seemed to be walking dreamily up a wall—actually, he had just slipped on an icy street in the upper 40's.

He blinked incredulously. In the background of the first picture there were half a dozen figures, mostly kids.

Among them was the tweedy woman.

In the background of the second, there was only one. It was the white-haired old man.

Thinking it over, Johnny discovered that he was scared. He had never actually enjoyed being the kind of buffoon who gets his shirttail caught in zippers, is trapped by elevators and revolving doors, and trips on pebbles; he had accepted it humbly as his portion, and in between catastrophes he'd had a lot of fun.

But suppose somebody was *doing* it to him?

A lot of it was not funny, look at it any way you like. There was the time the bus driver had closed the door on Johnny's foot and dragged him for three yards, bouncing on the pavement. He had got up with nothing worse than bruises—but what if that passenger hadn't seen him in time?

He looked at the clippings again. There they were, the same faces—the same clothing, even, except that the old man was wearing an overcoat. Even in the faded halftones, there was a predatory sparkle from his rimless eyeglasses; and the tweedy woman's sharp beak was as threatening as a hawk's.

Johnny felt a stifling sense of panic. He felt like a man waiting helplessly for the punchline of a long bad joke; or like a mouse being played with by a cat.

Something bad was going to happen next.

The door opened; somebody walked in. Johnny started, but it was only the Duke, brawny in a paint-smeared undershirt, with a limp cigarette in the corner of his mouth. The Duke had a rakish Errol Flynn mustache, blending furrily now into his day-old beard, and a pair of black, who-are-you-varlet brows. He was treacherous, clever, plausible, quarrelsome, ingenious, a great brawler and seducer of women—in short, exactly like Cellini, except he had no talent.

"Hiding?" said Duke, showing his big teeth.

Johnny became aware that, crouched in front of the closet that way, he looked a little as if he were about to dive into it and pull overcoats over his head. He got up stiffly, tried to put his hands in his pockets, and discovered he still had the clippings. Then it was too late. Duke took them gently, inspected them with a judicial eye, and stared gravely at Johnny. "Not flattering," he said. "Is that blood on your forehead?"

Johnny investigated; his fingers came away a little red, not much. "I fell down," he said uncomfortably.

"My boy," Duke told him, "you are troubled. Confide in your old uncle."

"I'm just—Look, Duke, I'm busy. Did you want something?"

"Only to be your faithful counselor and guide," said Duke, pressing Johnny firmly into a chair. "Just lean back, loosen the sphincters and say the first thing that comes into your mind." He looked expectant.

"Ugh," said Johnny.

Duke nodded sagely. "A visceral reaction. Existentialist. You wish to rid yourself of yourself—get away from it all. Tell me, when you walk down the street, do you feel the buildings are about to close on you? Are you being persecuted by little green men who come out of the woodwork? Do you feel an overpowering urge to leave town?"

"Yes," said Johnny truthfully.

Duke looked mildly surprised. "Well?" he asked, spreading his hands.

"Where would I go?"

"I recommend sunny New Jersey. All the towns have different names—fascinating. Millions of them. Pick one at random. Hackensack, Perth Amboy, Passaic, Teaneck, Newark? No? You're quite right—too suggestive. Let me see.

Something farther north? Provincetown, Martha's Vineyard —lovely this time of the year. Or Florida—yes, I can really see you, Johnny, sitting on a rotten wharf in the sunshine, fishing with a bent pin for pompano. Peaceful, relaxed, carefree . . ."

Johnny's fingers stirred the change in his pocket. He didn't know what was in his wallet—he never did—but he was sure it wasn't enough. "Duke, have you seen Ted Edwards this week?" he asked hopefully.

"No. Why?"

"Oh. He owes me a little money, is all. He said he'd pay me today or tomorrow."

"If it's a question of money—" said the Duke after a moment.

Johnny looked at him incredulously.

Duke was pulling a greasy wallet out of his hip pocket. He paused with his thumb in it. "Do you really want to get out of town, Johnny?"

"Well, sure, but—"

"Johnny, what are friends *for?* Really, I'm wounded. Will fifty help?"

He counted out the money and stuffed it into Johnny's paralyzed palm. "Don't say a word. Let me remember you just as you are." He made a frame of his hands and squinted through it. He sighed, then picked up the battered suitcase and went to work with great energy throwing things out of the dresser into it. "Shirts, socks, underwear. Necktie. Clean handkerchief. There you are." He closed the lid. He pumped Johnny's hand, pulling him toward the door. "Don't think it hasn't been great, because it hasn't. So on the ocean of life we pass and speak to one another. Only a look and a voice; then darkness and silence."

Johnny dug in his heels and stopped. "What's the matter?" Duke inquired.

"I just realized—I can't go now. I'll go tonight. I'll take the late train."

Duke arched an eyebrow. "But why wait, Johnny? When

the sunne shineth, make hay. When the iron is hot, strike. The tide tarrieth for no man."

"They'll see me leave," said Johnny, embarrassed.

Duke frowned. "You mean the little green men actually are after you?" His features worked; he composed them with difficulty. "Well, this is—Pardon me. A momentary aberration. But now don't you see, Johnny, you haven't got any time to lose. If they're following you, they must know where you live. How do you know they won't come here?"

Johnny, flushing, could think of no adequate reply. He had wanted to get away under cover of darkness, but that would mean another five hours at least. . .

"Look here," said Duke suddenly, "I know the very thing. Biff Feldstein—works at the Cherry Lane. Your own mother won't admit she knows you. Wait here."

He was back in fifteen minutes, with a bundle of old clothes and an object which turned out, on closer examination, to be a small brown beard.

Johnny put it on unwillingly, using gunk from a tube Duke had brought along. Duke helped him into a castoff jacket, color indistinguishable, shiny with grease, and clapped a beret on his head. The result, to Johnny's horrified gaze, looked like an old-time Village phony or a peddler of French postcards. Duke inspected him judicially. "It's magnificent, but it isn't war," he said. "However, we can always plant vines. *Allons!* I am grass; I cover all!"

Walking toward Sixth at a brisk pace, a hand firmly on Johnny's elbow, Duke suddenly paused. "Ho!" he said. He sprang forward, bent, and picked something up.

Johnny stared at it glassily. It was a five-dollar bill.

Duke was calmly putting it away. "Does that happen to you often?" Johnny asked.

"Now and again," said Duke. "Merely a matter of keeping the eyes in focus."

"Luck," said Johnny faintly.

"Never think it," Duke told him. "Take the word of an older and wiser man. You make your own luck in this world. Think of Newton. Think of O'Dwyer. Hand stuck in the jam jar? You asked for it. Now the trouble with you—"

Johnny, who had heard this theory before, was no longer listening. Look, he thought, at all the different things that had had to happen so that Duke could pick up that fiver. Somebody had to lose it, to begin with—say because he met a friend just as he was about to put the bill away, and stuffed it in his pocket instead so he could shake hands, and then forgot it, reached for his handkerchief—All right. Then it just had to happen that everybody who passed this spot between then and now was looking the other way, or thinking about something else. And Duke, finally, had to glance down at just the right moment. It was all extremely improbable, but it happened, somewhere, every day.

And also every day, somewhere, people were being hit by flowerpots knocked off tenth-story window ledges, and falling down manholes, and walking into stray bullets fired by law enforcement officers in pursuit of malefactors. Johnny shuddered.

"Oh-oh," said Duke suddenly. "Where's a cab? Ah—Cabby!" He sprang forward to the curb, whistling and waving.

Looking around curiously, Johnny saw a clumsy figure hurrying toward them down the street. "There's Mary Finigan," he said, pointing her out.

"I know," said Duke irascibly. The cab was just pulling in toward them, the driver reaching back to open the door. "Now here we go, Johnny—"

"But I think she wants to talk to you," said Johnny. "Hadn't we—"

"No time now," said Duke, helping him in with a shove. "She's taken to running off at the mouth—that's why I had to give her up. Get moving!" he said to the driver, and added to Johnny, "Among other things, that is . . . Here will be an old abusing of God's patience, and the King's English."

As they pulled away into traffic, Johnny had a last glimpse

of the girl standing on the curb watching them. Her dark hair was straggling down off her forehead; she looked as if she had been crying.

Duke said comfortably, "Every man, as the saying is, can tame a shrew but he that hath her. Now there, John boy, you have just had an instructive object lesson. Was it luck that we got away from that draggle-tailed ear-bender? It was not. . ."

But, thought Johnny, it was. What if the cab hadn't come along at just the right time?

"—in a nutshell, boy. Only reason you have bad luck, you go hunting for it."

"That isn't the reason," said Johnny.

He let Duke's hearty voice fade once more into a kind of primitive background music, like the muttering of the extras in a Tarzan picture when the Kalawumbas are about to feed the pretty girl to the lions. It had just dawned on him, with the dazzling glow of revelation, that the whole course of anybody's life was determined by improbable accidents. Here he stood, all five feet ten and a hundred thirty pounds of him—a billion-to-one shot from the word go. (What were the chances against any given sperm's uniting with any given ovum? *More* than a billion to one—unimaginable.) What if the apple hadn't fallen on Newton's head? What if O'Dwyer had never left Ireland? And what did free will have to do with the decision not to become, say, a Kurdish herdsman, if you happened to be born in Ohio?

. . . It meant, Johnny thought, that if you could control the random factors—the way the dice fall in a bar in Sacramento, the temper of a rich uncle in Keokuk, the moisture content of the clouds over Sioux Falls at 3:03 CST, the shape of a pebble in a Wall Street newsboy's sock—you could do anything. You could make an obscure painter named Johnny Bornish fall into the toy-boat pond in Central Park and get red paint all over his shoe and knock down a pushcart.

But why would you want to?

The airport waiting room was a little like a scene out of *Things to Come,* except that the people were neither white-robed, leisurely nor cool.

Every place on every bench was taken. Duke found a couple of square feet of floor space behind a pillar and settled Johnny there, seated on his upended suitcase.

"Now you're all set. Got your ticket. Got your magazine. Okay." Duke made an abrupt menacing gesture in order to look at his wrist-watch.

"Got to run. Now remember, boy—send me your address as soon as you get one, so I can forward your mail and so on. Oh: almost forgot." He scribbled on a piece of paper, handed it over. "Mere formality. Payable at any time. Sign here."

He had written, "I O U $50." Johnny signed, feeling a little more at home with Duke.

"Right. Oll korrect."

"Duke," said Johnny suddenly. "Mary's pregnant, isn't she?" His expression was thoughtful.

"It has been known to happen," said Duke good-humoredly.

"Why don't you give her a break?" Johnny asked with difficulty.

Duke was not offended. "How? Speak the truth to me, Johnny—do you see me as a happy bridegroom? Well—" He pumped Johnny's hand. "The word must be spoken that bids you depart—Though the effort to speak it should shatter my heart—Though in silence, with something I pine—Yet the lips that touch liquor must never touch mine!" With a grin that seemed to linger, like the Cheshire Cat's, he disappeared into the crowd.

II

UNCOMFORTABLY ASTRIDE his suitcase, solitary among multitudes, Johnny found himself thinking in words harder and longer at a time than he was used to. The kind of thinking he did when he was painting, or had painted, or was about to paint was another process altogether, and there were days on end when he did nothing else. He had a talent, Johnny Bornish. A talent is sometimes defined as a gift of the gods, a thing that most people, who have not had one, confuse with a present under a Christmas tree.

It was not like that at all. It tortured and delighted him, and took up so much room in his skull that a lot of practical details couldn't get in. Without exaggeration, it obsessed him, and when occasionally, as now, its grip relaxed, Johnny had the comical expression of a man who has just waked up to find his pocket picked and a row of hotfoot scars around his shoes.

He was thinking about luck. It was all right to talk about everybody making his own, and to a certain extent he supposed it was true, but Duke *was* the kind of guy who found money on the street. Such a thing had happened to Johnny only once in his life, and then it wasn't legal tender, but a Japanese coin—copper, heavy, about the size of a half-dollar with a chrysanthemum symbol on one side and a character on the other. He thought of it as his lucky piece; he had found it on the street, his last year in high school, and here—he took it out of his pocket—it still was.

. . . Which, when you came to think of it, was odd. He was not superstitious about the coin, or especially fond of it. He called it a lucky piece for want of a better name, because the word "keepsake" had gone out of fashion; and in fact he believed that his luck in the last ten years had been lousy. The coin was the only thing he owned that was anywhere near that old. He had lost three wristwatches, numberless fountain pens, two hats, three or four cigarette lighters, and genuine U. S. nickels and dimes by the handful. But here was the Japanese coin.

Now, how could you figure a thing like that, unless it was luck . . . or *interference?*

Johnny sat up straighter. It was a foolish notion, probably born of the fact that he hadn't had any lunch; but he was in a mood to read sinister significance into almost anything.

He already knew that the old man and the tweedy woman had been interfering in his life for at least five years, probably longer. Somehow, they were responsible for the "accidents" that kept happening to him—and *there* was a foolish and sinister notion for you, if you liked. Believing that, how could he help wondering about other odd things that had happened to him, no matter how small . . . like finding and keeping a Japanese coin?

With that kind of logic, you could prove anything. And yet, he couldn't rid himself of the idea.

Idly, he got up holding the coin and dropped it into a nearby waste can. He sat down on his suitcase again with a feeling of neurosis well quelled. If the coin somehow found its way back to him, he'd have evidence for thinking the worst of it; if it didn't, as of course it wouldn't, small loss.

"Excuse me," said a thinnish prim-faced little man in almost-clerical clothes. "I believe you dropped this. A Japanese coin. Quite nice."

Johnny found his tongue. "Uh, thank you. But I don't want it—you keep it."

"Oh, *no,*" said the little man, and walked stiffly away.

Johnny stared after him, then at the coin. It was lumpishly solid, a dirty-looking brown, nicked and rounded at the edges. Ridiculous!

His mistake, no doubt, had been in being too obvious. He palmed the coin, trying to look nonchalant. After a while he lit a cigarette, dropped it, and as he fumbled for it, managed to shove the coin under the leg of the adjoining bench.

He had taken one puff on the retrieved cigarette when a large hulk in a gray suit, all muscles and narrowed eyes, knelt beside him and extracted the coin. The hulk looked at it carefully, front and back, weighed it in his palm, rang it on the floor, and finally handed it over to Johnny. "This yours?" he asked in a gravelly voice.

Johnny nodded. The hulk said nothing more, but watched grimly until Johnny put the coin away in his pocket. Then he got up, dusted off his knees, and went away into the crowd.

Johnny felt a cold lump gather at the pit of his stomach. The fact that he had seen this same routine in at least half a dozen bad movies gave him no comfort; he did not believe in the series of natural coincidences that made it impossible to get rid of the neatly wrapped garbage, or the incriminating nylon stocking, or whatever.

He stood up. It was already twenty minutes after his plane's scheduled departure time. He *had* to get rid of the thing. It was intolerable to suppose that he couldn't get rid of it. Of course he could get rid of it.

The low false roof of the baggage counter looked promising. He picked up his suitcase and worked his way toward it, and got there just as the p. a. system burst forth with *"Flight number mnglang for Buzzclickville, now loading at Gate Lumber Lide."* Under cover of this clamor, Johnny swiftly took the coin out of his pocket and tossed it out of sight on the roof.

Now what? Was somebody going to fetch a ladder, and climb up there after the coin, and come down and hand it to him?

Nothing at all happened, except that the voice on the p. a. emitted its thunderous mutter again, and this time Johnny caught the name of his destination, Jacksonville.

Feeling better, he stopped at the newsstand for cigarettes. He paid for them with a half dollar, which was promptly slapped back into his palm.

"Flight mumble sixteen for Jagznbull, now loading at Gate Number Nine," said the p. a.

After a moment Johnny handed back the cigarettes, still staring at the Japanese coin that lay, infuriatingly solid, on his palm. . . He had had a fifty-cent piece in his pocket; it didn't seem to be there now; argal, he had thrown it up on top of the baggage counter. A natural mistake. Only, in ten years of carrying the coin around with him, he had never once mistaken it for a half-buck, or vice versa, until now.

"Flight number sixteen . . ."

The tweedy woman, Johnny realized with a slow chill crawling down his back, had been ahead of him in the art store, talking to a clerk. She couldn't have been following him—on the bus, in a cab, or any other way; there wouldn't have been time. She had known where he was going, and when he was going to get there.

It was as if, he thought, while the coin seemed to turn fishily cold and smooth in his fingers, it was just as if the two of them, the tweedy woman and the old man, had planted a sort of beacon on him ten years ago, so that wherever and whenever he went, he was a belled cat. It was as if they might be looking in a kind of radarscope, when it pleased them, and seeing the track of his life like a twisted strand of copper wire coiling and turning. . .

But of course there was no escape, if that was true. His track went winding through the waiting room and onto a particular aircraft and down again, where that plane landed, and into a particular room and then a particular restaurant, so that a day from now, a month, a year, ten years from now, they could reach out and touch him wherever he might be.

There was no escape, because there was a peculiarity built into this brown Japanese coin, a combination of random events that added up to the mirth-provoking result that he simply couldn't lose it.

He looked around wildly, thinking *Blowtorch. Monkey wrench. Sledge-hammer.* But there wasn't anything. It was a great big phony Things-to-Comeish airport wildcat waiting room, without a tool in it anywhere.

A pretty girl came out from behind the counter to his right, swinging up the hinged section of counter and letting it down again behind her. Johnny stared after her stupidly, then at the way she had come out. His scalp twitched. He stepped to the counter, raised the hinged section.

A bald man a few feet away stopped talking to wave a telephone handset at Johnny. "No admittance here, sir! No admittance!"

Johnny put the Japanese coin down at an angle on the place that supported the end of the hinged section. He made sure it was the Japanese coin. He wedged it firmly.

The bald man dropped his telephone and came toward him, hand outstretched.

Johnny slammed the hinged section down as hard as he could. There was a dull *bonk,* and an odd feeling of tension; the lights seemed to blur. He turned and ran. Nobody followed him.

The plane was a two-engined relic that looked faintly Victorian from the outside; inside, it was a slanting dark cavern with an astonishing number of seats crammed into it. It smelled like a locker room. Johnny stumbled down the narrow aisle to what seemed to be the only remaining place, next to a large dark gentleman in an awning-striped tie.

He sat down, a little awkwardly. He had had a peculiar feeling ever since he had bashed the coin with the counter section, and the worst of it was that he couldn't pin it down. It was a physical something-wrong feeling, like an upset stomach or too little sleep or a fever coming on, but it wasn't exactly any of those things. He was hungry, but not that hungry. He thought the trouble might be with his eyes, but whenever he picked out anything as a test, it looked perfectly normal and he could see it fine. It was in his skin, perhaps? a kind of not-quite-prickling that . . . No, it wasn't his skin.

It was a little like being drunk, at the fraction of an instant when you realize how drunk you are and regret it . . . it was like that, but not very much. And it was partly like the foreboding, stronger and more oppressive than before—*Something bad was going to happen.*

The pilot and copilot walked up the aisle and disappeared into the forward compartment. The door was shut; the stewardess, back in the tail, was poring over the papers on her clipboard. After a while the starters whined and the engines came to life; Johnny, who had flown only once before, and on a scheduled airline at that, was startled to find what a devil of a racket they made. There was another interminable wait, and then the plane was crawling forward, swinging its nose around, crawling a little faster, while an endless blank expanse of concrete slipped by—lumbering along, then, like some huge, preposterous, and above all flightless bird—and lifting incredibly, a few inches up, airborne, the runway falling back, tilted, dwindling until they were up, high above the mist on the water, steady as a hammock in the rasping monotone drone of the engines.

Something went *flip* at the corner of Johnny's vision. He turned his head.

Flop.

It was a little metallic disk that went *flip* up the carpet like a tiddlywink or a Mexican jumping bean, and paused for an instant while his jaw began to come loose at the hinge, and went *flop.* It lay on the carpet next to his seat, and went *hop.*

It landed on his knee, a little brown metallic disk with a chrysanthemum design, bent across the middle. He brushed at it. It hopped, and clung to his hand like a magnet to steel.

"Good heavens!" said an explosive voice in his ear.

Johnny had no attention to spare. He had taken hold of the coin with his other hand—a horrid feeling, it clung clammily to his fingers, and pulled away from his palm with reluctance—and now he was trying to scrape it off against the fabric of the seat. It was like trying to scrape off his own skin. He gave up and furiously began shaking his hand.

"Here, friend, don't do that!" The dark man in the next seat half rose, and there was a moment of confusion; Johnny heard a sharp click, and thought he saw something leap from the dark man's vest pocket. Then, for an instant, he had clinging to his fingers a brown Japanese coin *and* a pair of glittering pince-nez. And then the two had somehow twisted together in a nasty, writhing way that hurt his eyes to watch, and uncurled again—no coin, no pince-nez, but an impossible little leather change purse.

Had the coin ever been a coin at all? Was the change purse a change purse?

"Now look what you've done! *Ugh!*" The dark man, his face contorted with passion, reached gingerly fingers toward the purse. "Don't move, friend. Let me—"

Johnny pulled away a trifle. "Who are you?"

"F.B.I.," said the dark man impatiently. He flapped a billfold at Johnny; there was some kind of official-looking shield inside. "Now you have torn it, my God! Hold that still—just like that. Don't move." He pulled back his sleeves like a conjuror, and began to reach very cautiously for the little brown bit of leather that clung to Johnny's hand.

The thing twitched slightly in his fingers. The next moment, people all around them began getting up and crowding into the aisle, heading for the single washroom back in the tail of the plane.

Palpably, the plane tilted. Johnny heard the stewardess shrieking, "One at a time! One at a time! Take your seats, everyone—you're making the airplane tail-heavy!"

"Steady, steady," moaned the dark man. "Hold it absolutely still!"

Johnny couldn't. His fingers twitched again, and abruptly all the passengers in the aisle were tumbling the other way, fighting to get away from the dangerous tail. The stewardess came helplessly after them, squalling futile orders.

"Am I doing that?" Johnny gasped, staring in horror at the thing in his palm.

"The gadget is. Hold it steady, friend—"

But his hand twitched again, and abruptly all the passengers were back in their seats, quietly sitting as if nothing had happened. Then a chorus of shrieks arose. Looking out the window, Johnny saw a terrifying sea of treetops just below, where nothing but empty air had been the moment before. As the plane nosed up sharply, his hand moved again—

And the shrieks grew louder. Up ahead loomed a blue-violet wall of mountain, topless, gigantic.

His fingers twitched still again: and once more the plane was droning peaceably along between earth and heaven. The passengers were bored or sleeping. There was no mountain, and no trees.

Sweat was beaded on the dark man's forehead. "Now . . ." he said, gritting his teeth and reaching again.

"Wait a minute," said Johnny, pulling away again. "Wait —This is some kind of top secret thing, is it, that I'm not supposed to have?"

"Yes," said the dark man, agonized. "I tell you, friend, don't move it!"

The purse was slowly changing color, turning a watery violet around the edges.

"And you're from the F.B.I.?" Johnny asked, staring hard at the dark man.

"Yes! Hold it steady—"

"No," said Johnny. His voice had a disposition to tremble, but Johnny held it firmly in check. "You forgot about your ears," he said. "Or are they too hard to change?"

The dark man showed his teeth. "What are you talking about?"

"The *ears,*" Johnny said, "and the jawbone. No two people have ears alike. And before, when you were the old man, your neck was too thick. It bothered me, only I was too busy to think about it." He swallowed hard. "I'm thinking about it now. You don't want me to move this thing?"

"Right, friend, right."

"Then tell me what this is all about."

The dark man made placating gestures. "I can't do that, friend. I really can't. Look—"

The tiny weight shifted in Johnny's hand. "—out!" shouted the dark man.

Tiny flickerings gathered in the air around them. In the plane window, the clear blue of the sky abruptly vanished. Instead, Johnny saw a tumbling waste of gray cloud. Rain drummed against the window and the plane heeled suddenly as if a gust had caught it.

Scattered shrieks arose from up forward. Johnny swallowed a large lump, and his fingers twitched. The flickering came again.

The cloud and rain were gone; the sky was an innocent blue again. "*Don't* do that," said the dark man. "Listen, look: You want to know something? Watch me try to tell you." He moistened his lips and began, "When you have trouble—" but on the fourth word his throat seemed to tighten and lock. His lips went on moving, his eyes bulged with effort, but nothing came out.

After a moment he relaxed, breathing heavily. "You see?" he said.

"You can't talk," said Johnny. "About that. Literally."

"Right! Now, friend, if you'll just allow me—"

"Easy. Tell me the truth: is there any way you can get around this, whatever it is, this block or whatever?" He let his fingers twitch, deliberately, as he spoke. "Any gadget, or anything you can take?"

The dark man glanced nervously out the window, where blue sky had given way to purple twilight and a large sickle moon. "Yes, but—"

"There is? What?"

The man's throat tightened again as he tried to speak.

"Well, whatever it is, you'd better use it," said Johnny. He saw the dark man's face harden with resolution, and jerked his hand away just in time as the dark man grabbed—

III

THERE WAS a whirling moment, then the universe steadied. Johnny clutched at the seat with his free hand. The plane and all the passengers were gone. He and the dark man were sitting on a park bench in the sunshine. Two pigeons took alarm and flapped heavily away.

The dark man's face was twisted unhappily. "Now you have done it! Oh, what time is it, anyway?" He plucked two watches out of his vest and consulted them in turn.

"Wednesday, friend, at the latest! Oh, oh, they'll—" His mouth worked soundlessly.

"Wednesday?" Johnny managed. He looked around. They were sitting in Union Square Park, the only ones there. There were plenty of people on the streets, all hurrying, most of them women. It looked like a Wednesday, all right.

He opened his mouth, and shut it again carefully. He looked down at the limp bit of leather and metal in his hand. Start from the beginning. What did he know?

The coin, which had evidently been some kind of telltale or beacon, had in some way joined itself, after Johnny had damaged it, to some other instrument of the dark man's—apparently the gadget that enabled him to control probability, and move from one time to another, and small chores like that.

In their present fused state, the two gadgets were ungovernable—dangerous, the dark man seemed to think—and no good to anybody.

And that was absolutely all he knew.

He didn't know where the dark man and his companion had come from, what they were up to, anything that would be useful to know, and he wasn't getting any nearer finding out.

—Except that there was some way of loosening the dark man's tongue. Drugs, which were out of the question—liquor—

Well, he thought, sitting up a trifle straighter, there was no harm in trying, anyhow. It might not work, but it was the pleasantest thought he had had all afternoon.

He said, "Come on," and stood up carefully; but his motion must have been too abrupt, because the scene around them melted and ran down into the pavement, and they were standing, not in the park, but on the traffic island at Sheridan Square.

It looked to be a little after noon, and the papers on the stand at Johnny's elbow bore today's date.

He felt a little dizzy. Say it was about one o'clock: then he hadn't got out to the airport yet; he was on his way there now, with Duke, and if he could hop a fast cab, he might catch himself and tell himself not to go. . .

Johnny steadied his mind by a strenuous effort. He had, he told himself, one single, simple problem now in hand, and that was how to get to a bar. He took a careful step toward the edge of the island. The thing in his hand bobbled; the world reeled and steadied.

With the dark man beside him, Johnny was standing on the gallery of the Reptile Room of the Museum of Natural History. Down below, the poised shapes of various giant lizards looked extremely extinct and very dry.

Johnny felt the rising rudiments of a vast impatience. At this rate, it was clear enough, he would never get anywhere he wanted to go, because every step changed the rules. All right then; if Mahomet couldn't go to the mountain—

The dark man, who had been watching him, made a strangled sound of protest.

Johnny ignored him. He swung his hand sharply down. And up. And down.

The world swung around them like a pendulum, twisting and turning. Too far! They were on a street corner in Paris. They were in a dark place listening to the sound of machinery. They were in the middle of a sandstorm, choking, blinding—

They were sitting in a rowboat on a quiet river. The dark man was wearing flannels and a straw hat.

Johnny tried to move the thing in his hand more gently: it was as if it had a life of its own; he had to hold it back.

Zip!

They were seated on stools at a marble-topped counter. Johnny saw a banana split with a fly on it.

Zip!

A library, a huge low-ceilinged place that Johnny had never seen before.

Zip!

The lobby of the Art Theatre; a patron bumped into Johnny, slopping his demitasse.

Zip!

They were sitting opposite each other, the dark man and he, at a table in the rear of Dorrie's Bar. Dust motes sparkled in the late-afternoon sun. There was a highball in front of each of them.

Gritting his teeth, Johnny held his hand perfectly upright while he lowered it, so slowly that it hardly seemed to move, until it touched the worn surface of the table. He sighed. "Drink up," he said.

With a wary eye on the thing in Johnny's hand, the dark man drank. Johnny signaled the bartender, who came over with a faintly puzzled expression. "How long you guys been here?"

"I was just going to ask you," said Johnny at random. "Two more."

The bartender retired and came back looking hostile with the drinks, after which he went down to the farthermost end of the bar, turned his back on them and polished glasses.

Johnny sipped his highball. "Drink up," he told the dark man. The dark man drank.

After the third swift highball, the dark man looked slightly wall-eyed. "How you feeling?" Johnny asked.

"Fine," said the dark man carefully. "Jus' fine." He dipped two fingers into his vest pocket, drew out a tiny flat pillbox and extracted from it an even tinier pill which he popped into his mouth and swallowed.

"What was that?" said Johnny suspiciously.

"Just a little pill."

Johnny looked closely at him. His eyes were clear and steady; he looked exactly as if he had not drunk any highballs at all. "Let me hear you say 'The Leith police dismisseth us,' " said Johnny.

The dark man said it.

"Can you say that when you're drunk?" Johnny demanded.

"Don't know, friend. I never tried."

Johnny sighed. Look at it any way you liked, the man had been high, at least, before he swallowed that one tiny pill. And now he was cold sober. After a moment, glowering, he pounded on his glass with a swizzle-stick until the bartender came and took his order for two more drinks. "Doubles," said Johnny as an afterthought. When they arrived, the dark man drank one down and began to look faintly glassy-eyed. He took out his pillbox.

Johnny leaned forward. "Who's that standing outside?" he whispered hoarsely.

The dark man swiveled around. "Where?"

"They ducked back," said Johnny. "Keep watching." He brought his free hand out of his trousers pocket, where it had been busy extracting the contents of a little bottle of antihistamine tablets he had been carrying around since February. They were six times the size of the dark man's pills, but they were the best he could do. He slid the pillbox out from under the dark man's fingers, swiftly emptied it onto his own lap, dumped the cold tablets into it and put it back.

"I don't see anybody, friend," said the dark man anxiously. "Was it a man or—" He picked out one of the bogus tablets, swallowed it, and looked surprised.

"Have another drink," said Johnny hopefully. The dark man, still looking surprised, swilled it down. His eyes closed slowly and opened again. They were definitely glassy.

"How do you feel now?" Johnny asked.

"Dandy, thanks. *Vad heter denna ort?*" The dark man's face spread and collapsed astonishingly into a large loose, foolish smile.

It occurred to Johnny that he might have overdone it. "How was that again?" Swedish, it had sounded like, or some other Scandinavian language . . .

"Voss hot ir gezugt?" asked the dark man wonderingly. He batted his head with the heel of his hand several times. *"Favor de desconectar la radio."*

"The radio isn't—" began Johnny, but the dark man interrupted him. Springing up suddenly, he climbed onto the bench, spread his arms and began singing in a loud operatic baritone. The melody was that of the Toreador Song from

Carmen, but the dark man was singing his own words to it, over and over: *"Dove è il gabinetto?"*

The bartender was coming over with an unpleasant expression. "Cut that out!" Johnny whispered urgently. "You hear? Sit down, or I'll move this thing again!"

The dark man glanced at the object in Johnny's hand. "You don't scare me, bud. Go ahead and move it. *Me cago en su* highball." He began singing again.

Johnny fumbled three five-dollar bills out of his wallet—all he had—and shoved them at the bartender as he came up. The bartender went away.

"Well, why were you scared before, then?" Johnny asked, furiously.

"Simple," said the dark man. *"Vänta ett ögenblick,* it'll come back to me. Sure." He clapped a hand to his brow. *"Herr Gott im Himmel!"* he said, and sat down abruptly.

"Don't move it," he said. He was pale and sweat-beaded.

"Why not?"

"No control," whispered the dark man. "The instrument is tuned to you—sooner or later you're going to meet yourself. Two bodies can't occupy the same spacetime, friend." He shuddered. *"Boom!"*

Johnny's hand and wrist, already overtired, were showing a disposition to tremble. He had the hand propped against a bowl of pretzels, and that helped some, but not enough. Johnny was close to despair. The chief effect of the drinks seemed to have been to make the dark man babble in six or seven foreign tongues. The anti-drink pills were safely in his pocket; there was a fortune in those, no doubt, just as a by-product of this thing if he ever got out of it alive—but that seemed doubtful.

All the same, he checked with a glare the dark man's tentative move toward the object in his hand. His voice shook. "Tell me now, or I'll wave this thing until something happens. I haven't got any more patience! What are you after? What's it all about?"

"Un autre plat des pets de nonne, s'il vous plait, garçon," murmured the dark man.

"And cut that out," said Johnny. "I mean it!" Intentionally or not, his hand slipped, and he felt the table shudder under them.

Zip!

They were sitting at a narrow table in the Sixth Avenue Bickford's, full of the echoing clatter of inch-thick crockery.

"Well?" said Johnny, close to hysteria. The glasses on the table between them were full of milk, not whisky. Now he was in for it. Unless he could break the dark man's nerve before he sobered up—or unless, which was unlikely in the extreme, they happened to hit another bar—

"It's like this, friend," said the dark man. "I'm the last surviving remnant of a race of Lemurians, see, and I like to persecute people. I'm bitter, because you upstarts have taken over the world. You can't—"

"Who's the lady I saw you with?" Johnny asked sourly.

"Her? She's the last surviving remnant of the Atlanteans. We have a working agreement, but we hate each other even more than—"

Johnny's fingers were clammy with sweat around the limp leather that clung to them. He let his hand twitch, not too much.

Zip!

They were sitting facing each other on the hard cane seats of an almost empty subway train, rackety-clacking headlong down its dark tunnel like a consignment to hell. "Try again," said Johnny through his teeth.

"It's like this," said the dark man. "I'll tell you the truth. This whole universe isn't real, get me? It's just a figment of your imagination, but you got powers you don't know how to control, and we been trying to keep you confused, see, because otherwise—"

"Then you don't care if I do this!" said Johnny, and he made a fist around the leather purse and slammed it on his knee.

Zip!

A wind thundered in his ears, snatched the breath from his mouth. He could barely see the dark man, through a cloud of flying sleet, hunkered like himself on a ledge next to nowhere. "We're observers from the Galactic Union," the dark man shouted. "We're stationed here to keep an eye on you people on account of all them A-bomb explosions, because—"

"Or this!" Johnny howled, and jerked his fist again.

Zip!

They were sprawled on a freezing plain, staring at each other in the icy glitter of starlight. "I'll tell you!" said the dark man. "We're time travelers, and we got to make sure you never marry Piper Laurie, because—"

Gently, Johnny told himself.

Zip!

They were sliding side by side down the giant chute in the fun house at Jantzen's Beach in Portland, Oregon. "Listen!" said the dark man. "You're a mutant superman, see? Don't get sore—we had to test you before we could lead you into your glorious heritage of—"

As Johnny started to get to his feet, the movement jarred the thing in his hand, and—

Zip!

They were standing on the observation platform on top of the Empire State. It was a cold, raw day. The dark man was shivering—cold, or frightened enough to talk, or too frightened to stay drunk? His voice trembled: "Okay, this is it, friend. You aren't human—you're an android, but such a good imitation, you don't even know it. But we're your inventors, see—"

Gently: it was the little jumps that were dangerous, Johnny reminded himself.

Zip! They were in a revolving door, and *zip!* Johnny was on the staircase of his own rooming house, looking down at the dark man who was goggling up at him, trying to say something, and *zip!* they were standing beside a disordered banana cart while a cold chill ran up Johnny's spine, and—

"All right!" the dark man shouted. There was raw sincerity in his voice. "I'll tell you the truth, but *please*—"

Johnny's hand tilted in spite of himself.

Zip!

They were on the top deck of a Fifth Avenue bus parked at the curb, waiting for a load. Johnny lowered his hand with infinite care to the shiny rail top of the seat ahead. "Tell," he said.

The dark man swallowed. "Give me a chance," he said in an undertone. "I can't tell you—if I do, they'll break me, I'll never get a post again—"

"Last chance," said Johnny, looking straight ahead. *"One . . . Two . . ."*

"It's a livie," the dark man said, pronouncing the first *i* long. His voice was resigned and dull.

"A what?"

"Livie. Like movies. You know. You're an actor."

"What is this now?" said Johnny uneasily. "I'm a painter. What do you mean, I'm an ac—"

"You're an *actor, playing* a painter!" said the dark man. "You actors! Dumb cows! You're an actor! Understand? It's a *livie."*

"What is the livie about?" Johnny asked carefully.

"It's a musical tragedy. All about poor people in the slums."

"I don't live in the slums," said Johnny indignantly.

"In the *slums.* You want to tell me, or should I tell you? It's a big dramatic show. You're the comic *relief.* Later on you *die."* The dark man stopped short, and looked as if he wished he had stopped shorter. "A detail," he said. "Not important. We'll fix it up, next script conference." He put his hands to his temples suddenly. "Oh, why was I decanted?" he muttered. "Glorm will split me up the middle. He'll pulverize me. He'll shove me back into the—"

"You're serious?" said Johnny. His voice cracked. "What is this, I die? I die how?" He twitched uncontrollably.

Zip!

The Fifth Avenue bus was gone. They were sitting in the second row of a movie theater. The house lights had just gone up; the audience was shuffling out. Johnny seized the dark man by the shirt-front.

"I forget," said the dark man sullenly. "You fall off something, I think. Right before the end of the livie, when the hero gets to bed with the girl. You want to know who's the hero? Somebody you know. Duke—"

"Fall off what?" said Johnny, tightening his grip.

"Off a building. Into a trash can. Half."

"Comic relief?" said Johnny with an effort.

"Sure. Pratfalls You'll steal the livie! The lookers'll have heart attacks laughing!"

The sounds of the departing audience abruptly stopped. The walls and ceiling flickered alarmingly; when they steadied, Johnny saw with total bewilderment that they were in a different room altogether. It was nowhere he had ever been before—nowhere, he realized abruptly, with his heart racing, that he ever *could* have been before.

Out across the great silvery bowl, under a cloud-high ceiling, men were floating in the air like gnats, some drifting, some moving quickly around a bulbous metal shape that hung over the center of the huge room. Down below, twenty feet lower than the balcony on which they sat, there was a little puff of light and exploding shape—a brilliant unfolding that lasted only an instant, leaving a crazy memory of moving trees and buildings. After a moment, it happened again.

Johnny was aware that the dark man, beside him, had stiffened and somehow shrunk into himself.

He turned. Behind them, in the eerie stillness, a silvery man came striding through a doorway.

"Glorm," said the dark man, gasping, *"ne estis mia kulpo. Li—"*

Glorm said, *"Fermu vian truon."* He was slender and sinewy, dressed in something that looked like tin-foil. He had bulging eyes under a broad shelf of brow. He turned them on Johnny. "Now you vill give me d'in*stru*ment," he said.

Johnny found his breath. The bit of leather in his hand, he discovered, was now as rigid as if it were part of an invisible pillar in the air; but he tightened his grip on it, anyhow. "Why should I give it to you?" he demanded.

Glorm gestured impatiently. "Vait." He turned to look out over the enormous sunken bowl, and his voice suddenly echoed everywhere, somehow a hundred times magnified: *"Gi spinu!"*

Again came that flowering of color and movement under the hanging bulge of metal: but this time it sprang into full life, and didn't collapse again.

Fascinated, Johnny stared down over the balcony rim. The floor of the bowl was gone now, buried by a glittering marble street. On either side were white buildings, all porticos and pillars, and down at the end loomed something that looked like the Parthenon, only as big as the main UN building in New York.

The street was aboil with people, dwarfed by distance. They scattered as a four-horse chariot came hurtling past, then flowed together again. Johnny could hear them muttering angrily, like so many bees. There was a curious acrid scent in the air.

Puzzled, he glanced at Glorm and the dark man. "What's that?" he asked, pointing.

Glorm made a gesture. "Rome," said the dark man, shaking as if with a chill, "They're making a spectacle, back in 44 B.C. This here's the scene where Julius Caesar burns the place down because they won't make him Emperor."

Sure enough; the acrid scent was stronger; down below, a thin veil of gray-black smoke was beginning to arise. . .

"But he didn't," Johnny protested, stung. "That isn't even Rome—the Parthenon's in Athens."

"It used to be," said the dark man. His teeth were chattering. "We changed it. The last outfit that made livies there, they were okay on the little scenes, but they didn't understand spectacle. Glorm—" he cast a furtive glance at the silver man, and raised his voice slightly—"he understands spectacle."

"Let me get this straight now," said Johnny with a thick tongue. "You went to all the trouble of building that phony set, with that crazy Parthenon and all, when you could just go back in time and shoot the real thing?"

"Bona!" shouted Glorm's amplified voice. *"Gi estu presata!"* The scene down below whirled in upon itself and winked out.

Glorm turned impatiently to Johnny. "Now," he said. "You not un*der*stand. Dat vich you see dere *is* vat you call d'real ding. Ve not built set—built not set—not set—*Kiel oni gi diras?"*

" 'We didn't build no set,' " said the dark man.

"Putra lingvo! Ve din build no set. Ve made dat Romans build it. Dey din build no set—dey build Rome, dif*fer*ent. Un*der*stand? No-*body* din build no set! Real Rome! Real fire! Real dead! Real his*tory!"*

Johnny gaped at him. "You mean—you're changing history, just to make movies?"

"Livies," the dark man muttered.

"Livies, then. You must all be loopies. Where does that leave the people up in the future? Look—where are we now? What time?"

"Your calndar, uh, 4400-something. About twenty-five hundred years from your time."

"Twenty-five hundred—Well, what does it do to you, when you change the Romans all around?"

"Noddin'," said Glorm emphatically.

"Noddin'?" said Johnny, obtusely.

"Noddin' at all. Vat happens to dog ven you cut off his modder's tail?"

Johnny thought about it. "Noddin'."

"Korekti. You dink it is big job?"

Johnny nodded.

"It *is* big job. But ve do it tventy, forty times *every* year. You know how many people live on d'planet now?" Without pausing, he answered himself. "Tirty billion. You know how many go to livies? Half. Fifteen billion. Seven times more people dan live on d'planet in your time. Old, young. Stupid, smart. Livies got to en*ter*tain dem all. Not like your Hol*ly*vood. Dat vas not art, not spec*ta*cle. Ven d'people tink, deep down—" he tapped his head—"someting is true, den I make it true, and it *is* true! Dat is art! Dat is spec*tac*le!"

"You haven't changed New York much, anyway," said Johnny in self-defense.

Glorm's bulging eyes grew bulgier. "Not change!" He snorted, turned. His amplified voice rang out again: *"Donu al mi flugantan kvieton de Nov-Jorko natura!"*

There was a stirring of floating figures out around the hanging bulge of metal. Glorm cracked his knuckles impatiently. After a long moment the floor of the bowl blossomed again.

Johnny caught his breath.

The illusion was so perfect that the floor seemed to have dropped away: a thousand feet down, Manhattan Island lay spread in the morning sunlight; he could see ships at anchor in the harbor, and the clear glints of the Hudson and the East River running up northward into the mists over the Bronx.

The first thing he noticed was that the chaotic checkerboard of low buildings spread over the whole island: the cluster of skyscrapers at the southern tip, and the scattering at midtown, were missing.

"Guess vat year," said Glorm's voice.

He frowned. "About 1900? But that couldn't be right, he thought uneasily—there were too many bridges: more, even, than in his own time.

Glorm laughed heartily. "Dat vich you see is Nov-York, 1956—before ve change it. You dink you *in*vent sky*scrap*ers? Oh, no. Me *in*vent it."

"For *Wage-Slaves of Broadway,"* said the dark man reverently. "That was his first livie. What a spectacle!"

"Now you un*der*stand?" Glorm asked patronizingly. "Long time I vanted to tell dis to actor, see his face. Good —you un*der*stand now." His face was shining. "You are actor—I am producer, director. Producer, director is everyting. Actor is dirt! So you vill give me d'in*stru*ment."

"Won't," said Johnny weakly.

"You vill," Glorm said. "In a minute you have to let go."

Johnny discovered with shock that his hand was growing numb. So this was what they had all been stalling for, all this time. And now they'd got it. He *was* about to let go; he could feel it. So—

"Listen!" he said desperately. "What about the people in the future?—I mean your future. Do they make livies, too? If they do, are you an actor to them?"

Glorm's face tautened with fury. "Kracajo!" he said. "Vait. Vait *un*til—" He stared at the thing in Johnny's hand, and his fingers clenched.

Johnny's grip loosened. He was going to let go, and then what? Back to his own time, and more pratfalls, leading inexorably to—

His whole arm was tired. He was going to have to let go. . . . And there was nothing he could do about it. That endless chain of tinkerers, Gloms standing on each other's shoulders all the way up into the unguessable future—that was too big to change. It was, he supposed, no more frightening or terrible than other kinds of macrocosmic tyranny the human mind had imagined; it would be possible to live with it, if only his part weren't so unpleasant. . .

His hand dropped.

Smiling, Glorm reached out to the suspended bit of leather. His fingers did something to it that Johnny couldn't follow, and abruptly it sagged into his palm.

It shuddered and flickered there for a moment like a top running down. All at once it split into a brown coin and a pair of pince-nez. The flickering came again—a blue of bright shapes: fountain pen, notebook, watch, cigarette lighter—then both objects came to rest, tiny and metallic and dead.

Glorm put them into a fold of his clothing.

"Bona," he said indifferently over his shoulder. *"Resendu tion al Nov-Jorkon."*

Desperation limbered Johnny's tongue. He started talking before he even knew what he was going to say. "What if I don't stay in New York?"

Glorm paused, looking annoyed. *"Kio?"*

"You've got your gadget back," said Johnny, as the idea took shape in his head. "All right, but what are you going to do if I decide to move to Chicago, or someplace? Or get myself arrested and sent to jail? I mean, you can shuffle the probabilities around—but if I try hard enough, I can put myself where it's *impossible* to have what you want to have happen, happen." He took a deep breath. "See what I mean?"

"Plejmalpuro," said Glorm. From his expression, he saw.

"Listen," Johnny said. "Let me get the picture. This Duke you say is the hero—that's the Duke I know?" He got a nod from Glorm. "And that was part of the script, when he helped me get out of town?"

"Dress rehearsal," said the dark man. "You fall in a swamp in Florida—come up all over mud and leeches. A real boff."

Johnny shuddered, and turned his mind resolutely away from leeches and falls from high buildings. . . "What I want to know is, what was Duke's angle? Why did he think he wanted to get me out of town?"

They told him. The answer was brutally simple, and Johnny had been half afraid that he knew it already.

He waited until his nails unclenched from his palms, and he felt able to talk sensibly again. And even then, he found he had nothing to say. How could you talk to people who would do a thing like that and call it art, or entertainment? It was logical, he supposed, that a culture whose taste demanded Glorm's ruthless spec*tac*les should have such a concept of a "hero." It was also terrifying.

His time was running out again. But the answer to that one occurred to him, too.

If Duke were here, what would he say?

"Okay, look," Johnny said rapidly, "I'm just spitballing, you understand, talking off the top of my head—"

Glorm and the dark man leaned forward with interested, wary expressions.

"—but here's how I see it. Instead of this clown type for

your comedy relief, we have this suave man-of-the-world type. It's a switch. A really great, uh, producer-director could put it over. I can really see it. Take for instance—here, show me where it says in the script . . ."

Johnny materialized on the quiet side street a few steps from his door. He felt heavy and tired. The sun was still high over the tops of the old buildings; it was about 2:30—an hour and a half after Duke had left him at the airport.

He leaned against a railing and waited. Sure enough, here came Mary Finigan across the street, her hair uncombed, dark circles under her eyes.

"Go home, Mary," he said.

She was startled. "What's the matter, isn't he there? I mean, Duke, called me—he said he was at your place—"

"He's got an ax," said Johnny. "I'm telling you the truth. He was going to kill you in my apartment, with my Scout ax that I use for kindling, with my fingerprints on it."

When she was gone, Johnny went on around the corner and into the foyer. Duke was there with his hand in Johnny's mailbox. He turned around and swore, and his hand twitched a long fat envelope out of the box. "What the devil are you doing here, Johnny?"

"I decided not to go."

Duke leaned against the wall, grinning. "Well, every coming together again gives a foretaste of the resurrection. Whew!" He glanced at the envelope he was holding as if he had just noticed it. "Now I wonder what this might be."

"You know what it is," said Johnny without rancor. "Ted Edwards' fifty bucks that he owed me. That was what gave you the idea, when he told you he'd put it in the mail. Then this Mary business came up, and I suppose it just seemed to you like a God-given opportunity."

Duke's eyes were narrow and hard. "You know about that, too, do you? What were you planning to do about it, would you tell an old friend that?"

"Nothing," said Johnny. "Just give me my I O U, and we'll call it square."

Duke fished in his pocket for the folded scrap of paper and handed it over. He peered into Johnny's eyes, looking baffled. "Well, well. You're sure, are you?"

Johnny nodded and turned to go up the stairs.

"I believe you are," said Duke. He was shaking his head, arms akimbo. "Johnny, my boy, you're a character."

Johnny looked down at him for a moment. "You're another," he said.

Kris Neville

OLD MAN HENDERSON

Once, on request, I rewrote a story called "Old Man Henderson" three times, so you might think, in the end, it was the editor's story, too. But it wasn't.

He was content merely to clear away the barriers I had unwittingly set against my own vision and to be sure I did the best I was capable of. When he was done, no whisper of him remained.

He knew a trick that has been mastered only by very special men, men whose influence for good is always greater than any of us imagine.

He knew how to make himself invisible.

"JOEY, JOEY," Mrs. Mathews sighed, "haven't I told you and told you *not* to bring that animal in this house?"

"Awww, Mom," Joey said for what was probably the hundredth time since his father had brought Jasper home, "he won't hurt anything."

"I said, 'No,' and I mean just what I said! He st—smells."

Joey ruffled the green feathers on Jasper's neck and waited for the next line in the routine, which usually went, with minor variations, 'You just wait until your father gets home, young man, and *then* you'll be sorry.' Joey always thought it a tremendously ineffective approach to the issue under consideration. His father wouldn't be home from Mars for another three months yet, and by that time, she would have forgiven—or at least forgotten.

Mrs. Mathews, however, refused to run to her usual form today; she merely lowered her eyebrows, pursed her lips, and glared at him.

Jasper squirmed around in Joey's arms until he could look up at Mrs. Mathews with his big, bright, intelligent eyes, which were, at the moment, mildly reproachful.

Mrs. Mathews bolstered her relenting will. "You take him out of here this instant!"

Joey backed toward the door. "Can I play in the yard some more, then?"

Mrs. Mathews hid her enthusiasm for the idea behind sullen lips. "Well," she said, putting all the indecision she could muster into the syllable, "well, all right. For a little while longer. Then I want you to take a loaf of bread over to Old Man Henderson."

"Awwww, Mom," Joey whined. He did not like Old Man Henderson.

"I don't see why," he said in his party voice, trying to keep from going too far with the overt expression of his resentment, "you have to bake bread anyway. No one else ever does."

She replied, in a very even voice, "I like homemade bread."

Joey debated a 'Well, *I don't,*' which wasn't true, and wisely decided against it.

"Now take Jasper out of here, and let's have no more arguments."

"Yes, mother," Joey said.

When Mrs. Mathews called Joey, an hour and a half later, the bread was fresh from the oven. There were six sweet-smelling, golden-brown loaves of it. The melted butter she had rubbed in made them glisten.

"Go wash your hands," she directed.

After he had left the room, she crossed to the cupboard,

removed a section of plastic and wrapped the largest of the loaves tightly in it. Even through the insulation it felt delightfully warm in her hands. When you're as old as Old Man Henderson, she told herself, the warm center of the bread, dripping with butter, ought to taste very good to you. She put the loaf in a plastic bag.

"Hurry, Joey!" she called.

"I'm coming. I'm *coming!*"

Shortly he came.

"Here. I want you to take this now, and hurry, so he can get it before it gets cold."

She always made a special point of that: to see that she sent out his loaf just as soon as the bread came out of the oven.

"Now, hurry," she admonished again.

It was no more than right, she told herself, that we do little things for poor Old Man Henderson once in a while. After all, it wasn't as if it were charity (which she vaguely disapproved of) because he did have the government pension; it was just to show that they really hadn't forgotten him.

"Can Jasper go with me?"

"Now, Joey . . ."

"Aw, gee, *please?*"

"Well, I don't know," she said indecisively. Old Man Henderson was so old, she reflected, that he probably wouldn't notice the odor; and some people really didn't mind at all.

Joey shifted his feet. "He won't mind," he encouraged. He wanted to add, 'The way Old Man Henderson smells is a hundred times worse than Jasper.'

"All right," Mrs. Mathews agreed slowly. "And hurry, now."

At the door, Joey turned. "Mother—? If he wants me to stay a little while, may I?"

There! Mrs. Mathews reflected. That proved that if you raise a child properly (although at times he is bound to be exasperating beyond all measure and careless and inconsiderate and thoughtless), he is sure to do the proper thing when he has the chance.

And with adults, too, it was the same thing: wanting to do the proper thing. Of course you would expect adults to stop and visit with Old Man Henderson. 'Here comes the Story down the street,' they would say; and you knew immediately whom they meant. Although she, personally, would never say anything like that, or let anyone know how she really felt, she always found Old Man Henderson extremely tedious.

She smiled at her son. "But be sure to come back home in time for supper." She paused a fraction of a second and then added, "And Joey—be a nice boy and remember, he's an old man, so don't tire him out."

"I'll remember," Joey promised.

As soon as he stepped out into the yard (letting the door slam after him), he called to his pet.

"Here, Jasper, here, boy! You want to come with me?"

Jasper appeared to consider the question; after a moment, he shuffled to his feet and flapped his wings. "Kweet-kweet," he said. He came at an awkward run.

"Well, let's go, then."

It took Joey better than two hours to get to Old Man Henderson's.

The house was set well back from the street, and it had a broad, well-kept lawn with islands of blooming flowers inset against the greenness of the grass.

Joey could remember how mad his father had been when, last Halloween, some of the neighborhood boys had littered it with little scraps of paper and pulled up all the flowers. It had taken Old Man Henderson nearly all day just to get the paper picked up. His father had said to Joey, 'If a son of mine did a trick like that, I'd see to it he was whipped until he couldn't sit down.' And when his father discovered that Joey had helped to do it—! Every time Joey thought about that, his bottom side prickled with the memory.

Joey stood on the porch for a long moment, wondering if

it would be safe not to knock at all, but instead, throw the bread away somewhere and tell his mother he had delivered it. She would ask, 'And how did he like the bread?' and he could reply, 'Oh, he said to tell you that bakery bread couldn't come anywhere near yours.' But Joey was a little afraid to risk a lie, so he knocked at the door.

After scarcely a second, Old Man Henderson called, "Come in," in his reedy voice.

Reluctantly, Joey opened the door and entered.

The room was dim—or perhaps it just seemed to Joey that it was dim, coming in fresh from the sunlight—and it smelled, as he knew it would, of the dry, sweet-acrid odor of age.

Old Man Henderson blinked. "Ah, ah," he said. "Come in, boy, and set a while." He tried to keep his voice casual to keep from betraying the fact that he had been sitting there all afternoon hoping one of his young friends would drop by to talk to him.

"I've brought you some fresh bread," Joey replied non-committally.

"Ah, ah," Old Man Henderson said, "then you must be the Mathews boy." He had so many young friends that he sometimes confused their faces. There was the Jenkins lad, now, that looked a lot like this one.

"Well, well," he said, "so you've brought me some fresh bread, eh?"

"Yes."

"Ah, ah. Well, now, that's sure nice of you. Your mother makes fine bread. None better. Bakery bread can't come anywhere near hers— Now you be sure to tell her I said that, will you?"

Joey grunted.

"You want to bet something, boy? I'll bet that she just now finished baking that bread. Every time she bakes, she sends me a loaf while it's still nice and hot. Your mother's a fine woman. You ought to be proud to have a mother like that."

Joey stared hard at the old man. "It's not hot this time," he said. "It's cold."

"Oh," Old Man Henderson said.

"Yes," he said, "she forgot all about it until it was already cold."

Old Man Henderson moved his jaw twice, blinked his eyes, and said, "Don't you worry about that. It'll taste just as good, anyway. Here. Give it to me, and I'll put it in the kitchen, there, for supper."

He took the bread and shuffled out of the room.

Joey wanted to leave before he got back, but he knew he should stay at least a little while, in case his mother should remark, 'I hope Joey didn't tire you out, being over there all afternoon the other day.' If he left too quickly, Old Man Henderson would be sure to remember that.

When the old man came back, he was carrying a little plate of crisp chocolate cookies with coconut toppings.

"Here," Old Man Henderson said. "Take these, now, and sit down over there. In the comfortable chair."

Joey took the cookies without saying anything and sat down.

Old Man Henderson sat down in another chair and studied the boy of a bit, trying to think of something to say.

"How are things, my little man?" he finally asked.

"Fine."

"Fine, eh? Well, well . . ."

Old Man Henderson looked down at his feet and then looked up again, waiting for Joey to say something else. When it became apparent that Joey had no intention of saying anything, Old Man Henderson reopened the conversation.

"You know," he began, "when you came in just a minute ago, I was sitting here thinking . . . I was remembering back years and years ago. Must have been '51, '52 . . . yes, '52 . . . I believe it was . . . Well, one time, and I wasn't much older than you, then . . ." He didn't think Joey was listening very attentively. "Well," he finished lamely, "never mind about all that."

Old Man Henderson realized that the long ago of his youth was not as real and vivid as yesterday's sunset except to himself, and that growing boys do not like to listen to an old man ramble about his childhood. What they like, he told himself, are adventure stories, tales of drama and excitement.

He peered at Joey.

Let's see, he reflected, have I told this one? . . . Nothing is worse, he frequently told himself, than an old man who harps continually on a single theme.

But after a moment's study, he was sure that he had never told this boy. Still, he didn't want to rush things. He would wait for a point at which the story would fall naturally into the conversation so that it wouldn't seem he was trying to force it on the boy.

For the first time (his eyes were not as good as they once were), Old Man Henderson noticed the strange animal that had entered with Joey. Less out of curiosity and more as a topic of conversation, he said, "Well, ah, ah . . . And what's that you've got there?" Of late he had ceased to care very much about the strange new things in the outside world.

"Huh? Oh, just Jasper."

"Jasper, eh? Well, well."

Joey had finished the cookies and now he felt more expansive. "Yes, Daddy brought him back from Venus." Joey scratched Jasper's head. "He's very intelligent and affectionate. And an ideal pet for children." Then he added emphatically, as if Old Man Henderson had disagreed, "Daddy says so!"

'Why, why, now that's fine. That's very fine. Well, well . . . Come here, Jasper."

Jasper peered up at Joey as if for permission and then scampered across the room.

Absently, Old Man Henderson reached down and ruffled Jasper's feathers. "I've sure never seen anything like this one."

Jasper hopped into his lap.

"My!" he said, beginning for the first time to take other

than a conversational interest in the creature, for he always had a soft spot for affectionate animals. "Well, well. How do you like Old Man Henderson?"

Jasper nuzzled his hand and then looked up to study his face. "Kweeeeet," he said. He liked Old Man Henderson well enough.

"You should be very nice to him," the old man said.

"I am," Joey said. "Except once in a while. When he's mean."

"Ah, ah, yes," Old Man Henderson said.

Jasper had been following the conversation with his eyes and now, in the silence, he looked across at Joey.

At length, the old man said, "Ah, ah," half to himself. "Hummmm. Well. Venus you say?"

"Yes," Joey agreed. "We have to import food, and that's very expensive, but Daddy says it's worth it if *I* like him."

"Ah, ah. Seems to me I remember reading about them—whatever-you-call-'ems—now that I come to think of it."

Joey narrowed his eyes. Just last week his mother had said, 'It's a pity Old Man Henderson's too old to read any more, with so many exciting things happening every day, things he's always dreamed of seeing happen.'

"All right, then," Joey demanded, deleting an 'if you know so much' at the last moment, "how do Kweets manage to live on Earth, where the air's so different?"

Old Man Henderson opened and shut his mouth. He was suddenly confused. He tried to remember about that article—it *was* just the other day when he was reading it, wasn't it?—but he could not. "Why, why," he said. "Ahhhhhh, ahhhhhhhhh—"

"See there! You don't know!" Joey cried triumphantly.

Old Man Henderson had been looking at the boy. Now, he looked away. He studied the back of his heavy, veined hand as it glided over Jasper's soft, green feathers; there was a puzzled, half-frightened look on his face.

"So your Daddy gave him to you," he said at last. "And where is your Daddy now?"

"He's on Mars, doing engineering on the new Dome. I'll bet I've told you that a hundred times!"

Old Man Henderson blinked twice as if someone had slapped him almost hard enough to bring tears. "Of course," he said hastily. "I remember, now. Mars, you say. I . . . I . . . I . . . ah, ah, Mars? Hummmm."

He rubbed his withered hand along his leg.

"You know," he said, "when I was a young man, there hadn't even been a man to the *moon*." Already he could feel his confidence return. He had told the story quite a few times in the last fifty, seventy-five years. And he knew, too, that this young one would be sure to want to hear it, and that would make everything a-1 right again. "A couple of people had circled around it, but nobody had ever *landed* on it."

"Well, well," said Joey.

No one ever addressed him in that tone; people were always nice to him, and listened politely. Now, he could not quite understand it. He looked down at Jasper for reassurance.

"Ah, ah, yes. There hadn't been a single man to the moon . . . Well. You see that silver and gold plaque over the mantle, there?"

Joey did not turn to see.

But Old Man Henderson fell to studying it, and his eyes grew bright with the long ago and far away memory. Idly, one of his hands stroked Jasper's sleek feathers.

"Do you know who gave that to me?" he asked.

"Yes," Joey said. "The President of the United States gave it to you."

Slowly Old Man Henderson's mind drifted back to the room. That had been his sentence, and it sounded harsh and frightening to hear it coming from young lips in a voice twisting all the glory of it into ashes. He could scarcely believe that he had heard correctly.

"Yes, yes, that's right," he heard his voice tell the boy, and it sounded weary and dry with disappointment.

"And I'll tell you why you got it," Joey said loudly. There

was a queer excitement alive and throbbing in his body. He knew that the old man sitting before him was helpless before his words. He knew, also, that the old man would never protest to his mother. Not about this. It made him feel very big to be in a position to hurt Old Man Henderson without danger to himself.

"You got it because you were the first man to land on the moon!"

Old Man Henderson felt ice form somewhere below his heart. He quit petting the Kweet and sat unseeing, listening, in spite of himself, to his own words come twisting back at him in cruel burlesque.

"I've heard that story I'll bet a hundred times! Now let me tell you about it. How it felt when you first saw the long steel ship—" Joey began to mimic the reedy voice of Old Man Henderson—"*glistening* in the Florida sunlight."

Old Man Henderson gestured weakly and wanted to ask the boy, please, to stop, but Joey did not give him the chance.

"And how it felt when you took off, acceleration pushing you back in your couch. And how it felt when you first saw the moon right there almost under your feet . . .

"And the celebration they gave the three of you when you got back, and how the President gave you that—that *thing* up there with his own two hands, and how he said—"

"Please, please. I meant no harm."

Joey had stopped for breath. He was incoherent with excitement.

"And how you had Faith . . . ," and again his voice went to the upper register. " 'I always had *faith,* even when I was a little boy, that man couldn't be kept on Earth, that he was bound for the moon and then the planets and then the stars. I always had *faith!*'

"Nobody wants to listen to your silly old story any more. Can't you see that! *Nobody wants to listen!* You've told it and told it until we're all sick and tired of hearing it!

"When they see you coming down the street, they say,

'Here comes Old Man Henderson and his Story!' and they *laugh* at you when your back's turned!"

Joey had to stop for breath.

Old Man Henderson made no sound.

In his excitement, Joey waved his arms wildly. He upset the cookie dish and it shattered on the floor. Joey began again, and it was almost a scream.

"You don't seem to realize that nobody wants to hear about how you went to the moon. Why, anybody can go to the moon! I've been there twice, and Daddy and Mama have both been to Venus, and Daddy's on Mars putting up a Dome right now so people can live on it, and it's going to be a bigger Dome than the one on Venus, and all you talk about is how you went to the moon!"

Joey was crying, now.

"And you don't even know what a Kweet is, and you don't even know nothing about what we're doing!"

He turned and ran to the door. There, he stopped and looked back. He saw Old Man Henderson sitting very still, not saying anything, and suddenly he didn't feel glad any more.

"Come on, Jasper!" he screamed. "I'm getting out of here, away from that crazy old man!"

Jasper looked at Joey and said nothing. Then he turned his mute eyes to Old Man Henderson. He did not move.

For a moment, Joey did not know what to do; he began to feel the first rustlings of fear inside his mind. He turned and slammed the door behind him and began to run.

Jasper lay quietly in Old Man Henderson's lap. He looked up into the old face, the old face of loose folds of dry skin, but the face with the astonishingly bright eyes that brimmed with tears.

After a long time, Old Man Henderson put Jasper on the floor, stood up, and walked to Joey's chair. He got down on his knees and began to pick up pieces of the broken cookie dish.

Jasper walked over. "Kweet?" he asked, very, very softly.

William F. Nolan

HE KILT IT WITH A STICK

Tony was a good friend and a fine editor through the years of my pro career, and it means a great deal to me to be part of this memorial anthology. Back in 1952, when I made my first submissions, Tony encouraged me and aided me with sound editorial advice. He kept helping me over the years, making solid suggestions for Gamma *contributions, when I was managing editor of that short-lived magazine. In 1968 I dedicated my book* Three to the Highest Power *to Anthony Boucher, and the last word he wrote to me was "Amen"—this on a letter from Phyllis, telling me how much the dedication meant to him. This was just a few weeks before he died.*

A SUMMER NIGHT in Kansas City.

Ellen away, visiting her parents. The house on Forest empty, waiting.

Warm air.

A high, yellow moon.

Stars.

Crickets thrumming the dark.

Fireflies.

A summer night.

Fred goes to the Apollo on Troost to see a war film. It depresses him. All the killing. He leaves before it has ended, walking up the aisle and out of the deserted lobby and on past the empty glass ticket booth. Alone.

The sidewalk is bare of pedestrians.

It is late, near midnight, and traffic is very sparse along Troost. The wide street is silent. A truck grinds heavily away in the distance.

Fred begins to walk home.

He shouldn't. It is only two blocks: a few steps to the corner of 33rd, then down the long hill to Forest, then left along Forest to his house at the end of the block, near 34th. Not quite two blocks to walk. But too far for him. Too far.

Fred stops.

A gray cat is sleeping in the window of Rae's Drug Store. Fred presses the glass. *I could break the window—but that would be useless. The thing would be safe by then; it would leap away and I'd never find it in the store. The police would arrive and—No. Insane. Insane to think of killing it.*

The gray cat, quite suddenly, opens its eyes to stare at Fred Baxter. Unblinking. Evil.

He shudders, moves quickly on.

The cat continues to stare.

Foul thing knows what I'd like to do to it.

The hill, sloping steeply toward Forest, is tinted with cool moonlight. Fred walks down this hill, filled with an angry sense of frustration: he would very much have enjoyed killing the gray cat in the drug store window.

Hard against chest wall, his heart judders. Once, twice, three times. Thud thud thud. He slows, removes a tissue-wrapped capsule from an inside pocket. Swallows the capsule. Continues to walk.

Fred reaches the bottom of the hill, crosses over to Forest.

Trees now. Big fat-trunked oaks and maples, fanning their leaves softly over the concrete sidewalk. Much darker. Thick tree-shadow midnight dark, broken by three street lamps down the long block. Lamps haloed by green night insects.

Deeper.

Into the summer dark. . . .

When Fred Baxter was seven, he wrote: "Today a kitty kat bit me at school and it sure hurt a lot. The kitty was bad, so I kilt it with a stick."

When he was ten, and living in St. Louis, a boy two houses up told Fred his parents wanted to get rid of a litter. "I'll take care of it," Fred assured him—and the next afternoon, in Miller Lake, he drowned all six of the kittens.

At fifteen, in high school, Fred trapped the janitor's Tabby in the gymnasium locker room, choked it to death, and carried it downstairs to the furnace. He was severely scratched in the process.

As a college freshman, in Kansas City, Fred distributed several pieces of poisoned fish over the Rockhurst campus. The grotesquely twisted bodies of seven cats were found the next morning.

Working in the sales department of Hall Brothers, Fred was invited to visit his supervisor at home one Saturday—and was seen in the yard, playing with Frances, a pet Siamese. She was later found crushed to death, and it was assumed a car had run over the animal. Fred quit his job ten days later because his supervisor had cat hands.

Fred married Ellen Ferber when he was thirty, and she wanted to have children right away. Fred said no, that babies were small and furry in their blankets, and disturbed him. Ellen bought herself a small kitten for company while Fred was on the road. He didn't object—but a week after the purchase, he took a meat knife and dismembered the kitten, telling Ellen that it had "wandered away." Then he bought her a green parakeet.

ZZZZZZ Click

This is Frederick Baxter speaking and I . . . wait, the sound level is wrong and I'll— There, it's all right now. I can't tell anyone about this—but today I found an old Tom in an alley downtown, and I got hold of the stinking wretched animal, and I . . . .

ZZZZZZ Click

The heart trouble started when Fred was thirty-five.

"You have an unusual condition," the doctor told him. "You are, in effect, a medical oddity. Your chest houses a quivering-muscles heart—a fibrillator. Your condition can easily prove fatal. Preventive measures must be taken. No severe exercise, no overeating, plenty of rest."

Fred obeyed the man's orders—although he did not really trust a doctor whose cat eyes reflected the moon.

ZZZZZZ Click

. . . awful time with the heart. Really awful. The use of digitalis drives me to alcohol, which sends my heart into massive flutters. Then the alcohol forces me into a need for more digitalis. It is a deadly circle and I . . .

I have black dreams. A nap at noon and I dream of smothering. This comes from the heart condition. And because of the cats. They all fear me, now, avoid me on the street. They've *told* one another about me. This is fact. Killing them is becoming quite difficult . . . but I caught a big, evil one in the garden last Thursday and buried it. Alive. As I am buried alive in these black dreams of mine. I got excited, burying the cat—and this is bad for me. I must go on killing them, but I must *not* get excited. I must stay calm and not—here comes Ellen, so I'd better. . . .

ZZZZZZ Click

"What's wrong, Fred?"

It was two a.m. and Ellen had awakened to find him standing at the window.

"Something in the yard," he said.

The moon was flushing the grass with pale gold—and a dark shape scuttled over the lawn, breaking the pattern. A cat shape.

"Go to sleep," said his wife, settling into her pillow.

Fred Baxter stared at the cat, who stared back at him from the damp yard, its head raised, the yellow of the night moon now brimming the creature's eyes. The cat's mouth opened.

"It's sucking up the moonlight," Fred whispered.

Then he went back to bed.

But did not sleep.

Later, thinking about this, Fred recalled what his mother had often said about cats. "They perch on the chest of a baby," she'd said, "place their red mouth over the soft mouth of the baby and draw all the life from its body. I won't have one of the disgusting things in the house."

Alone in the summer night, walking down Forest Avenue in Kansas City, Fred passes a parked car, bulking black and silent in its gravel driveway. The closed car windows gleam deep yellow from the eyes inside.

Eyes?

Fred stops, looks back at the car.

It is packed with cats.

How many? Ten . . . a dozen. More . . . twenty maybe. All inside the car, staring out at me. Dozens of foul, slitted-yellow eyes . . . .

Fred can do nothing. He checks all four doors of the silent automobile, finds them locked. The cats stare at him.

Filthy creatures!

He moves on.

The street is oddly silent. Fred realizes why: the crickets have stopped. No breeze stirs the trees; they hang over him, heavy and motionless in the summer dark.

The houses along Forest are shuttered, lightless, closed against the night. Yet, on a porch, Fred detects movement.

Yellow eyes spark from porch blackness. A big dark-furred cat is curled into a wooden swing. It regards Fred Baxter.

Kill it!

He moves with purposeful stealth, leans to grasp a stout tree limb which has fallen into the yard. He mounts the porch steps.

The dark-furred cat has not stirred.

Fred raises the heavy limb. The cat hisses, claws extended, fangs balefully revealed. It cries out like a wounded child and vanishes off the porch into the deep shadow between houses.

Missed. Missed the rotten thing.

Fred moves down the steps, crosses the yard toward the walk. His head is lowered in anger. When he looks up, the walk is thick with cats. He runs into them, kicking, flailing the tree-club. They scatter, melting away from him as butter from a heated blade.

Thud. Thud, thud. Fred drops the club. His heart is rapping, fisting his chest. He leans against a tree, sobbing for breath. The yellow-eyed cats watch him from the street, from bushes, from steps and porches and the tops of cars.

Didn't get a one of them. Not a damn one. . . .

The fireflies have disappeared. The street lamps have dimmed into smoked circles above the heavy, cloaking trees. The clean summer sky is shut away from him—and Fred Baxter finds the air clogged with the sharp, suffocating smell of catfur.

He walks on down the block.

The cats follow him.

He thinks of what fire could do to them—long blades of yellow crisping flame to flake them away into dark ash—but he cannot burn them. . . . Burning them would be impossible. There are *hundreds*. That many at least.

They fill driveways, cover porches, blanket yards, pad in lion-like silence along the street. The yellow moon is in their eyes; sucked from the sky. Fred, his terror rising, arches his head to look upward.

The trees are alive with them!

His throat closes. He cannot swallow. Catfur cloaks his mouth. . . .

Fred begins to run down the concrete sidewalk, stumbling, weaving, his chest filled with a terrible winged beating.

A sound.

The scream of the cats.

Fred claps both hands to his head to muffle the stab and thrust of sound.

The house . . . must reach the house.

Fred staggers forward. The cat-masses surge in behind him as he runs up the stone walk to his house.

A cat lands on his neck. Mutely, he flings it loose—plunges up the wooden porch steps.

Key. Find your key and unlock the door. Get inside!

Too late.

Eyes blazing, the cats flow up and over him, a dark furry stifling weight as he pulls back the screen. Claws and needle teeth rip at his back, arms, face, legs . . . shred his clothing and skin. He twists wildly, beating at them. Blood runs into his eyes. . . .

The door is open. He falls forward, through the opening. The cats swarm after him in hot waves, covering his chest, sucking the breath from his body. Baxter's thin scream is lost in the sharp, rising, all-engulfing cry of the cats.

A delivery boy found him two days later, lying face down on the living room floor. His clothes were wrinkled. But untorn.

A cat was licking the cold white unmarked skin of Frederick Baxter's cheek.

Alan E. Nourse

THE CANVAS BAG

Virtually everyone who knew Tony Boucher during his years as editor of the Magazine of Fantasy and Science Fiction *was aware of the delight he took in gently and patiently prodding new writers into publication, and encouraging them to try to improve their work. He was more generous than perhaps any other editor in his thoughtful—and often detailed—suggestions for revisions of stories by rank newcomers; and then, praise heaven, he* remembered *the stories when they were resubmitted.*

"The Canvas Bag" was one of the first half-dozen stories I wrote, and the second of mine that Tony accepted for F&SF, after several painfully near-misses. The first story had been taken only after complete revision under his editorial guidance, but "The Canvas Bag" seemed to me to be just right as it was. Tony clearly agreed, for he accepted it within days of its submission, and asked for just one subtle change on the last page of the manuscript. He felt that the future Joe and Jeannie faced, implicit in the story's ending, should be made explicit by adding a word or two—a characteristically gentle editorial touch which magnified the story's impact by a factor of ten and made it, even today, one of my own favorites among my published stories.

THE TELEPHONE JANGLED just as Joe Baker got himself settled in the bathtub. He growled something poisonous and dashed the length of the rooming house hallway to his bare little room at the end, bathrobe flying, spattering water far and wide as he reached for the offending instrument. Then Jeannie's voice was tinkling in his ear; his annoyance vanished, and his heart skipped twice in dreadful premonition.

Jeannie was laughing. "I must have dragged you out of the shower! You sound like you've hurdled barriers."

"Many barriers," said Joe, slapping at the trickle of water meandering down his leg. His feet were planted in an expanding puddle. "There's nothing wrong—is there?"

"Nothing drastic." Jeannie's voice was warm. "I'll have to be late tonight, is all. Maybe an hour or more—I don't know. Frankie's decided that *this* is the night to finish the inventory. No other night will do. And you know Frankie."

Joe shook the water out of his ears and consigned Frankie to the eighth circle of the nether world. A chill of disappointment stabbed through him all out of proportion to the importance of an hour's delay in their dinner date. But then, he was sure he heard the same disappointment in Jeannie's voice and felt somewhat mollified. It was almost as if she knew what a special date it was going to be. "How about nine, then? I'll meet you there."

"We should be finished by then. I'll be hungry, too."

"Sky's the limit tonight. Even on barriers to hurdle." He wondered vaguely how a girl who spent all day dishing out food could bear to look at it at night, much less eat it.

Jeannie's laugh was echoing in his ears as he hung up. He blinked sourly around the room. An *extra* hour to kill. He could hardly bear it. It was a drab room with a single window that stared out on the main street catching the hot Indiana sun. Not a bad room if you liked cheap boarding houses. From the window he could see the whole town before him. He stared down for a moment or two before turning away, allowing his mind to drift back to his first impression of it the day he'd dropped off the freight car six weeks before.

A grubby little dump town, he had thought. A good place

to stop for the night and move on. They probably wouldn't favor gentlemen of the road around here anyway. Nothing unusual, his thinking that—the usual chain of thoughts that went through his mind when he hit a little Midwest town with its dusty streets and its dirty frame houses. It was even an ordinary-looking diner where he had been sitting, deciphering the hectographed bill-of-fare when the girl behind the counter had come over, and he had looked up and seen Jeannie.

He gave a little laugh now and fished clean clothes from the bureau. A starched shirt had always been a trial for Joe; he struggled into it manfully, grinning at himself in the mirror. So very much could happen in six short weeks! One's ideas of towns and people and everything could change so rapidly. He whistled a little tune, regarding his broad tanned face and unkempt brown hair as he whirled the tie. Not a bad face, Joe Baker. Not bad at all. You could see how a gal might go for it. And tonight she simply *had* to go for it. He'd never asked a girl to marry him before in his whole life. She couldn't refuse, not tonight.

But the thought of mariage made him feel a bit strange. It was bound to happen sometime, he had told himself. A man can't tramp the roads forever. Someday the time would come to stop. It had always been sometime in the dim, distant future with Joe. But it wasn't any more. Tonight the time had come.

And then his eye fell on the little blue canvas bag on the floor in the corner.

He blinked at the bag. The bag blinked back at him. He gave a nervous laugh and kicked the bag. It went skidding across the floor.

"Good-by, Bag," he said gleefully. "I won't need *you* any more. Our drifting days are over."

For a girl who had inventoried all evening, Jeannie was bright and chipper when Joe met her coming out of the diner. She was one of those curious girls who seem to have totally unlimited energy and become the more beautiful the wearier they are. She was slender and dark with wide gray eyes set in a narrow elfin face. Like a queen, Joe thought, as she came down the steps, or at least a princess. She kissed him lightly, and he slipped his arm around her as they walked around back to her old coupé. "He's an old tyrant, that Frankie," she was saying.

"Let me take you away from all this," said Joe gallantly. "Let me take you on the wings of the wind. The Pleasure Palace awaits."

She laughed, and Joe slipped easily into the driver's seat.

"The Spoon for dinner?" Jeannie asked.

"The Spoon? Not tonight. This is *our* night, kiddie, nothing but the best." He looked down at her and kissed her on the nose. "You know that place on the point—down by the bend of the river? Steaks an inch thick, they say, and dancing on the terrace." He slid the car out into the road traffic. "Tonight we celebrate."

"It's very, very expensive, I've heard."

"Eat, drink, and be merry."

Worry flickered in her gray eyes. "You're—you're not heading out again, are you, Joe?"

He smiled. " 'Fraid not. Not a chance. I'm thinking of retiring from the road."

She snuggled closer and threw her head back happily. "For good?"

"For good."

"Then we *do* have something to celebrate."

The place was crowded when they arrived, but the waiter found them a table for two looking out on the broad river. Across the room the orchestra was playing quietly when they ordered, and soon they were in each other's arms, whirling gracefully to the music. It was a strange world for Joe—a warm soft world of love and sweet smells and great cleanliness, and he could hardly focus his thoughts as the girl pressed her soft cheek to his. He had missed so much, all these years of drifting from town to town, never satisfied, never stopping. He had waited for years, and now he was sure, beyond doubt that the long years of waiting had been entirely worth it.

"I've got a secret, Jeannie," he whispered as they moved into the shadows of the terrace.

"Don't tell me," she whispered back.

"Why not?"

"Because then it wouldn't be a secret, would it?"

"But some secrets are for two people, they aren't any good for just one." Her ear was inches from his lips. "I love you, Jeannie. Did you know that?"

She nodded.

"I want you to marry me."

He thought he felt her arms tighten for a moment, and they danced silently, close together in a wonderful haze that required no words. But when she turned her face up to him, her eyes were sober and troubled. "Are you sure you want that?" she asked.

"I'm not fooling, Jeannie."

She turned her face away. "Oh, I know you're not, Joe, but do you *know* what you want to do? Do you really want to stop drifting, take a house, settle down for good? Do you really think you could do that?"

"I wouldn't be asking you if I hadn't thought it through, would I?" There was a puzzled note in his voice, and he frowned. Something deep inside him had gone cold, a strange sort of pain he had never felt before. "I've been on the road for a long time, I know; but a man gets tired of drifting after a while. Sooner or later he finds a girl that makes it all seem silly." His words faltered; somehow, he couldn't get the right ones to come out. The coldness in his chest deepened. "Look, Jeannie, the road is a hard life, there isn't any softness or friendship or happiness out there. Why would anybody choose it? Why should I ever want to go back?"

He broke off realizing that he was raising his voice. He blinked at Jeannie in dismay, and she looked away, shaking her head and guiding them back to their seats. She looked up at him strangely. "You don't have to convince me, Joe. I believe it." She paused. "I wonder if *you* believe it."

His voice choked in his throat. "I only know how I feel, and I know it's true. I wouldn't have asked you otherwise."

She nodded, staring at the checkered tablecloth. Then she looked him straight in the eyes. "I want you to tell me something, Joe," she said quietly. "I want you to tell me how old you are."

Joe stared at her and very slowly set down his glass. Something was drumming in his head, a frightful deafening sound that chilled him to the bone. "Why, I'm . . . thirty-ish, or so," he said vaguely, wrinkling his forehead. "Thirty-one, I think, or thirty-two." He blinked at her. "I don't know, it's somewhere around there."

"But can't you *remember,* Joe?" Her eyes were wide.

"Well, of course I can, I suppose! I had a birthday last February." The drumming in his ears grew louder. "No, that was Pete Hower's birthday. We were on the road together. Funny guy, Pete, he—"

"Please, Joe"

A chill ran up his back. It was as if he had suddenly glanced over his shoulder and seen a vast pit opening up behind him. He saw Jeannie's worried face, and he wracked his brains trying to remember, but his mind met with nothing save abysmal blankness. He stared at her in alarm. "Jeannie, *I can't remember!"*

"Oh, Joe! Think! You've got to!"

"But what difference does it make?"

"Joe—" The girl's voice was trembling, close to tears. "Think, Joe. Go back. Back to where you were before you came here, and where you went before that. Here—here's some paper. Write it down. Try to remember, Joe."

He took the pencil numbly. Slowly, from the drumming in his head things were beginning to creep into his mind, incredible things. "I—I just came East from Fargo six weeks ago," he faltered. "Hopped a freight. Ran into some trouble with the cops and had a fight. And then I'd been in Minot for a while before that."

"How long?"

"Couple of months. I was working my way East, thought I'd work the docks for a while."

"And where were you before Minot?"

"Santa Monica. Cab-driving job. I almost got killed; that chilled me on the coast. Came up from San Diego before that; hit Dago on a tramp steamer that had come through the canal from Vera Cruz. And then before that there was the war."

A horrible thought flashed through Joe Baker's mind. A fiendish voice was screaming in his ear: *Which war, Joe, which war?*

Suddenly, in a terrifying flash, he remembered. The muddy fog cleared from his mind, and his memory whirled back and back, and his face went white.

There was the fighting in Anzio, and the storming of Monte Casino—

And there was the girl in Pittsburgh who'd cleaned him out that night at Jardine's—that seemed like a century ago! And the logging up in Canada before that—

And the long depression years before that in the hobo jungles—

And the job he'd lost when his boss went down in the crash—

And the run-in with the Boston cops in the boot-legging deal which couldn't go wrong—

And the cattle-herding jaunt down through Wyoming and Colorado and Oklahoma before that—how long was that trip? Four years? Must have been, with all the time he'd wasted in Denver—

Joe Baker stared at the girl across the table from him, his mind screaming. He could almost see the blue canvas bag by his side, he could feel the excitement again as he had packed it full, ready for another move, and another, and another. . . . With a sudden horrified rush he picked up the paper and pencil and began scratching down places, times, distances, something clutching in his chest as he wrote:

The mustering out after the armistice, and the long trip home from France—

The days drifting through Europe after the turn of the century—

The shouting, savage cavalry charges against the Spanish in Cuba—

The bitter hatred of the Kansas farmers when the railroads went through—

The hum of hoofbeats on the Nevada prairie, the wild screams of the Indian raiders—

The crash of artillery, the bitter sharp voice of the long-rifles at Chickamauga—

He remembered them. He remembered them all.

Joe Baker sat back in his chair finally, his hands trembling. It was utterly incredible, of course. But it was true. He'd just never thought of it before. He'd drifted from town to town, from job to job, anywhere the moment seemed to suggest. Drifted, and stopped for a while, and drifted again. He'd never thought of the past, for the past was filled with pain and loneliness, and such things seldom encourage reminiscing. It had simply never occurred to him to stop and think how long he'd drifted, nor what might happen if he ever tried to stop.

And he had drifted for a hundred and fifty years.

He stared at the girl's frightened face. "You knew—somehow you knew."

She nodded. "I didn't know what it was. I knew you were *different,* somehow. At first I thought it was just that you'd been traveling a long time, that it was a part of a personality you'd built up on the road. I felt it the first moment I saw you. And then I began to realize that the difference was something else. But I didn't realize how long you've been going—"

"But my face!" he cried. "My body! How could it be possible? Why is it that I'm not old, shriveled, dead?"

"I don't, know."

"But it couldn't happen!"

Jeannie shook her head weakly. "There's something else far more important."

"What's that?"

"What makes you do it."

"I tell you *I don't know.*"

"But you *must* have remembered the time passing!" she burst out.

Joe shook his head. "I just never stopped to think. Why should I have? There've never been friends, or family, or anyone to hang onto along the way. It never mattered what time it was, or what day it was. All that mattered was whether it was winter or summer, whether it was hot or cold, whether I was full or hungry. Jeannie, does it matter now? I love you, I want to stop, now, I want to marry you."

They were dancing again, and she was fighting to hold back the tears, clinging to him like a lost child. "Yes, yes—tomorrow, Joe—We can get the papers. Don't ever go away from me, Joe. Oh, I'm afraid."

"Don't be, don't be."

"I can't help it. I'm afraid tomorrow—"

He put a finger to her lips. "Tomorrow we'll get a license. Then we'll be married. I've never wanted to stop before. But I do now, more than anything on Earth. And I will."

The drive back into town was very quiet.

It was late when he returned to his room. He dreaded to return. If there were only something they could *do,* some place to go *now,* while he knew he could! But there was nothing to do until tomorow, and he was cold with fear. He walked into the room and snapped on the lights and the coldness tightened in his chest.

His eyes fell on the blue canvas bag.

It was old and threadbare and exceedingly dusty. The dust from a thousand long roads of a thousand countries was ground into its fiber, and it seemed a thing alive, a living entity with a power of its own worn deep into its creases and leatherwork. An ordinary old-fashioned traveling bag, really; over the years he had become attached to it with an unreasoning fondness. It was his home, his only solid, dependable connection with the world through which he had been drifting like a ghost. A sound, sturdy friend, always there, carrying his few possessions. He had tramped miles, once, to recover it when it had been left behind. Once it had been stolen, and he had killed a man to get it back.

And now he hated it.

Even as he looked at it, the drums were beating in his ears again—his own pulse? He didn't know. He stared at the bag, and phantoms began to flicker through his mind tormenting him. The miles had been long and dusty, but they had been free miles. He had been lonely, desperately lonely, but always, he had been free. And now. . . .

He took the bag up on his lap, unzippered it, and watched it fall open into the familiar creases. Once there had been buttons on it, long ago. Now a zipper replaced the buttons, but it was still the same old bag. Inside there were odds and ends. A pack of cigarettes, slightly mildewed, and an ancient straight-razor. A couple of unused rifle shells, a pair of stick-on rubber soles for his shoes, a shabby torn bandanna. Like an overpowering wind the memories filtered under the glistening star blanket. And now he would stop, throw away the bag, go off and settle down in a house, take work in the quarry outside town every day. . . . Once stopped, he could never drift again.

The coldness deepened. Nervously he dropped the bag on the floor, kicked it across the room. It was nonsense to think that way. He hated the road and all the loneliness it had meant. He *wouldn't* go back, not with a girl like Jeannie to keep him from ever being lonely again.

The chill grew into panic. He sat down on the bed, trembling. He was afraid. He was fighting now, and a voice was whispering in his ear, *You've got to go, Joe, you can't stop, never, never—run now, before you hurt her any more! You can never stop drifting, Joe.*

He gripped the bedstead until his knuckles turned white. Why? He strained his memory trying to think back, trying to remember how it had started so long ago. It was as though a great hand were pushing him, drawing him toward the canvas bag, urging him to pack it up, take it and race away, like the wind, onto the road again. But he didn't want to go; he wanted a wife, a home.

Home, Joe? You hated your home!

No, no, he thought. A line of sweat was standing out on his upper lip. I didn't hate it, I was young, I didn't understand, I didn't know.

You threw a curse on your home, Joe. Remember? You screamed it in your mother's face, you reviled her and packed your canvas bag.

I didn't know what I was doing he thought. I was foolish. I couldn't have known.

But you said it, Joe. Remember what you said?

No!

I'll never come home if I live a thousand years.

He clutched at the bag. His hand anchored on the grip, and he felt it start tugging at him. He let out a cry and threw it on the floor. Frantically he jerked the telephone from the hook, dialed Jeannie's number and heard her sleepy voice.

"Jeannie, you've got to help me," he choked. "Come over, please, I can't help myself."

There had been other times he'd tried. He remembered them now, horrible struggles that had nearly killed him with torment until he gave up. He had never believed in ghosts and witchcraft and curses, but something was forcing him now, something within him so cold, so dark and powerful that he could never hope to fight it. He sat on the edge of the bed, gritting his teeth, and the voice was crying louder and louder, *You can never stop, Joe, no matter what happens, you'll never have a home again, never, never, never.*

The room was empty when she arrived. She choked back a sob, closed the door behind her, and leaned exhausted against the wall. She was too late. The dresser drawers were ripped open, a dirty sock lay under the bed, a handkerchief was crumpled on the bureau. He was gone, and so was the canvas bag.

Her eye fell on a folded white paper on the floor. She picked it up with trembling fingers and recognized it. With a little cry she plunged it into her pocket and fled down the front stairs, her coat flying behind her as she ran.

The street was dark and deserted. A light shone across the street, and another, up near the end of town, made a baleful yellow blotch in the darkness. She ran faster, her heels snapping harshly on the dry pavement, until she turned into a lighted building at the end of the street.

A sleepy clerk looked up at her and blinked.

"Was—was a young man in here?"

The clerk nodded suspiciously. "Bus to Chicago. Getting ready to leave?"

She threw her money down, and snatched up the little white ticket. Seconds later she was running down the bus lane to the large coach with CHICAGO across the front. She stumbled up the steps, and then she saw him.

He was sitting near the back, eyes closed, face deathly white. In his arms he was clutching his blue canvas bag, and his whole body was trembling. Slowly she moved back, sank down in the seat beside him. "Oh, Joe, Joe—"

"Jeannie, I'm sorry, I just can't help it."

"I know, Joe."

He looked at her, his eyes widening. She shook her head, and took his heavy hand in hers. Then he saw the ticket.

"Jeannie—"

"Hush. Don't say it."

"But you don't know what you're doing! We can never have a home, darling, *never.* No matter how hard we try. Think of the long, homeless roads, Jeannie, all over the world, on and on, maybe even to the stars."

She smiled, nodding gently. "But at least you won't be lonely now."

"Jeannie, *you can't.*"

"I can," she said and rested her head quietly against his shoulder.

Chad Oliver

PILGRIMAGE

Nearly twenty years ago Tony Boucher (and Mick McComas) bought the first story I ever sold, for the Magazine of Fantasy and Science Fiction. *I knew then, of course, that Tony was a great editor. Nothing has ever changed that opinion.*

Any fool can reject a story—or buy one, for that matter. That does not make him an editor. The wonderful thing about Tony, in both his editing and his reviewing, was that he made a writer want to write and gave him the courage to go on. He took no cheap shots. He had a cultivated taste both for the original and the traditional. When he bounced a story, he did it with exquisite tact. When a story needed fixing, he could tell you how to fix it. When he bought a story, you knew that you had written something that appealed to a man you respected.

Tony was a man of high intelligence, but he was also a man of fun. I remember our times together as times of laughter. Once in a while Chuck Beaumont and I would write a wild farce just for the sheer joy of it. We would tell one another, "Tony will love it." Sometimes he did and sometimes he didn't, but he always heard the music.

Wherever he may be, there will be laughter there. And when someone comes up with a happy idea, there will surely be a voice to say, "Tony will love it."

THERE WAS SOMETHING desperately wrong with Grandpa Erskine and everyone in Pryorville knew it. It was not, of course, the mere fact that Grandpa was a hopeless crackpot; *that* had been obvious for fifty years, and Grandpa's radical eccentricities were as much a part of the Pryorville Way of Life as barbecues, charades, and the girl next door.

This time it was far more alarming.

For one thing, Grandpa was happy. He beamed benevolently at small children and his normally acid remarks had lost much of their sting. For another, Grandpa was actually working despite his firm and loudly proclaimed opinion that industriousness was the one infallible mark of a feeble mind. It was true that no one could quite figure out what Grandpa was doing, but he *was* working. And, most sinister of all, Grandpa had been caught in the act of being enthusiastic about the forthcoming annual Pryorville Pilgrimage. In the light of his candid manifesto that the Pilgrimage represented mankind's closest approach yet to the Ultimate Boredom, this was downright frightening.

Two days before the Pilgrimage all of these symptoms were much in evidence and it was apparent that a crisis was near. Grandpa Erskine woke up at the crack of dawn and did not even bother to take a potshot at the squawking blue jay in the tree outside his window with the air-rifle he kept on hand for that express purpose. He slapped down the hall in his antediluvian slippers, gently cursing the throw-rugs on the slick wood floor, and sailed into the bathroom. He lathered his face and shaved the gleaming pink with a straight razor, after which he applied a liberal portion of Wild Stag Lotion; since Cousin Bess particularly despised the smell of Wild Stag, saying that it made her bilious, he managed to splatter a good deal of the stuff here and there around the room. He employed two black oval brushes to slick back his rather lank white hair, carefully combed his white chin-beard, and marched back into the hall stark naked.

There were numerous pious slogans hanging in little brown frames on the flowered yellow wallpaper. Grandpa detested them all, but he reserved his most devastating scowl for the one that read: A GOOD WOMAN WITH A GOOD BABY IN A GOOD HOUSE MAKES A GOOD MAN GODLY. About an acre of wall-space was taken up by a rogues' gallery of faded photographs of past members of the Erskine clan with assorted wives and children. A fair number of the men were dressed in Confederate uniforms and fearsome black beards. All the women wore high-necked dresses, unbecoming hair styles, and perpetually stern looks of all-inclusive disapproval. The children were stiff, scared, and scrubbed. Grandma was there too, on the lower right. Grandpa thought she looked a little tired.

Once in his room, Grandpa dressed with a care that almost amounted to fussiness. He pulled on his tight black trousers and looped the suspenders over his soft white shirt. He neatly knotted a black string tie, buttoned up his silk-lined vest, and shrugged into his black frock coat. He sat down on the bed and after considerable heaving and cursing managed to pull on his polished cowboy boots. He topped off the ensemble with a wide-brimmed black hat, admired his reflection in the cracked mirror, and stepped over to the bookcase. He tugged at his beard a moment, considering. He had gotten excellent results in the past with *The Life of the Marquis de Sade* and also with James Joyce's *Ulysses,* but only with the town's few literate people. He reached for Lawrence's *Lady Chatterley's Lover,* which was reliable, but then changed his mind and chose a large volume entitled *General Sherman: American Hero.* He chuckled gleefully to himself. General Sherman was surefire.

Grandpa emerged from the room with the book under his arm. He clumped down the winding stairs, pausing on the landing to listen. Yes, he heard the babble of female voices; the ladies were up and about. Grandpa took a deep breath and burst into song as he continued down the stairs, giving quite a spirited rendition of "The Battle Hymn of the Republic."

The feminine voices ceased abruptly.

Grandpa marched into the living room, removed his hat, and bowed magnificently. "A good morning to you, Cousin

Bess," he said, "and to you, my *dear* Mrs. Jackson. Where the hell is my breakfast?"

Cousin Bess, a large henlike woman who played the part of a Pioneer Wife in the Pilgrimage, did not bat an eye. Mrs. Jackson, who was on the Steering Committee and built along the general lines of a lead pencil, fluttered her small fan and blushed.

"The coffee is on the stove," Cousin Bess said.

Grandpa sighed. "Is chivalry dead?" he asked. "Has it come to this—that a gentleman must fry his own eggs?"

"You are no gentleman," Cousin Bess said. "I declare."

Grandpa clamped his hat back on his head. "I shall dine at the hotel and air my grievances among the white trash," he announced. "As a Pioneer Wife, my dear, you would be sacrificed to the Indians at the drop of a wagon wheel."

"Well, I declare," said Cousin Bess.

"Well, I declare," echoed Mrs. Jackson.

"I too declare," Grandpa said and stomped outside, slamming the heavy door behind him.

He paused on the large porch, stepped behind one of the white pillars to get out of the breeze, and fired up a good black cigar. He puffed on it contentedly, climbed down the porch steps, and set off toward town.

Grandpa felt fine.

He would have a good breakfast and four cups of coffee and then he could settle down to the day's work.

His only problem was that he was not yet exactly sure where he would steal the television set.

Far above the town, where the blue of the sky gave way before the star-sprinkled blackness of space, the great ship waited. It moved only enough to compensate for the rotation of the Earth. Its mission was almost complete but its scientists were still curious. It was standard practice, of course, to work through a native, and preferably one who was ready and willing to violate his culture's taboos for a suitable reward. But the old codger's choice of payment had been singularly odd. . . .

It would not literally be true to say that Pryorville was alive with preparations for the Pilgrimage, but it could not be denied that the town was definitely less dead than usual. The old Bayou Hotel (built in 1839) was freshly painted and the long iron railing that ran along the balcony gleamed in the morning sun. Every female in town was putting the finishing touches on her more or less authentic plantation costume and the log corral was suffering from its annual influx of horses for the parade. There were antique automobiles parked along the streets and even an old Conestoga wagon drawn up near the bridge outside of town. Confederate flags hung from every other window.

Grandpa marched through all this faded glory, his copy of *General Sherman: American Hero* clutched tightly under his arm. His lilting voice preceded him down the street and the strange words of "The Battle Hymn of the Republic" blistered the spring air like a blasphemy. It was not that Grandpa had any use for Yankees; he was not as odd as all that. It was simply that he liked to annoy people. The town's smugness and hypocrisy got under his hide. He sang the Yankee song for the same reason that he contrived to weave a little when he walked. Pryorville was dry as a bone—not even beer could be sold in the county—and a man had to look a trifle tipsy to maintain his self-respect.

And there *was* an unholy light in his eyes, a light of anticipation. It made everybody nervous.

Grandpa encountered the mayor, who was all dressed up in his cowboy suit and six-shooter. The mayor tried to ignore him, but Grandpa was a hard man to ignore. Grandpa managed to get in a few digs about shady oil operations before the man could get away. He then cornered Mrs. Audrey Busby in front of the hotel. Mrs. Busby was already decked out in her squawboots and Navaho jewelry.

"Ah, Mrs. Busby," Grandpa said, bowing low. "How is the vacuum cleaner working out in the old wigwam?"

Mrs. Busby pursed her thin lips, "You ought not to make fun of the Red Man," she said.

"I wasn't," he assured her.

"We could all learn a great deal from the Noble Savage," Mrs. Busby informed him. "He knew how to live in harmony with Nature. He was an unspoiled child of the wilderness. He lived in freedom with the creatures of the woodlands."

"The only good Indian," Grandpa told her coldly, "is a dead Indian."

While Mrs. Busby dug into her bag of Indian lore to find a suitable retort, Grandpa stamped into the hotel dining room and was delighted to spot Allan Garner breakfasting alone at a small table under a large chandelier. Allan was a local attorney and the town's leading advocate of States' Rights. He had been known to cry when "Dixie" was played.

"Mind if I join you?" Grandpa asked, sitting down.

Allan eyed the book which Grandpa plopped on the table without visible enthusiasm.

Grandpa enjoyed a splendid breakfast of ham, eggs, biscuits, and hominy, in the course of which he touched on many topics. He pointed out the superiority of General Grant to General Lee and discussed at length the role of the Supreme Court in American society.

"Say what you will, sir," Allan Garner said, "plantation life Before the War was a gracious and dignified way of life. Now, mind you, I don't hold with slavery in any form—"

"You just want free labor so you can sip your mint juleps in peace, hey?"

"I don't drink," Allan Garner said.

"A pity," Grandpa observed. "It is a custom that has been known to change people into human beings."

"One day, sir, you will go too far."

For some reason, that remark sent Grandpa into a paroxysm of laughter. He was still cackling happily to himself after Allan had stormed out of the hotel.

Over his final cup of coffee, Grandpa decided that the ideal place to steal a television set would be his own house. To be sure, the set belonged to Cousin Bess, but that was a minor detail.

He settled his bill and strolled back up to the white house he shared with Cousin Bess. He let himself through the metal gate into the back yard, gazing without affection at the clucking hens in the fenced-off area. There were three self-satisfied cats under the back porch and Grandpa paused to pay his respects. He admired cats; they were an independent lot. The cats would survive, he thought, no matter what happened.

Silently, he opened the screen door of the back porch and stepped inside. As long as Cousin Bess was awake, she was talking—to herself if necessary, although there were almost always kinfolk around. It made the whole thing ridiculously easy. He located Cousin Bess by her voice and calculated that she was in the kitchen making sandwiches with Sister May. Grandpa took off his boots and slipped through the high-ceilinged hall to what had once been the music room. There was still a piano, but the room's focus was now the small TV set. Grandpa unplugged it, hefted the set with a grunt, and hauled it silently to the back porch. He put on his boots again and carried the set to the garage behind the chicken house. He put the set on the floor of his car and covered it with a mouldy feed bag. He climbed into his car —the only Volkswagen in town—and backed into the street.

He gunned the buglike little car along the highway, heading northeast. He was soon outside the limits of Pryorville and three miles beyond town he turned down a side road into the cool piny woods. He drove six miles and then, just before he came to the boat dock on Catfish Bayou, he turned off again down an obscure dirt road that wound through the underbrush to an old shack at the water's edge. The shack had been a fishing camp that belonged to Old Man McGee, but since McGee's death it had been unused. Grandpa stopped long enough to unload the TV set on what was left of the pier, then got back in his car and drove on to Perry's Boat Dock. He rented a rowboat from Junior Perry, declined an offer of worms and a cane pole, and rowed out into the bayou, puffing on his cigar. When he rounded the bend and was out of sight, he landed at Old Man McGee's and loaded the pilfered TV set into the boat. Then he set out again.

The air was heavy and rich with the smells of scummy water, fish, and rotting vegetation. He rowed his way between great cypress trees, their gnarled roots twisting like snakes in the black shallow water. The sun was hot on his back but there was enough of a breeze to make things tolerable.

Grandpa rowed for almost an hour, cussing steadily, and finally arrived at one of the dreary little islands that dotted the bayou when the water was low. He tied the boat to a stump, heaved the TV set to his shoulder, and stepped out onto squishy, spongy soil. He followed the faint trail he had made to the center of the island, and placed the TV set on a dry flat rock. He mopped his brow.

It was done. The last payment had been made. He already had his reward, of course, but a bargain was a bargain—and anyhow the ship people controlled the power source.

A day and a half to go now.

He looked up, shading his eyes against the sun. He could see nothing. Since the first contact, the ship had remained invisible, only sending down a small sphere at night to pick up the loot that Grandpa brought to the island.

Well, no matter.

They were there.

Grandpa returned to his rowboat, cast off, and began the long pull back to Perry's Boat Dock.

That night, while a fat yellow moon bathed the piny woods in silver, the spaceship lowered the spherical pickup to the island in Catfish Bayou, retrieved the TV set, and hauled it aboard. The scientists took it apart, studied it, entered its number in a field catalogue, and stored it with the rest of the ethnological specimens from Earth.

The Pilgrimage was still a full day off, but already the ship's officers and men were clustered around the viewers that were trained on the streets of Pryorville far below. The primary function of the viewers was to gather social and cultural data on the natives but the pictures were being watched now with more than scientific enthusiasm. After all, you just didn't run across a native with a twisted mind like Grandpa's very often. . . .

The day of the Pilgrimage dawned with a polished copper sun beginning its long climb into a cloudless blue sky. It was a pleasant spring day, warm but not hot, and the tourists drove into Pryorville in gratifying numbers. Most of them were from Texas and Louisiana, but there were some from Oklahoma and other nearby states.

Pryorville had an interesting history and the Pilgrimage made the most of it. Before the arrival of the white men, the piny woods country had been the home of the Caddo Indians. Then, because of its position on the Catfish Bayou, Pryorville had become an important steamboat shipping center. Wagon trains brought in loads of buffalo hides and these were piled on the old stern-wheelers and carried to New Orleans via the Red River. Pryorville had boomed, with graceful Southern mansions and saloons going up in about equal numbers. It even boasted a famous murder case, when a local woman of something less than spotless reputation, Sapphire Sadie, had been killed by a wealthy Yankee.

Unhappily for Pryorville, the farsighted city fathers had looked upon the new railroad as a passing fad and had refused permission when it wished to extend its service to the Pryorville area. The railroad had gone through Deputy instead, and as a result Pryorville had been left with its steamboats and its memories. It became a town that resolutely faced the past; it died on the vine. Every year in the spring, the antique-filled old houses were opened up to the tourists, a play was put on about Sapphire Sadie, and there was a parade that served as a kind of historical pageant of the romanticized past of Pryorville.

The town lived for the Pilgrimage. In fact, the Pilgrimage *was* an accurate reflection of what Pryorville had become: artificial, prim, bloodless.

And today was the day.

Everyone was in costume.

Sandwiches were piled high at the concessions.

Cousin Bess was putting the finishing touches on the full homespun dress and bonnet of a Pioneer Wife. Her usually sluggish blood raced in her veins. She was a confirmed and vocal admirer of what she often referred to as the pioneer spirit, and she only felt really *alive* once a year at the Pilgrimage.

The mayor was already in the saddle. He rode a splendid bay stallion but the total effect was somewhat marred by the mayor's rotund body and flopping white hat. He was all decked out in his idea of a cowboy suit, which he affected because it gave him a good excuse to pack a gun. He rode happily up and down the street, practicing his chain-lightning draw and firing blank cartridges at all the tourists. His old Colt boomed like a cannon and the mayor was in his element. He was firmly convinced that he was a born glacial-eyed gunman.

Mrs. Audrey Busby, her aches and pains forgotten, was not only dressed like an Indian—in her own mind, she *was* an Indian. From squawboots to feather headdress, she was a walking museum. Her painted face was frozen into complete immobility. She talked in very short sentences. She looked at the town around her with something like contempt. Not for her the confining houses and crowded streets of the paleface world! No, she was free, free as the wind, and all she wanted was to get back to her wigwam—or was it a wickiup?

Allan Garner, a trim dark-haired figure in his black suit and string tie, was standing in the hotel looking out the window. He was not overly impressed with what he saw. To him, although he had lived there all his life, Pryorville represented the decay of the South. The old way of life had never been the same After the War—he thought of it as the War Between the States, of course. His heart was with the plantation he had never had. He longed for the gracious life, when ladies and gentlemen could sit out on a great white porch beneath the stars and listen to the far-off strumming of the banjos. He viewed the Pilgrimage as a poor substitute for the real thing, but it was better than nothing.

Men, women, and children lined Main Street, waiting.

The parade was due to start at ten o'clock.

At precisely five minutes before ten, Grandpa Erskine slipped into the attic of the house he shared with Cousin Bess. He went directly to a curious machine he had hidden in a packing case. He stroked his white beard, slapped his thigh, and closed a gleaming toggle switch.

In the spaceship far above the streets of Pryorville, the lights dimmed briefly as a mighty surge of power was drained from the atomic plant and directed through the machine in Grandpa Erskine's attic. Almost every man on the ship crowded around the viewers, grinning. This was going to be a parade worth seeing. . . .

At a few minutes after ten, the parade came into view. The tourists and Pryorville citizens lining Main Street gave a hearty cheer. They could hear the music from the Pryorville High School Band. The high-stepping girls in their boots and short satin skirts came first, smiling at the whistles from the crowd.

Then the band marched by.

In the last row, the tuba-players looked a trifle nervous.

Behind the tuba-players came the Indians.

At first, the crowd did not notice anything out of the ordinary. They laughed and waved at the Indians. They pointed and gawked. Two boys strained their lungs and gave out with what they fondly imagined to be war-whoops. One gentleman dressed up like a gambler pulled out a small pistol and fired it into the air.

Then the people took a closer look and a sudden silence fell. If there was one thing that an Indian in a parade was *not* supposed to look like, it was a genuine Indian. But these . . . .

There were five Indian men. They walked barefoot down the tarred street. They wore simple skin breechclouts and their brown skins were elaborately tatooed. Their black hair had been pulled out, leaving the head bald except for scalp locks. Two of the men carried hardwood war clubs spiked with garfish teeth. Two others carried bows, and the fifth man had a stone-tipped lance and a small oval shield.

Two Indian women followed the men. They were on the stocky side and they wore wrap-around cloth skirts, shell necklaces, and nothing else.

It was obvious that Mrs. Audrey Busby would not appear in public dressed like *that*.

The Indians had a healthy smell about them. They walked down Main Street as if they owned the place. When one of the local women passed out on the sidewalk, one brave fingered his scalping knife thoughtfully but did not break formation.

From the porch of the white house on the corner there came a cackle of satisfied laughter. Grandpa Erskine leaned back in his wicker rocking chair and watched the authentic Pryorville history march by in the parade.

There was a battered, muddy wagon pulled by fly-covered oxen. A woman with a bandana tied over her gray hair cracked a long black whip and cussed the oxen with a skill that brought an appreciative smile to Grandpa's lips. A freckle-faced boy leaned out of the back of the wagon and used Main Street as a heaven-sent latrine. Out in front of the wagon a grizzled man rode along with a very long rifle balanced on his saddle. When a dog ran into the street and barked, the man casually put a slug through its head.

Oh, they were all there: the dirt-caked buffalo hunters staring at the young girls with frank hunger, the cowboys firing bullets into shop windows, the weary red-eyed Confederate soldiers.

And Sapphire Sadie was there, riding in a handsome carriage. In person, she was a far cry from the dainty lady in the white dress who played her part in the play. Sapphire Sadie was all woman, and there was no possible doubt about her profession.

Long before the parade had run its course, the audience had vanished. There was a mass exodus of tourists and the Pryorville citizens locked themselves in their houses.

The show went on, however.

Firewater began to flow freely. The Indians set up camp in a vacant lot and the squaws began to cook the dead dog. Sapphire Sadie set up shop in the Bayou Hotel and there were great gusts of ribald laughter from the poker table. The cowboys and the buffalo hunters began a house-to-house canvass looking for Southern belles. There were two excellent gunfights within half an hour, the more fatal of which was conducted with shotguns at twenty paces. The soldiers wandered around wearily, looking for their regiment.

On the porch of the house he no longer shared with Cousin Bess, Grandpa rubbed his hands together gleefully. "Tarnation," he said, fumbling for a cigar. "There'll be a hot time in the old town tonight!"

Grandpa had only one minor regret.

He wished that he could have witnessed the other end of the great time somersault.

The men on the spaceship could witness it, and did. It was a fundamental natural law that matter could be neither created nor destroyed. If certain persons were snatched out of the past by the Selective Temporal Dislocator—Grandpa insisted on calling it a Time Machine—then certain contemporary persons had to be sent back along the time stream to replace them. Great care was taken, of course, to make certain that no modern person was sent into an uncongenial era. It might perhaps cause a small amount of inconvenience to the natives, but Grandpa had earned his reward by his faithful collection of ethnological specimens. The STD would not function after the ship's power source was removed; for those concerned it was going to be a one-way trip. The ship's crew had enjoyed the parade, but the other end of the line was even better. They clustered around the Temporal Viewers with rare enthusiasm. . . .

Cousin Bess came to with a start. The last thing she remembered clear was dressing in her Pioneer Wife outfit of homespun dress and bonnet for the parade. Then there had been that awful buzzing in her ears—a touch of the sun, likely.

There came a clump of heavy boots on the porch. *Porch?* Where was she? This log cabin—

The door banged open and a dirty man with a fierce black beard swept into the cabin like a hurricane. Cousin Bess had never seen the man before in her life.

"Howdy gal!" he boomed, squinting in the cabin's gloom and swatting her playfully on her Pioneer Wife Posterior. "Whar's chow?"

"Chow?" Cousin Bess echoed.

The man's face clouded up like a storm. "Yuh mean chow ain't ready? You lookin' for a whuppin', Lucy?"

"Lucy?" queried Cousin Bess, backing against the wall. "I fear there has been some terrible mistake. I declare I just don't know . . . ."

"Damnation!" The man slammed his filthy hat down on the floor. He peered at her narrowly. "Why, you ain't Lucy! Has that no-good she-coyote done run off *again?* Whar is she?"

"I'm sure I don't know, sir. My name is Cousin Bess—that's what they call me—and I'm from Pryorville. This Lucy person—"

The man raged through the cabin, peering under the bed and into the closets. He came back and confronted Cousin Bess darkly. "I don't take kindly to your helpin' to rustle off my wife, woman," he said. "Ain't you got no damned sense of *decency?*"

Cousin Bess put her hands on her ample hips. "I assure you I have never even *heard* of this Lucy creature of yours. And you mind your tongue, sir, when you talk to a lady!"

The man cleared his whiskered throat and spat accurately on the dirt floor. He walked up to Cousin Bess and pinched her shoulder thoughtfully, as though sizing up a prize cow. "Lady, huh? Wal, Bess, I ain't never been one to hold a grudge. A swap is a swap, that's what I always say. My name is Amos, Amos Carrico, and I'll be right happy to have you for my woman until Lucy comes back. Gimme a kiss."

Cousin Bess pressed her back into the wall, ignoring the splinters. She covered her face with her hands, blushing. "Now, Amos—"

Amos Carrico let loose a bellow of laughter. "Shy, huh? Well, that's a change! Never you mind, Bess. Lots of time for that sort of thing later. But a man's got to eat, ain't that so? I reckon you're a mite confused yet, so I'll rustle grub. You sidle on out and gut that pig I killed. And we'll need firewood too, I reckon."

"Gut?" Cousin Bess faltered. "Pig?"

Amos put his hamlike hands on his hips and surveyed her curiously. "What's the matter with you, woman? You're actin' plumb strange. Git on out thar afore I take a stick to yuh."

"Stick," said Cousin Bess. She considered fainting but thought better of it—Amos might chop her up for dinner. A horrible certainty was growing in her mind. God knew this was not the sort of life she had imagined for a Pioneer Wife, but she had better watch her step. And Amos wouldn't be a *bad* looking man, once you got rid of those filthy clothes and that ugly beard. . . .

She bowed her head submissively and weaved out the door.

How did one go about gutting a pig, anyway?

Mrs. Audrey Busby felt like a malted milk.

Every step she took jolted her from stem to stern and her feet were bleeding. She shook her head, feeling as though there were innumerable cobwebs in her brain. Realism in a parade was all very well, but things were obviously getting out of hand. . . .

When she finally managed to focus her eyes, the first thing she saw was a half-naked tattooed Indian riding in front of her on a spotted pony. Riding! And she was walking, eating his dust, and with a pack on her back at that!

"You!" she cried. "You up there!"

The brave pulled up his pony and looked back. His eyes were black as midnight and his face showed the unhappy results of a bout with smallpox. At first, he said nothing. Then he rode back and looked at Mrs. Busby closely. He stared at her for a long minute and then burst out laughing.

"What's so funny?" Mrs. Busby demanded.

The Indian leaned down and fingered her elaborate feather headdress. He gawked at her Navaho jewelry and her tattered squawboots. He eyed her white skin suspiciously. He said something to her that was obviously a question, but it was in no language she knew.

"Speak English, you," Mrs. Busby said.

The brave turned up his nose, snorted, and kicked his pony. The horse plodded on, leaving Mrs. Busby in the dust. She looked around, remembering that strange buzzing in her ears. It was a desolate, trackless land that she saw. In the distance she heard the mournful howl of what she hoped was only a coyote.

The Indian was pulling away from her, and he did not look back.

Well! Mrs. Busby wiped the sweat out of her eyes and began to run to catch up. It just wouldn't *do* to be left out here all alone in this horrible wasteland. She cried a little but brightened visibly when she saw the village.

Of course, the women weren't wearing proper clothing at all, which was going to be awkward. Mrs. Busby giggled slightly. Still, whatever had happened, these *were* Indians.

"Wait for me!" she called, running forward with one hand holding on her feather headdress.

Now, if she could just remember whether one called them wigwams or wickiups. . . .

The man who had once been the mayor of Pryorville suddenly found himself at one end of a long, dusty street. A blazing sun burned down from a cloudless blue sky. False-fronted stores and roaring saloons lined the street.

Saloons? In Pryorville? By God, they were carrying this Pilgrimage thing too far!

The mayor hitched up his cowboy pants and jammed his big hat down more firmly over his eyes. He felt decidedly odd. Somewhere along the way, he had lost his horse. Fine thing. Had to be expected though, with all the foreign riff-raff in town.

Funny. This wasn't Pryorville at all—

At the other end of the street, a dark figure was walking slowly toward him. The figure was bent slightly into an all-too-familiar crouch. He had a gun tied down on his hip.

The mayor stood absolutely still, too terrified to move. His own Colt was in his holster but the mayor had abruptly lost his interest in gunfights. He affixed a wan smile to his face and watched the man coming toward him.

The other man came closer. A tall, skeletal man. A man standing almost six feet tall and he couldn't have weighed over 115 pounds. He was neatly dressed in an expensive felt sombrero and a funereal black suit. He coughed slightly, sounding like death itself. He stopped. His eyes were cold as ice.

"My God," the mayor whispered, "it's Doc Holliday. Aren't you dead?"

"Not yet," Doc said quietly. "How about you?"

"Who, me?" The mayor's hands were trembling violently and he took care to keep them far, far away from the butt of his Colt. "No, I'm not dead. At least, I don't *think* I am."

"Hard to tell sometimes," Doc observed. "Quite a Colt you got there, stranger."

The mayor swallowed hard. "That old thing?" He laughed weakly. "Just carry it for laughs. Just loaded with blanks, you know. With blanks. *Blanks.*"

"Man ought not to pack hardware like that unless he figures on using it."

"True," said the mayor agreeably. "Oh, very true." With infinite caution he loosened his gun belt and let it fall into the dust of the street. "Truer words were never spoken. Perhaps you would—ah—care for a drink, Doc old man?"

"I could use a quart or two," said Doc Holliday. "That's

right neighborly of you, stranger. Yes, I definitely feel that I could handle a quart or two."

"So could I," said the mayor.

He followed the thin gunman into the nearest saloon, wondering idly what the political situation was in this town. In any event, it would certainly do no harm to have Doc Holliday on his side. . . .

For one wild moment, after the buzzing in his ears had stopped, Allan Garner thought that he had died and gone to a Dixie Valhalla. There it was, just as he had seen it in his dreams: a magnificent white mansion high on a green hill, stately pillars lining a long, cool porch, the sound of birds in the great magnolia trees.

He felt a choking sensation in his chest. He couldn't imagine what had happened, and he didn't care. He knew he was in the Old South—knew it by the sight and sound and feel of it. Dear old Dixie!

He was here; that was all that mattered.

Look away, look away . . .

Ah, a lovely girl moving gracefully across the green lawn. A lovely Southern belle, all crinoline and cotton—

Look away, look away . . .

And listen! The banjos ringing down in the slave quarters, the happy darkies who knew their place singing and laughing, no NAACP to stir them up and make trouble—

Oh, it was heaven!

But it was all so far away, up there on the great green hill. Why was he down here in the valley? A sudden cold sweat broke out on the palms of his hands. He looked down at himself. No, he was still himself, thank God, still Allan Garner, still dressed in the black suit and string tie he had been wearing for the Pilgrimage. But—

He turned around and saw it. An old rotting shack with gaping holes for windows and the boards warping off its sagging sides. A skinny chicken scraping in the hard dirt of the yard. A smell of something rancid from the kitchen.

He knew what it was. You didn't have to draw any pictures for Allan Garner.

It was *his house.*

He began to sob hysterically. Oh, the ignominy of it!

"A sharecropper!" he screamed. "A sharecropper!"

He fell to the earth, whimpering. And somehow he *knew.*

"Grandpa Erskine," he cried, beating his fists into the hard-packed dirt. "Oh, you evil old man. Oh, you traitor to the Cause. . . ."

Meanwhile, the gentleman in question was having a high old time. He was all dressed up in his finest suit, his beard was freshly trimmed and combed, and he reeked of Wild Stag Lotion. He sat jovially at the poker table—it had been a prized antique belonging to Cousin Bess but there was no need to worry about *her* any longer—and raked in the chips.

Grandpa snapped his fingers. "More firewater," he said.

A grinning Indian complied, helping himself to a shot as he did so.

"It's yore deal, Sapphire," drawled a grizzled buffalo hunter, neatly dropping an ash from his cigar on the rug.

Sapphire Sadie adjusted her shawl to let more flesh peek through and shuffled the cards with expert, perfumed fingers.

Outside, the shooting and the hollering was still going on.

Grandpa was radiant with satisfaction. He felt, somewhat inaccurately, that a lifetime of toil had reaped a truly bountiful harvest.

"Mighty nice little town you got here," a cowboy said, studying his cards. "Mighty neighborly."

"You're dang tootin'," Grandpa beamed. "Oh, we've had our ups and downs, and I'd be the first to admit it. But we're up now, and we're gonna stay up. All we ever needed was a mite of new blood." He fired up a fresh cigar. "Let's have another round of that firewater, Sitting Bull."

The Indian staggered toward the bottle, singing an obscure but definitely happy song.

The spaceship had completed its mission. Far above the Earth its great jets flamed and the ship flashed back into the darkness that was its home. Behind it, had there been anyone to hear, there lingered the soft warm silver of celestial laughter.

Mack Reynolds

GUN FOR HIRE

I never met anybody in the writing dodge who didn't like Tony Boucher. I don't mean that they didn't exist. They had to, because Tony was one of the least wishy-washy people going and you don't get everybody *to love you if you've got guts. But I never met any of them and to hell with them . . . Back in the days when I was selling him quite a few things, during the* Magazine of Fantasy and Science Fiction *editorship, they were usually humor pieces. Tony was always a great believer that there should be more humor in science fiction . . . The two of us were instrumental, back in 1951, in trying to launch a premature Science Fiction Writers of America organization at the science fiction convention in Portland, but what he really wanted was a union of science fiction group and the Mystery Writers of America for added weight . . . As everyone knows, Tony carried quite a bit of social consciousness and I wish he could see some of the yarns I'm trying to spin today . . . At any rate the present story tries to cover a bit of humor, both crime and science fiction, and a touch of socioeconomic background.*

JOE PRANTERA called softly, "Al." The pleasurable, comfortable, warm feeling began spreading over him, the way it always did.

The older man stopped and squinted, but not suspiciously, even now.

The evening was dark, it was unlikely that the other even saw the circle of steel that was the mouth of the shotgun barrel, now resting on the car's window ledge.

"Who's it?" he growled.

Joe Prantera said softly, "Big Louis sent me, Al."

And he pressed the trigger.

And at that moment, the universe caved inward upon Joseph Marie Prantera.

There was nausea and nausea upon nausea.

There was a falling through all space and through all time. There was doubling and twisting and twitching of every muscle and nerve.

There was pain, horror and tumultuous fear.

And he came out of it as quickly and completely as he'd gone in.

He was in, he thought, a hospital and his first reaction was to think, *This here California. Everything different.* Then his second thought was *Something went wrong. Big Louis, he ain't going to like this.*

He brought his thinking to the present. So far as he could remember, he hadn't completely pulled the trigger. That at least meant that whatever the rap was it wouldn't be too tough. With luck, the syndicate would get him off with a couple of years at Quentin.

A door slid open in the wall in a way that Joe had never seen a door operate before. *This here California.*

The clothes on the newcomer were wrong, too. For the first time, Joe Prantera began to sense an alienness—a something that was awfully wrong.

The other spoke precisely and slowly, the way a highly educated man speaks a language which he reads and writes fluently but has little occasion to practice vocally. "You have recovered?"

Joe Prantera looked at the other expressionlessly. Maybe the old duck was one of these foreign doctors, like.

The newcomer said, "You have undoubtedly been through

a most harrowing experience. If you have any untoward symptoms, possibly I could be of assistance."

Joe couldn't figure out how he stood. For one thing, there should have been some kind of police guard.

The other said, "Perhaps a bit of stimulant?"

Joe said flatly, "I wanta lawyer."

The newcomer frowned at him. "A lawyer?"

"I'm not sayin' nothin'. Not until I get a mouthpiece."

The newcomer started off on another tack. "My name is Lawrence Reston-Farrell. If I am not mistaken, you are Joseph Salviati-Prantera."

Salviati happened to be Joe's mother's maiden name. But it was unlikely this character could have known that. Joe had been born in Naples and his mother had died in childbirth. His father hadn't brought him to the States until the age of five and by that time he had a stepmother.

"I wanta mouthpiece," Joe said flatly, "or let me outta here."

Lawrence Reston-Farrell said, "You are not being constrained. There are clothes for you in the closet there."

Joe gingerly tried swinging his feet to the floor and sitting up, while the other stood watching him, strangely. He came to his feet. With the exception of a faint nausea, which brought back memories of that extreme condition he'd suffered during . . . during what? He hadn't the vaguest idea of what had happened.

He was dressed in a hospital-type nightgown. He looked down at it and snorted and made his way over to the closet. It opened on his approach, the door sliding back into the wall in much the same manner as the room's door had opened for Reston-Farrell.

Joe Prantera scowled and said, "These ain't my clothes."

"No, I am afraid not."

"You think I'd be seen dead wearing this stuff? What is this, some religious crackpot hospital?"

Reston-Farrell said, "I am afraid, Mr. Salviati-Prantera, that these are the only garments available. I suggest you look out the window there."

Joe gave him a long, chill look and then stepped to the window. He couldn't figure the other. Unless he was a fruitcake. Maybe he was in some kind of pressure cooker and this was one of the fruitcakes.

He looked out, however, not on the lawns and walks of a sanitarium but upon a wide boulevard of what was obviously a populous city.

And for a moment again, Joe Prantera felt the depths of nausea.

This was not his world.

He stared for a long, long moment. The cars didn't even have wheels, he noted dully. He turned slowly and faced the older man.

Reston-Farrell said compassionately, "Try this, it's excellent cognac."

Joe Prantera stared at him, said finally, flatly, "What's it all about?"

The other put down the unaccepted glass. "We were afraid first realization would be a shock to you," he said. "My colleague is in the adjoining room. We will be glad to explain to you if you will join us there."

"I wanta get out of here," Joe said.

"Where would you go?"

The fear of police, of Al Rossi's vengeance, of the measures that might be taken by Big Louis on his failure, were now far away.

Reston-Farrell had approached the door by which he had entered and it reopened for him. He went through it without looking back.

There was nothing else to do. Joe dressed, then followed him.

In the adjoining room was a circular table that would have accommodated a dozen persons. Two were seated there now, papers, books and soiled coffee cups before them. There had evidently been a long wait.

Reston-Farrell, the one Joe had already met, was tall and drawn of face and with a chainsmoker's nervousness. The other was heavier and more at ease. They were both, Joe estimated, somewhere in their middle fifties. They both looked like docs. He wondered, all over again, if this was some kind of pressure cooker.

But that didn't explain the view from the window.

Reston-Farrell said, "May I present my colleague, Citizen Warren Brett-James? Warren, this is our guest from . . . from yesteryear, Mr. Joseph Salviati-Prantera."

Brett-James nodded to him, friendly, so far as Joe could see. He said gently, "I think it would be Mr. Joseph Prantera, wouldn't it? The maternal lineage was almost universally ignored." His voice too gave the impression he was speaking a language not usually on his tongue.

Joe took an empty chair, hardly bothering to note its alien qualities. His body seemed to *fit* into the piece of furniture, as though it had been molded to his order.

Joe said, "I think maybe I'll take that there drink, Doc."

Reston-Farrell said, "Of course," and then something else Joe didn't get. Whatever the something else was, a slot opened in the middle of the table and a glass, so clear of texture as to be all but invisible, was elevated. It contained possibly three ounces of golden fluid.

Joe didn't allow himself to think of its means of delivery. He took up the drink and bolted it. He put the glass down and said carefully, "What's it all about, huh?"

Warren Brett-James said soothingly. "Prepare yourself for somewhat of a shock, Mr. Prantera. You are no longer in Los Angeles—"

"Ya think I'm stupid? I can see that."

"I was about to say, Los Angeles of 1960. Mr. Prantera, we welcome you to Nuevo Los Angeles."

"Ta where?"

"To Nuevo Los Angeles and to the year—" Brett-James looked at his companion. "What is the date, Old Calendar?"

"2133," Reston-Farrell said. "A.D. 2133 they would say."

Joe Prantera looked from one of them to the other, scowling. "What are you guys talking about?"

Warren Brett-James said softly, "Mr. Prantera, you are no longer in the year 1960, you are now in the year 2133."

He said, uncomprehendingly, "You mean I been, like, unconscious for—" He let the sentence fall away as he realized the impossibility.

Brett-James said gently, "Hardly for one hundred and seventy years, Mr. Prantera."

Reston-Farrell said, "I am afraid we are confusing you. Briefly, we have *transported* you, I suppose one might say, from your own era to ours."

Joe Prantera had never been exposed to the concept of time travel. He had simply never associated with anyone who had ever even remotely considered such an idea. Now he said, "You mean, like, I been asleep all that time?"

"Not exactly," Brett-James said, frowning.

Reston-Farrell said, "Suffice to say, you are now one hundred and seventy-three years after the last memory you have."

Joe Prantera's mind suddenly reverted to those last memories and his eyes narrowed dangerously. He felt suddenly at bay. He said, "Maybe you guys better let me in on what's this all about."

Reston-Farrell said, "Mr. Prantera, we have brought you from your era to perform a task for us."

Joe stared at him, and then at the other. He couldn't believe he was getting through to them. Or, at least, that they were to him.

Finally he said, "If I get this, you want me to do a job for you."

"That is correct."

Joe said, "You guys know the kind of jobs I do?"

"That is correct."

"Like hell you do. You think I'm stupid? I never even seen you before." Joe Prantera came abruptly to his feet. "I'm gettin' outta here."

For the second time, Reston-Farrell said, "Where would you go, Mr. Prantera?"

Joe glared at him. Then sat down again, as abruptly as he'd arisen.

"Let's start all over again. I got this straight, you brought me, some screwy way, all the way . . . here. O.K., I'll buy that. I seen what it looks like out that window—" The real comprehension was seeping through to him even as he talked. "Everybody I know, Jessie, Tony, the Kid, Big Louis, everybody, they're dead. Even Big Louis."

"Yes," Brett-James said, his voice soft. "They are all dead, Mr. Prantera. Their children are all dead, and their grandchildren."

The two men of the future said nothing more for long minutes while Joe Prantera's mind whirled its confusion.

Finally he said, "What's this bit about you wanting me to give it to some guy?"

"That is why we brought you here, Mr. Prantera. You were . . . you are, a professional assassin."

"Hey, wait a minute, now."

Reston-Farrell went on, ignoring the interruption. "There is small point in denying your calling. Pray remember that at the point when we . . . *transported* you, you were about to dispose of a contemporary named Alphonso Annunziata-Rossi. A citizen, I might say, whose demise would probably have caused small dismay to society."

They had him pegged all right. Joe said, "But why me? Why don't you get some heavy from now? Somebody knows the ropes these days."

Brett-James said, "Mr. Prantera, there are no professional assassins in this age, nor have there been for over a century and a half."

"Well, then do it yourself." Joe Prantera's irritation over this whole complicated mess was growing. And already he was beginning to long for the things he knew—for Jessie and Tony and the others, for his favorite bar, for the lasagne down at Papa Giovanni's. Right now he could have welcomed a calling down at the hands of Big Louis.

Reston-Farrell had come to his feet and walked to one of the large room's windows. He looked out, as though unseeing. Then, his back turned, he said, "We have tried, but it is simply not in us, Mr. Prantera."

"You mean you're yella?"

"No, if by that you mean afraid. It is simply not within us to take the life of a fellow creature—not to speak of a fellow man."

Joe snapped: "Everything you guys say sounds crazy. Let's start all over again."

Brett-James said, "Let me do it, Lawrence." He turned his eyes to Joe. "Mr. Prantera, in your own era, did you ever consider the future?"

Joe looked at him blankly.

"In your day you were confronted with national and international, problems. Just as we are today and just as nations were a century or a millennium ago."

"Sure, O.K., so we had problems. I know whatcha mean —like wars, and depressions and dictators and like that."

"Yes, like that," Brett-James nodded.

The heavy-set man paused a moment. "Yes, like that," he repeated. "That we confront you now indicates that the problems of your day were solved. Hadn't they been, the world most surely would have destroyed itself. Wars? Our pedagogues are hard put to convince their students that such ever existed. More than a century and a half ago our society eliminated the reasons for international conflict. For that matter," he added musingly, "we eliminated most international boundaries. Depressions? Shortly after your own period, man awoke to the fact that he had achieved to the point where it was possible to produce an abundance for all with a minimum of toil. Overnight, for all practical purposes, the whole world was industrialized, automated. The second industrial revolution was accompanied by revolutionary changes in almost every field, certainly in every science. Dictators? Your ancestors found, Mr. Prantera, that it is difficult for a man to be free so long as others are still enslaved. Today the democratic ethic has reached a pinnacle never dreamed of in your own era."

"O.K., O.K.," Joe Prantera growled. "So everybody's got

it made. What I wanta know is what's all this about me giving it ta somebody? If everything's so great, how come you want me to knock this guy off?"

Reston-Farrell bent forward and thumped his right index finger twice on the table. "The bacterium of hate—a new strain—has found the human race unprotected from its disease. We had thought our vaccines immunized us."

"What's that suppose to mean?"

Brett-James took up the ball again. "Mr. Prantera, have you ever heard of Ghengis Khan, of Tamerlane, Alexander, Caesar?"

Joe Prantera scowled at him emptily.

"Or, more likely, of Napoleon, Hitler, Stalin?"

"Sure I heard of Hitler and Stalin," Joe growled. "I ain't stupid."

The other nodded. "Such men are unique. They have a drive . . . a drive to power which exceeds by far the ambitions of the average man. They are genii in their way, Mr. Prantera, genii of evil. Such a genius of evil has appeared on the current scene."

"Now we're getting somewheres," Joe snorted. "So you got a guy what's a little ambitious, like, eh? And you guys ain't got the guts to give it to him. O.K. What's in it for me?"

The two of them frowned, exchanged glances. Reston-Farrell said, "You know, that is one aspect we had not considered."

Brett-James said to Joe Prantera, "Had we not, ah, taken you at the time we did, do you realize what would have happened?"

"Sure," Joe grunted. "I woulda let old Al Rossi have it right in the guts, five times. Then I woulda took the plane back to Chi."

Brett-James was shaking his head. "No. You see, by coincidence, a police squad car was coming down the street just at that moment to arrest Mr. Rossi. You would have been apprehended. As I understand Californian law of the period, your life would have been forfeit, Mr. Prantera."

Joe winced. It didn't occur to him to doubt their word.

Reston-Farrell said, "As to reward, Mr. Prantera, we have already told you there is ultra-abundance in this age. Once this task has been performed, we will sponsor your entry into present day society. Competent psychiatric therapy will soon remove your present—"

"Waita minute, now. You figure on gettin me candled by some head shrinker, eh? No thanks, Buster. I'm going back to my own—"

Brett-James was shaking his head again. "I am afraid there is no return, Mr. Prantera. Time travel works but in one direction, *with* the flow of the time stream. There can be no return to your own era."

Joe Prantera had been rocking with the mental blows he had been assimilating, but this was the final haymaker. He was stuck in this squaresville of a world.

Joe Prantera on a job was thorough.

Careful, painstaking, competent.

He spent the first three days of his life in the year 2133 getting the feel of things. Brett-James and Reston-Farrell had been appointed to work with him. Joe didn't meet any of the others who belonged to the group which had taken the measures to bring him from the past. He didn't want to meet them. The fewer persons involved, the better.

He stayed in the apartment of Reston-Farrell. Joe had been right, Reston-Farrell was a medical doctor. Brett-James evidently had something to do with the process that had enabled them to bring Joe from the past. Joe didn't know how they'd done it, and he didn't care. Joe was a realist. He was here. The thing was to adapt.

There didn't seem to be any hurry. Once the deal was made, they left it up to him to make the decisions.

They drove him around the town, when he wished to check the traffic arteries. They flew him about the whole vicinity. From the air, Southern California looked much the same as it had in his own time. Oceans, mountains, and to a lesser extent, deserts, are fairly permanent even against man's corroding efforts.

It was while he was flying with Brett-James on the second day that Joe said, "How about Mexico? Could I make the get to Mexico?"

The physicist looked at him questioningly, "Get?" he said.

Joe Prantera said impatiently, "The getaway. After I give it to this Howard Temple-Tracy guy. I gotta go on the run, don't I?"

"I see." Brett-James cleared his throat. "Mexico is no longer a separate nation, Mr. Prantera. All North America has been united into one unit. Today, there are only eight nations in the world."

"Where's the nearest?"

"South America."

"That's a helluva long way to go on a get."

"We hadn't thought of the matter being handled in that manner."

Joe eyed him in scorn. "Oh, you didn't, huh? What happens after I give it to this guy? I just sit around and wait for the cops to put the arm on me?"

Brett-James grimaced in amusement. "Mr. Prantera, this will probably be difficult for you to comprehend, but there are no police in this era."

Joe gaped at him. "No police! What happens if you gotta throw some guy in stir?"

"If I understand your idiom correctly, you mean prison. There are no prisons in this era, Mr. Prantera."

Joe stared. "No cops, no jails. What stops anybody? What stops anybody from just going into some bank, like, and collecting up all the bread?"

Brett-James cleared his throat. "Mr. Prantera, there are no banks."

"No banks! You gotta have banks!"

"And no money to put in them. We found it a rather antiquated method of distribution well over a century ago."

Joe had given up. Now he merely stared.

Brett-James said reasonably, "We found we were devoting as much time to financial matters in all their endless ramifications—including bank robberies—as we were to productive efforts. So we turned to more efficient methods of distribution."

On the fourth day, Joe said, "O.K., let's get down to facts. Summa the things you guys say don't stick together so good. Now, first place, where's this guy Temple-Tracy you want knocked off?"

Reston-Farrell and Brett-James were both present. The three of them sat in the living room of the latter's apartment, sipping a sparkling wine which seemed to be the prevailing beverage of the day. For Joe's taste it was insipid stuff. Happily, rye was available to those who wanted it.

Reston-Farrell said, "You mean, where does he reside? Why, here in this city."

"Well, that's handy, eh?" Joe scratched himself thoughtfully. "You got somebody can finger him for me?"

"Finger him?"

"Look, before I can give it to this guy I gotta know some place where he'll be at some time. Get it? Like Al Rossi. My finger, he works in Rossi's house, see? He lets me know every Wednesday night, eight o'clock, Al leaves the house all by hisself, O.K., so I can make plans, like, to give it to him." Joe Prantera wound it up reasonably. "You gotta have a finger."

Brett-James said, "Why not just go to Temple-Tracy's apartment and, ah, dispose of him?"

"Jest walk in, eh? You think I'm stupid? How do I know how many witnesses hangin' around? How do I know if the guy's carryin' heat?"

"Heat?"

"A gun, a gun. Ya think I'm stupid? I come to give it to him and he gives it to me instead."

Dr. Reston-Farrell said, "Howard Temple-Tracy lives alone. He customarily receives visitors every afternoon, largely potential followers. He is attempting to recruit members to an organization he is forming. It would be quite simple for you to enter his establishment and dispose of him. I assure you, he does not possess weapons."

Joe was indignant. "Just like that, eh?" he said sarcastically. "Then what happens? How do I get out of the building? Where's my get car parked? Where do I hide out? Where do I dump the heat?"

"Dump the heat?"

"Get rid of the gun. You want I should get caught with the gun on me? I'd wind up in the gas chamber so quick—"

"See here, Mr. Prantera," Brett-James said softly. "We no longer have capital punishment, you must realize."

"O.K. I still don't wanta get caught. What *is* the rap these days, huh?" Joe scowled. "You said they didn't have no jails any more."

"This is difficult for you to understand, I imagine," Reston-Farrell told him, "but, you see, we no longer punish people in this era."

That took a long, unbelieving moment to sink in. "You mean, like, no matter what they do? That's crazy. Everybody'd be running around giving it to everybody else."

"The motivation for crime has been removed, Mr. Prantera," Reston-Farrell attempted to explain. "A person who commits a violence against another is obviously in need of medical care. And, consequently, receives it."

"You mean, like, if I steal a car or something, they just take me to a doctor?" Joe Prantera was unbelieving.

"Why would anybody wish to steal a car?" Reston-Farrell said easily.

"But if I *give it* to somebody?"

"You will be turned over to a medical institution. Citizen Howard Temple-Tracy is the last man you will ever kill, Mr. Prantera."

A chillness was in the belly of Joe Prantera. He said very slowly, very dangerously, "You guys figure on me getting caught, don't you?"

"Yes," Brett-James said evenly.

"Well then, figure something else. You think I'm stupid?"

"Mr. Prantera," Dr. Reston-Farrell said, "there has been as much progress in the field of psychiatry in the past two centuries as there has in any other. Your treatment would be brief and painless, believe me."

Joe said coldly, "And what happens to you guys? How do you know I won't rat on you?"

Brett-James said gently, "The moment after you have accomplished your mission, we plan to turn ourselves over to the nearest institution to have determined whether or not we also need therapy."

"Now I'm beginning to wonder about you guys," Joe said. "Look, all over again, what'd'ya wanta give it to this guy for?"

The doctor said, "We explained the other day, Mr. Prantera. Citizen Howard Temple-Tracy is a dangerous, atavistic, evil genius. We are afraid for our institutions if his plans are allowed to mature."

"Well if you got things so good, everybody's got it made, like, who'd listen to him?"

The doctor nodded at the validity of the question. "Mr. Prantera, *Homo sapiens* is a unique animal. Physically he matures at approximately the age of thirteen. However, mental maturity and adjustment is often not fully realized until thirty or even more. Indeed, it is sometimes never achieved. Before such maturity is reached, our youth are susceptible to romantic appeal. Nationalism, chauvinism, racism, the supposed glory of the military, all seem romantic to the immature. They rebel at the orderliness of present society. They seek entertainment in excitement. Citizen Temple-Tracy is aware of this and finds his recruits among the young."

"O.K., so this guy is dangerous. You want him knocked off before he screws everything up. But the way things are, there's no way of making a get. So you'll have to get some other patsy. Not me."

"I am afraid you have no alternative," Brett-James said gently. "Without us, what will you do? Mr. Prantera, you do not even speak the language."

"What'd'ya mean? I don't understand summa the big words you eggheads use, but I get by O.K."

Brett-James said, "Amer-English is no longer the language spoken by the man in the street, Mr. Prantera. Only students of such subjects any longer speak such tongues as Amer-English, French, Russian or the many others that once confused the race with their limitations as a means of communication."

"You mean there's no place in the whole world where they talk American?" Joe demanded, aghast.

Dr. Reston-Farrell controlled the car. Joe Prantera sat in the seat next to him and Warren Brett-James sat in the back. Joe had, tucked in his belt, a .45 caliber automatic, once displayed in a museum. It had been more easily procured than the ammunition to fit it, but that problem too had been solved.

The others were nervous, obviously repelled by the very conception of what they had planned.

Inwardly, Joe was amused. Now that they had got in the clutch, the others were on the verge of chickening out. He knew it wouldn't have taken much for them to cancel the project. It wasn't any answer though. If they allowed him to call it off today, they'd talk themselves into it again before the week was through.

Besides, already Joe was beginning to feel the comfortable, pleasurable, warm feeling that came to him on occasions like this.

He said, "You're sure this guy talks American, eh?"

Warren Brett-James said, "Quite sure. He is a student of history."

"And he won't think it's funny I talk American to him, eh?"

"He'll undoubtedly be intrigued."

They pulled up before a large apartment building that overlooked the area once known as Wilmington.

Joe was coolly efficient now. He pulled out the automatic, held it down below his knees and threw a shell into the barrel. He eased the hammer down, thumbed on the safety, stuck the weapon back in his belt and beneath the jacketlike garment he wore.

He said, "O.K. See you guys later." He left them and entered the building.

An elevator—he still wasn't used to their speed in this era—whooshed him to the penthouse duplex occupied by Citizen Howard Temple-Tracy.

There were two persons in the reception room but they left on Joe's arrival, without bothering to look at him more than glancingly.

He spotted the screen immediately and went over and stood before it.

The screen lit and revealed a heavy-set, dour of countenance man seated at a desk. He looked into Joe Prantera's face, scowled and said something.

Joe said, "Joseph Salviati-Prantera to interview Citizen Howard Temple-Tracy."

The other's shaggy eyebrows rose. "Indeed," he said. "In Amer-English?"

Joe nodded.

"Enter," the other said.

A door had slid open on the other side of the room. Joe walked through it and into what was obviously an office. Citizen Temple-Tracy sat at a desk. There was only one other chair in the room. Joe Prantera ignored it and remained standing.

Citizen Temple-Tracy said, "What can I do for you?"

Joe looked at him for a long, long moment. Then he reached down to his belt and brought forth the .45 automatic. He moistened his lips.

Joe said softly, "You know what this here is?"

Temple-Tracy stared at the weapon. "It's a handgun, circa, I would say, about 1925 Old Calendar. What in the world are you doing with it?"

Joe said, very slowly, "Chief, in the line you're in these days you needa heavy around with wunna these. Otherwise, Chief, you're gunna wind up in some gutter with a lotta holes in you. What I'm doin', I'm askin' for a job. You need a good man knows how to handle wunna these, Chief."

Citizen Howard Temple-Tracy eyed him appraisingly. "Perhaps," he said, "you are right at that. In the near future, I may well need an assistant knowledgeable in the field of violence. Tell me more about yourself. You surprise me considerably."

"Sure, Chief. It's kinda a long story, though. First off, I better tell you you got some bad enemies, Chief. Two guys special, named Brett-James and Doc Reston-Farrell. I think one of the first jobs I'm gonna hafta do for you, Chief, is to give it to those two."

Margaret St. Clair

BRIGHTNESS FALLS FROM THE AIR

People will say a lot of nice things about Tony Boucher, but perhaps nobody will think to mention what I considered one of his most delightful characteristics, his beautiful tact. I never knew anybody who could handle difficult situations better: I suppose it came from his amiability, which was a basic thing. He was a keen and perceptive critic, but I never heard him make a nasty remark about anyone, or hurt anybody's feelings. It was this tact and perceptiveness that made him so much in demand as a master of ceremonies. He was a wonderfully amiable man.

KERR USED TO GO into the tepidarium of the identification bureau to practice singing. The tepidarium was a big room, filled almost from wall to wall by the pool of glittering preservative, and he liked its acoustics. The bodies of the bird people would drift a little back and forth in the pellucid fluid as he sang, and he liked to look at them. If the tepidarium was a little morbid as a place to practice singing, it was (Kerr used to think) no more morbid than the rest of the world in which he was living. When he had sung for as long as he thought good for his voice—he had no teacher—he would go to one of the windows and watch the luminous trails that meant the bird people were fighting again. The trails would float down slowly against the night sky as if they were made of star dust. But after Kerr met Rhysha, he stopped all that.

Rhysha came to the bureau one evening just as he was going on duty. She had come to claim a body. The bodies of the bird people often stayed in the bureau for a considerable time. Ordinary means of transportation were forbidden to the bird people because of their extra-terrestrial origin, and it was hard for them to get to the bureau to identify their dead. Rhysha made the identification—it was her brother—paid the bureau's fee from a worn purse, and indicated on the proper form the disposal she wanted made of the body. She was quiet and controlled in her grief. Kerr had watched the televised battles of the bird people once or twice, but this was the first time he had ever seen one of them alive and face to face. He looked at her with interest and curiosity, and then with wonder and delight.

The most striking thing about Rhysha was her glowing, deep turquoise plumage. It covered her from head to heels in what appeared to be a clinging velvet cloak. The coloring was so much more intense than that of the bodies in the tepidarium that Kerr would have thought she belonged to a different species than they.

Her face, under the golden top-knot, was quite human, and so were her slender, leaf-shaped hands; but there was a fantastic, light-boned grace in her movements such as no human being ever had. Her voice was low, with a 'cello's fullness of tone. Everything about her, Kerr thought, was rare and delightful and curious. But there was a shadow in her face, as if a natural gaiety had been repressed by the overwhelming harshness of circumstance.

"Where shall I have the ashes sent?" Kerr asked as he took the form.

She plucked indecisively at her pink lower lip. "I am not sure. The manager where we are staying has told us we must leave tonight, and I do not know where we will go. Could I come to the bureau again when the ashes are ready?"

It was against regulations, but Kerr nodded. He would keep the capsule of ashes in his locker until she came. It would be nice to see her again.

She came, weeks later, for the ashes. There had been several battles of the bird people in the interval, and the pool in the tepidarium was full. As Kerr looked at her, he wondered how long it would be before she too was dead.

He asked her new address. It was a fantastic distance away, in the worst part of the city, and after a little hesitation he told her that if she could wait until his shift was over he would be glad to walk back with her.

She looked at him doubtfully. "It is most kind of you, but —but an earthman was kind to us once. The children used to throw stones at him."

Kerr had never thought much about the position of the non-human races in his world. If it was unjust, if they were badly treated, he had thought it no more than a particular instance of the general cruelty and stupidity. Now anger flared up in him.

"That's all right," he said harshly. "If you don't mind waiting, that is."

Rhysha smiled faintly. "No, I don't mind," she said.

Since there were still some hours to go on his shift, he took her into a small reception room where there was a chaise lounge. "Try to sleep," he said.

A little before three he came to rouse her, and found her lying quiet but awake. They left the bureau by a side door.

The city was as quiet at this hour as it ever was. All the sign projectors, and most of the street lights, had been turned off to save power, and even the vast, disembodied voices that boomed out of the air all day long and half the night were almost silent. The darkness and quiescence of the city made it seem easy for them to talk as they went through the streets.

Kerr realized afterwards how confident he must have been of Rhysha's sympathy to have spoken to her as freely as he did. And she must have felt an equal confidence in him, for after a little while she was telling him fragments of her history and her people's past without reserve.

"After the earthmen took our planet," she said, "we had nothing left they wanted. But we had to have food. Then we discovered that they liked to watch us fight."

"You fought before the earthmen came?" Kerr asked.

"Yes. But not as we fight now. It was a ritual then, very formal, with much politeness and courtesy. We did not fight to get things from each other, but to find out who was brave and could give us leadership. The earth people were impatient with our ritual—they wanted to see us hurting and being hurt. So we learned to fight as we fight now, hoping to be killed.

"There was a time, when we first left our planet and went to the other worlds where people liked to watch us, when there were many of us. But there have been many battles since then. Now there are only a few left."

At the cross street a beggar slouched up to them. Kerr gave him a coin. The man was turning away with thanks when he caught sight of Rhysha's golden top-knot. "God-damned Extey!" he said in sudden rage. "Filth! And you, a man, going around with it! Here!" He threw the coin at Kerr.

"Even the beggars!" Rhysha said. "Why is it, Kerr, you hate us so?"

"Because we have wronged you," he answered, and knew it was the truth. "Are we always so unkind, though?"

"As the beggar was? Often . . . it is worse."

"Rhysha, you've got to get away from here."

"Where?" She answered simply. "Our people have discussed it so many times! There is no planet on which there are not already billions of people from earth. You increase so fast!

"And besides, it doesn't matter. You don't need us, there isn't any place for us. We cared about that once, but not any more. We're so tired—all of us, even the young ones like me—we're so tired of trying to live."

"You mustn't talk like that," Kerr said harshly. "I won't

let you talk like that. You've got to go on. If we don't need you now, Rhysha, we will."

From the block ahead of them there came the wan glow of a municipal telescreen. Late as the hour was, it was surrounded by a dense knot of spectators. Their eyes were fixed greedily on the combat that whirled dizzily over the screen.

Rhysha tugged gently at Kerr's sleeve. "We had better go around," she said in a whisper. Kerr realized with a pang that there would be trouble if the viewers saw a "man" and an Extey together. Obediently he turned.

They had gone a block further when Kerr (for he had been thinking) said, "My people took the wrong road, Rhysha, about two hundred years ago. That was when the council refused to accept, even in principle, any form of population control. By now we're stifling under the pressure of our own numbers, we're crushed shapeless under it. Everything has had to give way to our one basic problem, how to feed an ever-increasing number of hungry mouths. Morality has dwindled into feeding ourselves. And we have the battle sports over the telecast to keep us occupied.

"But I think—I believe—that we'll get into the right road again sometime. I've read books of history, Rhysha. This isn't the first time we've chosen the wrong road. Someday there'll be room for your people, Rhysha, if only—" he hesitated—"if only because you're so beautiful."

He looked at her earnestly. Her face was remote and bleak. An idea came to him. "Have you ever heard anyone sing, Rhysha?"

"Sing? No, I don't know the word."

"Listen, then." He fumbled over his repertory and decided, though the music was not really suited to his voice, on Tamino's song to Pamina's portrait. He sang it for her as they walked along, as loudly as he dared.

Little by little Rhysha's face relaxed. "I liked that," she said when the song was over. "Sing more, Kerr."

"Do you see what I was trying to tell you?" he said at last, after many songs. "If we could make songs like that, Rhysha, isn't there hope for us?"

"For you, perhaps. Not us," Rhysha answered. There was anger in her voice. "Stop it, Kerr. I do not want to be waked."

But when they parted she clasped hands with him and told him where they could meet again. "You are really our friend," she said without coquetry.

When he next met Rhysha, Kerr said, "I brought you a present. Here." He handed her a parcel. "And I've some news, too."

Rhysha opened the little package. An exclamation of pleasure broke from her lips. "Oh, lovely! What a lovely thing! Where did you get it, Kerr?"

"In a shop that sells old things, in the back." He did not tell her he had given ten days' pay for the little turquoise locket. "But the stones are lighter than I realized. I wanted something that would be the color of your plumage."

Rhysha shook her head. "No, this is the color it should be. This is right." She clasped the locket around her neck and looked down at it with pleasure. "And now, what is the news you have for me?"

"A friend of mine is a clerk in the city of records. He tells me a new planet, near gamma Cassiopeiae, is being opened for colonization.

"I've filed the papers, and everything is in order. The hearing will be held on Friday. I'm going to appear in behalf of the Ngayir, your people, and ask that they be allotted space on the new world."

Rhysha turned white. He started toward her; but she waved him away. One hand was still clasping her locket, that was nearly the color of her plumage.

"It hurts so," she said, "it hurts so—to hope."

The hearing was held in a small auditorium in the basement of the Colonization building. Representatives of a dozen groups spoke before Kerr's turn came.

"Appearing on behalf of the Ngayir," the arbitrator read

from a form in his hand, "S 3687 Kerr. And who are the Ngayir, S-Kerr? Some Indian group?"

"No, sir," Kerr said. "They are commonly known as the bird people."

"Oh, a conservationist!" The arbitrator looked at Kerr not unkindly. "I'm sorry, but your petition is quite out of order. It should never have been filed. Immigration is restricted by executive order to terrestrials. . . ."

Kerr dreaded telling Rhysha of his failure, but she took it with perfect calm.

"After you left I realized it was impossible," she said.

"Rhysha, I want you to promise me something. I can't tell you how sure I am that humanity is going to need your people sometime. It's true, Rhysha. I'm going to keep trying. I'm not going to give up.

"Promise me this, Rhysha: promise me that neither you nor the members of your group will take part in the battles until you hear from me again."

Rhysha smiled. "All right, Kerr."

Preserving the bodies of people who have died from a variety of diseases is not without its dangers. Kerr did not go to work that night or the next or for many nights. His dormitory chief, after listening to him shout in delirium for some hours, called a doctor, who filled out a hospital requisition slip.

He was gravely ill, and his recovery was slow. It was nearly five weeks before he was released.

Howard Schoenfeld

BUILT UP LOGICALLY

"You'll be pleased, I hope," Anthony Boucher wrote me during his co-editorship of the Magazine of Fantasy and Science Fiction, *"to hear that we've been getting a lot of strongly favorable reaction on 'Built Up Logically' [my first contribution to the magazine]. A few dullards mutter Hey, what is this, but the more typical reaction is simply* Wheee!"

Could any writer resist an editor who took the trouble to write such glowing accounts of his work? I didn't have the good luck to meet Mr. Boucher, but I'll never forget him.

"THE UNIVERSAL PANACEA," Frank said, lighting a cigar. "Have one."

I took it.

"Light up, man."

"It's great, man."

We walked up Fifth Avenue toward 14th Street.

"Stop," Frank said. We came to a halt.

Frank put his hand out in front of him and moved it back and forth a couple of times, inventing the rabbit. Getting the feel of the creature's fur, he built it up logically from the feel. It was the only animal that could have produced that particular feel, and I was proud of him for thinking of it.

"Marvelous," I said, looking at it.

The rabbit sat on its haunches, a bundle of white fur with pink eyes. Dilating its nostrils, it hopped away from us, disappearing into an open doorway. I'd never seen a more ingenious invention.

"Amazing," I said.

"Nothing really," Frank said. "Watch this."

Frank was a tall, thin-lipped man with a round forehead. Beads of perspiration appeared on his forehead. His face became taut, then relaxed.

"Feel anything?" he asked.

My brain tingled curiously. Something was being impinged on it. It was the consciousness of rabbits, their place in the scheme of things. I knew they'd been with us always.

Frank grinned.

"Not only you, but practically every man, woman and child in the world thinks that now. Only I know differently."

It was uncanny.

We got in a cab and went up to The Three Sevens, a night club on 52nd Street. Inside, the place was crowded with jazz enthusiasts, listening to the Sevens. At the bar a man in a grey overcoat was reading a manuscript to a blonde girl in her teens. I went over and listened.

This was what he read:

"The Universal Panacea," Frank said, lighting a cigar. "Have one."

I took it.

"Light up, man."

"It's great, man."

We walked up Fifth Avenue toward 14th Street.

"Stop," Frank said. We came to a halt.

Frank put his hand out in front of him and moved it back and forth a couple of times, inventing the rabbit. Getting the feel of the creature's fur, he built it up logically from the feel. It was the only animal that could have produced that particular feel, and I was proud of him for thinking of it.

"Stop," I yelled. "For Christ's sake, stop!"

The man in the grey overcoat turned around and faced me. "What's eating you, bud?"

"That manuscript you're reading," I said. "It's mine."

He looked me up and down contemptuously.

"So you're the guy."

There was something disquietingly familiar about him.

"Say. Who are you?"

For an answer he doubled up his first and socked the blonde sitting next to him. She thudded and teetered on the bar stool before falling off. She hit the floor with a resounding thump.

"Wood," he said, looking down at her. "Solid wood."

I tapped the girl's back with the toe of my shoe. There was no doubt about it. She was wooden to the core.

"How would you like to have to sit in a night club and read to a piece of wood?" he asked, disgustedly.

"I wouldn't," I admitted.

"All your characters are wooden," he said.

His voice was strangely familiar.

"Say. Who are you?"

He grinned and handed me his card. It said:

HILLBURT HOOPER ASPASIA	
Birdsmith	Author

For a moment I stared at him in startled disbelief. Then I saw it was true. The man in the grey overcoat was—myself.

"You're getting in over your head," he said.

He was beginning to be a pain in the neck.

I think I'll just write him out of the story right now . . .

The man in the grey overcoat got up and walked out of the club.

I looked around to see what had happened to Frank. He had taken advantage of my preoccupation to step out of the characterization I'd given him and adopt one of his own choice, jazz musician. He was sitting in on the jam session with the Sevens, holding a trumpet he'd found somewhere. The Sevens paused, giving him the opportunity to solo. He arose and faced the audience.

Frank now found himself in the embarrassing position of not knowing how to play the instrument. This, of course, was the consequence of having stepped out of character without my permission. The audience waited expectantly.

Frank looked at me pleadingly.

I grinned and shook my head, no.

I will leave him in this humiliating situation for a while as a punishment for getting out of control in the middle of the story.

The bartender tapped me on the shoulder. He nodded toward the rear of the club. A tall redhead in a low cut evening dress was standing in front of a door labelled "Manager." She motioned me to join her. I threaded my way between the crowded tables.

"Aren't you Aspasia, the writer?" she asked.

She was about nineteen and as sleek as a mink.

"I am."

Her eyes sparkled.

"I'm Sally La Rue," she said. "The manager's daughter." Her body was an enticing succession of trim curves under her black dress. "I have something you may be interested in."

I didn't doubt it for a minute.

"It's an invention of dad's. You might like to do an article about it."

"I might at that," I said, looking at her.

She smiled shyly.

"I'd do anything to help dad," she said simply.

She took my hand and led me into the office. It was a large room with two windows facing 51st Street. In the center of it was a metallic contraption resembling a turbine. Attached to it were a mass of complicated wiring, several rheostats, and two retorts containing quicksilver.

"What is it?" I asked.

"A time machine," Sally said, dramatically.

I looked at the device.

"Does it work?"

"Of course it works. Would you like to try it?"

I said I would.

"Past or future?"

"Future."

"How about 5,000 years?"

"That'll be fine."

Sally adjusted a dial. Then she stepped over to the wall and pulled a switch.

The turbine roared. Blue lightning flashed between the retorts and vaporized the quicksilver into a green gas. The room became luminous. An indicator hit the 5,000 mark. Sally released the switch.

"Here we are," she said.

I dashed over to the windows to see what the world of the future was like.

"It's the same," Sally said, guessing my thought.

I looked out on 51st Street. Nothing had changed.

"That's the beauty of the machine," Sally explained. "It moves the whole world through time rather than just one part of it."

"The stars," I said. "Surely their positions have changed."

"No. It moves the whole universe through time. Everything."

"I see."

"Isn't it wonderful?"

Thinking it over I couldn't say it was. I didn't say it was.

"You'll do the article, won't you?" she asked eagerly.

Her body was rippling with excitement beneath her black dress. I noticed her father kept a couch in his office.

"Well. If you really want me to," I said. "Yes."

"Would you like to go forward another 5,000 years?" she asked.

I glanced at the couch.

"Not right now," I said.

She was engrossed in the machine.

"I think I'll set it for 1,000,000 A.D."

I looked at her, then at the couch. Then I remembered I'd left Frank in an awkward spot some 5,000 years and odd minutes ago.

"I'll be right back," I said. "Wait for me here, will you?"

She had her hand on the switch. She smiled.

"Of course," she said. "Darling."

I left her at her dad's time machine playfully thrusting the universe a million years into the future.

Frank was in the bandstand with the Sevens, where I'd left him, facing an expectant audience. When he saw me he waved the trumpet at me before returning it to its case. He motioned the audience to be quiet.

Frank tilted his head sideways, cupped his ear in his hand, and invented the piano. Getting the sound of the instrument's notes, he built it up logically from the sound. It was the only instrument that could have produced that particular sound and I was glad to see him invent it, though I was getting a little tired of the trick.

One of the Sevens sat down and started playing a boogie-woogie number. Frank came over and stood beside me. "What do you think of it?" he asked.

"It's great, man."

He handed me a cigar.

We lit up.

Behind me a familiar voice said:

"Ask him to invent something original."

"Like what?" I asked without turning.

"Something socially conscious. Like a new sex, perhaps."

Somebody's hand was in my pocket.

"How about that, Frank?" I asked.

"Your subconscious is showing," Frank said, looking over my shoulder.

The hand was withdrawn.

I reached inside my pocket and brought out the card that had been left in it. It said:

> guess who and you can have me
> (over)

I turned the card over with fingers thát trembled just a little. It said:

> HILLBURT HOOPER ASPASIA
> Birdsmith Author

The voice behind me and the hand in my pocket were my own again!

Turning, I caught a glimpse of the man in the grey overcoat hurrying toward the door marked "Manager." He paused in front of it and glanced at me. I nodded. With my approval he went in and closed the door behind him. Once inside, he joined the redhead, Sally La Rue.

I congratulated myself on projecting myself in the story in two characterizations. Owing to my foresight I will now be able to enjoy the person of Sally La Rue without interference from the censors, and, at the same time, continue my narrative.

I turned to Frank.

"Let's drop in on the Baron's party," I said.

"Good idea."

We went outside, got in a cab, and went uptown to the Baron's apartment house.

Inside, the party was going full blast. The Baron, as usual, was on the studio couch, passed out. The guests were in various states of inebriation. When I entered, the room became quiet for a moment.

In the lull a girl whispered:

"There's Aspasia, the writer."

"He ought to trade himself in on a new model," someone else said. "He looks like a caricature of himself."

"More like a cliché with feet."

"Have you read his latest story?"

"No."

"It's a direct steal from *Built Up Logically* by H. H. Aspasia."

"You don't say."

Blushing, I pretended an interest in the Baron's Mondrian collection. One of the girls said:

"I met his psychiatrist last week. He said he never knew which of his split personalities was analyzing which of Aspasia's."

"How awful."

"Yes, but significant."

"Very."

"What else did he say?"

"Basically maladjusted. Almost non-neurotic."

"Tendencies toward normalcy, too, I'll bet."

"I wouldn't be surprised."

"How perfectly abominable."

"Yes, but significant."

"Very."

"I almost feel sorry for him."

"I wonder if it's safe being here with him?"

"He's only partly with us you know."

"Poor guy. Probably lives in a world of reality."

"No doubt about it."

"Do you think psychiatry can help him?"

"Possibly. There have been cures."

"Notice the way he's staring at the Baron's Mondrians. It's significant, don't you think?"

"Very."

A feeling of boredom was beginning to come over me. I liked nobody at the party. I decided to bring it to an end . . .

The guests, laughing and talking, gathered up their belongings, and left in groups of two and three. Only Frank and I and the passed-out Baron remained.

Frank stood in the center of the room, his head cocked to one side, listening.

"What is it?" I asked.

"Sh-h-h-h," Frank said. "Listen."

I listened.

"Hear it?"

I shook my head.

"What is it?"

"The pulse beat of the universe. I can hear it."

"My God," I said.

He stood there listening to the pulse beat of the universe.

"Marvelous," I said.

"Yes," he said. "But not for you."

Frank tilted his head sideways, cupped his ear in his hand, and invented the universe. Getting the sound of its pulse beat, he built it up logically from the sound. It was the only universe that could have produced that particular pulse beat, and I was amazed at his blasphemy in creating it.

"Stop," I demanded.

My demand went unheeded.

The universe and its contents appeared.

Frank's face tautened. Beads of perspiration broke out on his forehead. Then he relaxed. His grin was ominous.

With a start of fear I realized my predicament. In inventing the universe and its contents Frank had also invented me.

I was in the unheard-of position of having been created by a figment of my own imagination.

"Our roles are reversed," Frank said. "I've not only

created you, but all your works, including this narrative. Following this paragraph I will assume my rightful role as author of the story and you will assume yours as a character in it."

Aspasia's face blanched.

"This is impossible," he said.

"Not impossible," I said. "I've done it. I, Frank, have done it. I'm in control of the story. I've achieved reality at last."

Aspasia's expression was bitter. "Yes. At my expense."

"You're the first author in history to achieve a real status in fiction," I pointed out.

Aspasia sneered.

"Happens every day."

I shrugged.

"Survival of the fittest. Serves you right for giving me more creative power than you have. What did you expect?"

"Gratitude," Aspasia said, nastily. "And a little loyalty."

"Gratitude, my eye. You're the bird who made me stand in front of a night club audience for 5,000 years with a trumpet I couldn't play. Most humiliating experience of my life."

"You deserved it for getting out of character," Aspasia said, a trifle petulantly.

"That," I said, "gives me an idea."

As a punishment for humiliating me in The Three Sevens I will now give Aspasia a little dose of his own medicine. During his authorship of the story Aspasia neglected completely to give himself a description. He will now have no alternative but to accept the one I give him.

I allowed him to guess my intention.

"No," Aspasia begged. "No. Don't do it."

But I did.

Aspasia's harelip grimaced frightfully. He placed a gnarled hand to his pockmarked and cretinous face, squinting at me through bloodshot, pig eyes. Buttons popped from his trousers as his huge belly sagged. Beetling, black eyebrows moved up and down his receding forehead. Bat ears stuck outward from his head.

"You fiend," he gasped. "You ungrateful fiend."

There was murder in his eyes.

I knew then it was going to be one or the other of us sooner or later. In self-defense I had no alternative but to beat Aspasia to it.

I was standing near the door. Turning the lights out, I stepped into the hall and closed the door behind me, leaving Aspasia in the dark with the sleeping Baron.

By a coincidence arranged by me as the author of the story, a neighbor of the Baron's was in the hall walking toward the steps. I joined him. Halfway down the steps we heard a shot fired in the Baron's apartment. My companion dashed back up. There was no need for me to follow him. I knew what he would find.

I had arranged that the Baron, awakening suddenly, would mistake Aspasia for a burglar in the darkness of the room, and fire a bullet into his brain.

Upstairs, Aspasia lay dead on the floor.

I walked down the steps to the sidewalk. Across the street I sat heavily on the front stoop of a brownstone house. Dog tired, I rested my head against the step railing and went to sleep.

While Frank is asleep I, Aspasia, will take advantage of the opportunity to reassume my role as author of the story.

Although I am quite dead in my characterization as Hillburt Hooper Aspasia, the companion and victim of Frank, the reader will be relieved to know I am alive and unharmed in my other characterization as Aspasia, the man in the grey overcoat.

For the second time that night I congratulated myself on my foresight in projecting myself in the story in two characterizations.

As the man in the grey overcoat I was last seen entering the manager's office in The Three Sevens with the redhead, Sally La Rue.

Sally lay on the couch in her dad's office, her red head cradled against the white of her arm, looking upward at me contentedly.

The stars in her eyes were shining.

"Dear Aspasia," Sally said, huskily.

"Is there a typewriter here?" I asked.

"On the desk," Sally said.

I sat at the desk.

"Hurry, darling," Sally said.

I nodded, inserted a sheet of paper in the typewriter, and went on with the story:

The lights were on in the Baron's apartment. Staring at the form on the floor, the Baron recognized it as his lifelong friend, Hillburt Hooper Aspasia. In a burst of anguish, the Baron flung the pistol that had killed his friend out the window.

By a coincidence arranged by me as the legitimate author of the story, the pistol exploded on landing, sending a bullet into the brain of Frank who was still asleep across the street on the front stoop of a brownstone house.

Frank slumped forward and rolled into the gutter, dead, a grim monument and warning to all characters with rebellious spirits. I grinned and added the last two words to the story: THE END.

Robert Silverberg

WARM MAN

I was something of a boy wonder of science fiction in the 1950s, with a hundred stories and a couple of novels in print before I was old enough to vote. Tony Boucher, who had such a keen interest in curious phenomena of all sorts, thought it would be charming to have a story by this prodigy in F&SF. The prodigy thought so too—most of his stories had been submitted there before selling elsewhere. All during 1956 Tony and I worked on the project of getting a story of mine into the magazine; but, prodigy or no, I wasn't yet ready for its pages, and Tony wasn't about to relax his editorial standards for the sake of slipping me in. Then "Warm Man" came out of the typewriter, late in the year, and I knew I'd make it at last. Yes, Tony said, the ice is broken. I don't know which of us was happier—he that he had finally been able to bag his prodigy, or I that I had managed to please science fiction's most selective arbiter of literary merit. It was, at any rate, a wonderously heady thing to find my name on that elegant contents page a few months later.

No one was ever quite sure just when Mr. Hallinan came to live in New Brewster. Lonny Dewitt, who ought to know, testified that Mr. Hallinan died on December 3, at 3:30 in the afternoon, but as for the day of his arrival no one could be nearly so precise.

It was simply that one day there was no one living in the unoccupied split-level on Melon Hill, and then the next *he* was there, seemingly having grown out of the woodwork during the night, ready and willing to spread his cheer and warmth throughout the whole of the small suburban community.

Daisy Moncrieff, New Brewster's ineffable hostess, was responsible for making the first overtures toward Mr. Hallinan. It was two days after she had first observed lights on in the Melon Hill place that she decided the time had come to scrutinize the newcomers, to determine their place in New Brewster society. Donning a light wrap, for it was a coolish October day, she left her house in early forenoon and went on foot down Copperbeech Road to the Melon Hill turnoff, and then climbed the sloping hill till she reached the split-level.

The name was already on the mailbox: DAVIS HALLINAN. That probably meant they'd been living there a good deal longer than just two days, thought Mrs. Moncrieff; perhaps they'd be insulted by the tardiness of the invitation? She shrugged and used the doorknocker.

A tall man in early middle age appeared, smiling benignly. Mrs. Moncrieff was thus the first recipient of the uncanny warmth that Davis Hallinan was to radiate throughout New Brewster before his strange death. His eyes were deep and solemn, with warm lights shining in them; his hair was a dignified gray-white mane.

"Good morning," he said. His voice was deep, mellow.

"Good morning. I'm Mrs. Moncrieff—*Daisy* Moncrieff, from the big house down on Copperbeech Road. You must be Mr. Hallinan. May I come in?"

"Ah—please, no, Mrs. Moncrieff. The place is still a chaos. Would you mind staying on the porch?"

He closed the door behind him—Mrs. Moncrieff later claimed that she had a fleeting view of the interior and saw unpainted walls and dust-covered bare floors—and drew one of the rusty porch chairs for her.

"Is your wife at home, Mr. Hallinan?"

"There's just me, I'm afraid. I live alone."

"Oh." Mrs. Moncrieff, discomforted, managed a grin none the less. In New Brewster *everyone* was married; the idea of a bachelor or a widower coming to settle there was strange, disconcerting . . . and just a little pleasant, she added, surprised at herself.

"My purpose in coming was to invite you to meet some of your new neighbors tonight—if you're free, that is. I'm having a cocktail party at my place about six, with dinner at seven. We'd be so happy if you came!"

His eyes twinkled gaily. "Certainly, Mrs. Moncrieff. I'm looking forward to it already."

The ne plus ultra of New Brewster society was impatiently assembled at the Moncrieff home shortly after 6, waiting to meet Mr. Hallinan, but it was not until 6:15 that he arrived. By then, thanks to Daisy Moncrieff's fearsome skill as a hostess, everyone present was equipped with a drink and with a set of speculations about the mysterious bachelor on the hill.

"I'm sure he must be a writer," said Martha Weede to liverish Dudley Heyer. "Daisy says he's tall and distinguished and just *radiates* personality. He's probably here only for a few months—just long enough to get to know us all, and then he'll write a novel about us."

"Hmm. Yes," Heyer said. He was an advertising executive who commuted to Madison Avenue every morning; he had an ulcer, and was acutely conscious of his role as a stereotype. "Yes, then he'll write a sizzling novel exposing suburban decadence, or a series of acid sketches for *The New Yorker*. I know the type."

Lys Erwin, looking desirable and just a bit disheveled after her third martini in thirty minutes, drifted by in time to overhear that. "You're *always* conscious of *types*, aren't you, darling? You and your gray flannel suit?"

Heyer fixed her with a baleful stare but found himself, as usual, unable to make an appropriate retort. He turned away, smiled hello at quiet little Harold and Jane Dewitt, whom he pitied somewhat (their son Lonny, age 9, was a shy, sensitive child, a total misfit among his playmates) and confronted the bar, weighing the probability of a night of acute agony against the immediate desirability of a Manhattan.

But at that moment Daisy Moncrieff reappeared with Mr. Hallinan in tow, and conversation ceased abruptly throughout the parlor while the assembled guests stared at the newcomer. An instant later, conscious of their collective *faux pas*, the group began to chat again, and Daisy moved among her guests, introducing her prize.

"Dudley, this is Mr. Davis Hallinan. Mr. Hallinan, I want you to meet Dudley Heyer, one of the most talented men in New Brewster."

"Indeed? What do you do, Mr. Heyer?"

"I'm in advertising. But don't let them fool you; it doesn't take any talent at all. Just brass, nothing else. The desire to delude the public, and delude 'em good. But how about you? What line are you in?"

Mr. Hallinan ignored the question. "I've always thought advertising was a richly creative field, Mr. Heyer. But, of course, I've never really known at first hand—"

"Well, I have. And it's everything they say it is." Heyer felt his face reddening, as if he had had a drink or two. He was becoming talkative, and found Hallinan's presence oddly soothing. Leaning close to the newcomer, Heyer said, "Just between you and me, Hallinan, I'd give my whole bank account for a chance to stay home and *write*. Just write. I want to do a novel. But I don't have the guts; that's my trouble. I know that come Friday there's a $350 check waiting on my desk, and I don't dare give that up. So I keep writing my novel up here in my head, and it keeps eating me away down here in my gut. *Eating*." He paused, conscious that he had said too much and that his eyes were glittering beadily.

Hallinan wore a benign smile. "It's always sad to see talent hidden, Mr. Heyer. I wish you well."

Daisy Moncrieff appeared then, hooked an arm through Hallinan's, and led him away. Heyer, alone, stared down at the textured gray broadloom.

Now why did I tell him all that? he wondered. A minute after meeting Hallinan, he had unburdened his deepest woe to him—something he had not confided in anyone else in New Brewster, including his wife.

And yet—it had been a sort of catharsis, Heyer thought. Hallinan had calmly soaked up all his grief and inner agony, and left Heyer feeling drained and purified and warm.

Catharsis? Or a blood-letting? Heyer shrugged, then grinned and made his way to the bar to pour himself a Manhattan.

As usual, Lys and Leslie Erwin were at opposite ends of the parlor. Mrs. Moncrieff found Lys more easily, and introduced her to Mr. Hallinan.

Lys faced him unsteadily, and on a sudden impulse hitched her neckline higher. "Pleased to meet you, Mr. Hallinan. I'd like you to meet my husband Leslie. *Leslie!* Come here, please?"

Leslie Erwin approached. He was twenty years older than his wife, and was generally known to wear the finest pair of horns in New Brewster—a magnificent spread of antlers that grew a new point or two almost every week.

"Les, this is Mr. Hallinan. Mr. Hallinan, meet my husband, Leslie."

Mr. Hallinan bowed courteously to both of them. "Happy to make your acquaintance."

"The same," Erwin said. "If you'll excuse me, now—"

"The louse," said Lys Erwin, when her husband had returned to his station at the bar. "He'd sooner cut his throat than spend two minutes next to me in public." She glared bitterly at Hallinan. "I don't deserve that kind of thing, do I?"

Mr. Hallinan frowned sympathetically. "Have you any children, Mrs. Erwin?"

"Hah! He'd never give me any—not with *my* reputation! You'll have to pardon me; I'm a little drunk."

"I understand, Mrs. Erwin."

"I know. Funny, but I hardly know you and I like you. You seem to *understand.* Really, I mean." She took his cuff hesitantly. "Just from looking at you, I can tell you're not judging me like all the others. I'm not really *bad*, am I? It's just that I get so *bored*, Mr. Hallinan."

"Boredom is a great curse," Mr. Hallinan observed.

"Damn right it is! And Leslie's no help—always reading his newspapers and talking to his brokers! But I can't help myself, believe me." She looked around wildly. "They're going to start talking about us in a minute, Mr. Hallinan. Every time I talk to someone new they start whispering. But promise me something—"

"If I can."

"Someday—someday soon—let's get together? I want to *talk* to you. God, I want to talk to someone—someone who understands why I'm the way I am. Will you?"

"Of course, Mrs. Erwin. Soon." Gently he detached her hand from his sleeve, held it tenderly for a moment, and released it. She smiled hopefully at him. He nodded.

"And now I must meet some of the other guests. A pleasure, Mrs. Erwin."

He drifted away, leaving Lys weaving shakily in the middle of the parlor. She drew in a deep breath and lowered her décolletage again.

At least there's one decent man in this town now, she thought. There was something *good* about Hallinan—good, and kind, and understanding.

Understanding. That's what I need. She wondered if she could manage to pay a visit to the house on Melon Hill tomorrow afternoon without arousing too much scandal.

Lys turned and saw thin-faced Aiken Muir staring at her slyly, with a clear-cut invitation on his face. She met his glance with a frigid, wordless *go to hell.*

Mr. Hallinan moved on, on through the party. And, gradually, the pattern of the party began to form. It took shape like a fine mosaic. By the time the cocktail hour was over and dinner was ready, an intricate, complex structure of interacting thoughts and responses had been built.

Mr. Hallinan, always drinkless, glided deftly from one New Brewsterite to the next, engaging each in conversation, drawing a few basic facts about the other's personality, smiling politely, moving on. Not until after he moved on did the person come to a dual realization: that Mr. Hallinan had said quite little, really, and that he had instilled a feeling of warmth and security in the other during their brief talk.

And thus while Mr. Hallinan learned from Martha Weede of her paralyzing envy of her husband's intelligence and of her fear of his scorn, Lys Erwin was able to remark to Dudley Heyer that Mr. Hallinan was a remarkably kind and understanding person. And Heyer, who had never been known to speak a kind word of anyone, for once agreed.

And later, while Mr. Hallinan was extracting from Leslie Erwin some of the pain his wife's manifold infidelities caused him, Martha Weede could tell Lys Erwin, "He's so gentle—why, he's almost like a saint!"

And while little Harold Dewitt poured out his fear that his silent 9-year-old son Lonny was in some way subnormal, Leslie Erwin, with a jaunty grin, remarked to Daisy Moncrieff, "That man must be a psychiatrist. Lord, he knows how to talk to a person. Inside of two minutes he had me telling him all my troubles. I feel better for it, too."

Mrs. Moncrieff nodded. "I know what you mean. This morning, when I went up to his place to invite him here, we talked a little while on his porch."

"Well," Erwin said, "if he's a psychiatrist he'll find plenty of business here. There isn't a person here riding around without a private monkey on his back. Take Heyer, over there—he didn't get that ulcer from happiness. That scatterbrain Martha Weede, too—married to a Columbia professor who can't imagine what to talk to her about. And my wife Lys is a very confused person too, of course."

"We all have our problems," Mrs. Moncrieff sighed. "But I feel much better since I spoke with Mr. Hallinan. Yes: *much* better."

Mr. Hallinan was now talking with Paul Jambell, the architect. Jambell, whose pretty young wife was in Springfield Hospital slowly dying of cancer. Mrs. Moncrieff could well imagine what Jambell and Mr. Hallinan were talking about.

Or rather, what Jambell was talking about—for Mr. Hallinan, she realized, did very little talking himself. But he was such a *wonderful* listener! She felt a pleasant glow, not entirely due to the cocktails. It was good to have someone like Mr. Hallinan in New Brewster, she thought. A man of his tact and dignity and warmth would be a definite asset.

When Lys Erwin woke—alone, for a change—the following morning, some of the past night's curious calmness had deserted her.

I have to talk to Mr. Hallinan, she thought.

She had resisted two implied and one overt attempts at seduction the night before, had come home, had managed even to be polite to her husband. And Leslie had been polite to her. It was most unusual.

"That Hallinan," he had said. "He's quite a guy."

"You talked to him too?"

"Yeah. Told him a lot. Too much, maybe. But I feel better for it."

"Odd," she said. "So do I. He's a strange one, isn't he? Wandering around that party, soaking up everyone's aches. He must have had half the neuroses in New Brewster unloaded on his back last night."

"Didn't seem to depress him, though. More he talked to people, more cheerful and affable he got. And us, too. You look more relaxed than you've been in a month, Lys."

"I *feel* more relaxed. As if all the roughness and ugliness in me was drawn out."

And that was how it had felt the next morning, too. Lys woke, blinked, looked at the empty bed across the room.

Leslie was long since gone, on his way to the city. She knew she had to talk to Hallinan again. She hadn't got rid of it all. There was still some poison left inside her, something cold and chunky that would melt before Mr. Hallinan's warmth.

She dressed, impatiently brewed some coffee, and left the house. Down Copperbeech Road, past the Moncrieff house where Daisy and her stuffy husband Fred were busily emptying the ashtrays of the night before, down to Melon Hill and up the gentle slope to the split-level at the top.

Mr. Hallinan came to the door in a blue checked dressing gown. He looked slightly seedy, almost overhung, Lys thought. His dark eyes had puffy lids and a light stubble sprinkled his cheeks.

"Yes, Mrs. Erwin?"

"Oh—good morning, Mr. Hallinan. I—I came to see you. I hope I didn't disturb you—that is—"

"Quite all right, Mrs. Erwin." Instantly she was at ease. "But I'm afraid I'm really extremely tired after last night, and I fear I shouldn't be very good company just now."

"But you said you'd talk to me alone today. And—oh, there's so much more I want to tell you!"

A shadow of feeling—*pain? fear?* Lys wondered—crossed his face. "No," he said hastily. "No more—not just yet. I'll have to rest today. Would you mind coming back—well, say Wednesday?"

"Certainly, Mr. Hallinan. I wouldn't want to disturb you."

She turned away and started down the hill, thinking: *he had too much of our troubles last night. He soaked them all up like a sponge, and today he's going to digest them—*

Oh, what am I thinking?

She reached the foot of the hill, brushed a couple of tears from her eyes, and walked home rapidly, feeling the October chill whistling around her.

And so the pattern of life in New Brewster developed. For the six weeks before his death, Mr. Hallinan was a fixture at any important community gathering, always dressed impeccably, always ready with his cheerful smile, always uncannily able to draw forth whatever secret hungers and terrors lurked in his neighbors' souls.

And invariably Mr. Hallinan would be unapproachable the day after these gatherings, would mildly but firmly turn away any callers. What he did, alone in the house on Melon Hill, no one knew. As the days passed, it occurred to all that no one knew much of anything about Mr. Hallinan. He knew *them* all right, knew the one night of adultery twenty years before that still racked Daisy Moncrieff, knew the acid pain that seared Dudley Heyer, the cold envy glittering in Martha Weede, the frustration and loneliness of Lys Erwin, her husband's shy anger at his own cuckoldry—he knew these things and many more, but none of them knew more of him than his name.

Still, he warmed their lives and took from them the burden of their griefs. If he chose to keep his own life hidden, they said, that was his privilege.

He took walks every day, through still-wooded New Brewster, and would wave and smile to the children, who would wave and smile back. Occasionally, he would stop, chat with a sulking child, then move on, tall, erect, walking with a jaunty stride.

He was never known to set foot in either of New Brewster's two churches. Once Lora Harker, a mainstay of the New Brewster Presbyterian Church, took him to task for this at a dull dinner party given by the Weedes.

But Mr. Hallinan smiled mildly and said, "Some of us feel the need. Others do not."

And that ended the discussion.

Toward the end of November a few members of the community experienced an abrupt reversal of their feelings about Mr. Hallinan—weary, perhaps, of his constant empathy for their woes. The change in spirit was spearheaded by Dudley Heyer, Carl Weede, and several of the other men.

"I'm getting not to trust that guy," Heyer said. He knocked dottle vehemently from his pipe. "Always hanging around soaking up gossip, pulling out dirt—and what the hell for? What does *he* get out of it?"

"Maybe he's practising to be a saint," Carl Weede remarked quietly. "Self-abnegation. The Buddhist Eightfold Path."

"The women all swear by him," said Leslie Erwin. "Lys hasn't been the same since he came here."

"I'll say she hasn't," said Aiken Muir wryly, and all of the men, even Erwin, laughed, getting the sharp thrust.

"All I know is I'm tired of having a father-confessor in our midst," Heyer said. "I think he's got a motive back of all his goody-goody warmness. When he's through pumping us he's going to write a book that'll put New Brewster on the map but good."

"You always suspect people of writing books," Muir said. *"Oh, that mine enemy would write a book . . . !"*

"Well, whatever his motives I'm getting annoyed. And that's why he hasn't been invited to the party we're giving on Monday night." Heyer glared at Fred Moncrieff as if expecting some dispute. "I've spoken to my wife about it, and she agrees. Just this once, dear Mr. Hallinan stays home."

It was strangely cold at the Heyers' party that Monday night. The usual people were there, all but Mr. Hallinan. The party was not a success. Some, unaware that Mr. Hallinan had not been invited, waited expectantly for the chance to talk to him, and managed to leave early when they discovered he was not to be there.

"We should have invited him," Ruth Heyer said after the last guest had left.

Heyer shook his head. "No. I'm glad we didn't."

"But that poor man, all alone on the hill while the bunch of us were here, cut off from us. You don't think he'll get insulted, do you? I mean, and cut us from now on?"

"I don't care," Heyer said, scowling.

His attitude of mistrust toward Mr. Hallinan spread through the community. First the Muirs, then the Harkers, failed to invite him to gatherings of theirs. He still took his usual afternoon walks, and those who met him observed a slightly strained expression on his face, though he still smiled gently and chatted easily enough, and made no bitter comments.

And on December 3, a Wednesday, Roy Heyer, age 10, and Philip Moncrieff, age 9, set upon Lonny Dewitt, age 9, just outside the New Brewster Public School, just before Mr. Hallinan turned down the school lane on his stroll.

Lonny was a strange, silent boy, the despair of his parents and the bane of his classmates. He kept to himself, said little, nudged into corners and stayed there. People clucked their tongues when they saw him in the street.

Roy Heyer and Philip Moncrieff made up their minds they were going to make Lonny Dewitt say something, or else.

It was *or else*. They pummeled him and kicked him for a few minutes; then, seeing Mr. Hallinan approaching, they ran, leaving him weeping silently on the flagstone steps outside the empty school.

Lonny looked up as the tall man drew near.

"They've been hitting you, haven't they? I see them running away now."

Lonny continued to cry. He was thinking, *There's something funny about this man. But he wants to help me. He wants to be kind to me.*

"You're Lonny Dewitt, I think. Why are you crying? Come, Lonny, stop crying! They didn't hurt you that much."

They didn't, Lonny said silently. *I like to cry.*

Mr. Hallinan was smiling cheerfully. "Tell me all about it. Something's bothering you, isn't it? Something big, that makes you feel all lumpy and sad inside. Tell me about it, Lonny, and maybe it'll go away." He took the boy's small cold hands in his own, and squeezed them.

"Don't want to talk," Lonny said.

"But I'm a friend. I want to help you."

Lonny peered close and saw suddenly that the tall man told the truth. He wanted to help Lonny. More than that: he *had* to help Lonny. Desperately. He was pleading. "Tell me what's troubling you," Mr. Hallinan said again.

OK, Lonny thought. *I'll tell you.*

And he lifted the floodgates. Nine years of repression and torment came rolling out in one roaring burst.

I'm alone and they hate me because I do things in my head and they never understood and they think I'm queer and they hate me I see them looking funny at me and they think funny things about me because I want to talk to them with my mind and they can only hear words and I hate them hate them hate hate hate—

Lonny stopped suddenly. He had let it all out, and now he felt better, cleansed of the poison he'd been carrying in him for years. But Mr. Hallinan looked funny. He was pale and white-faced, and he was staggering.

In alarm, Lonny extended his mind to the tall man. And got:

Too much. Much too much. Should never have gone near the boy. But the older ones wouldn't let me.

Irony: the compulsive empath overloaded and burned out by a compulsive sender who'd been bottled up.

. . . like grabbing a high-voltage wire . . .

. . . he was a sender, I was a receiver, but he was too strong . . .

And four last bitter words: *I . . . was . . . a . . . leech . . .*

"Please, Mr. Hallinan," Lonny said out loud. "Don't get sick. I want to tell you some more. Please Mr. Hallinan."

Silence.

Lonny picked up a final lingering wordlessness, and knew he had found and lost the first one like himself. Mr. Hallinan's eyes closed and he fell forward on his face in the street. Lonny realized that it was over, that he and the people of New Brewster would never talk to Mr. Hallinan again. But just to make sure he bent and took Mr. Hallinan's limp wrist.

He let go quickly. The wrist was like a lump of ice. *Cold*—burningly cold. Lonnie stared at the dead man for a moment or two.

"Why, it's dear Mr. Hallinan," a female voice said. "Is he—"

And feeling the loneliness return, Lonny began to cry softly again.

Jack Vance

GREEN MAGIC

In the middle forties Tony and I were near-neighbors, living about a block apart in Berkeley. We did not become acquainted, however, until ten years later, I think at Poul Anderson's house. Thenceforth we were often in contact, though rather irregularly—I think because our styles of amusing ourselves never quite meshed. Tony loved his poker games; I don't know one card from another. Tony was an opera buff; I espouse the no less archaic field of classical jazz. Tony was gastronomically adventurous; I slavishly eat the things I like. I've always felt that we might have become very good friends had there been a single aspect of existence, besides general conviviality, to bring us together. Certainly I've always enjoyed his company.

I don't dare recount any anecdotes.

HOWARD FAIR, LOOKING OVER the relics of his great uncle Gerald McIntyre, found a large ledger entitled:

WORKBOOK & JOURNAL
Open at Peril!

Fair read the journal with interest, although his own work went far beyond ideas treated only gingerly by Gerald McIntyre.

"The existence of disciplines concentric to the elementary magics must now be admitted without further controversy," wrote McIntyre. "Guided by a set of analogies from the white and black magics (to be detailed in due course), I have delineated the basic extension of purple magic, as well as its corollary, Dynamic Nomism."

Fair read on, remarking the careful charts, the projections and expansions, the transpolations and transformations by which Gerald McIntyre had conceived his systemology. So swiftly had the technical arts advanced that McIntyre's expositions, highly controversial sixty years before, now seemed pedantic and overly rigorous.

"Whereas benign creatures: angels, white sprites, merrihews, sandestins—are typical of the white cycle; whereas demons, magners, trolls and warlocks are evinced by black magic; so do the purple and green cycles sponsor their own particulars, but these are neither good nor evil, bearing, rather, the same relation to the black and white provinces that these latter do to our own basic realm."

Fair re-read the passage. The "green cycle"? Had Gerald McIntyre wandered into regions overlooked by modern workers?

He reviewed the journal in the light of this suspicion, and discovered additional hints and references. Especially provocative was a bit of scribbled marginalia: "More concerning my latest researches I may not state, having been promised an infinite reward for this forbearance."

The passage was dated a day before Gerald McIntyre's death, which had occurred on March 21, 1898, the first day of spring. McIntyre had enjoyed very little of his "infinite reward," whatever had been its nature . . . Fair returned to a consideration of the journal, which, in a sentence or two, had opened a chink on an entire new panorama. McIntyre provided no further illumination, and Fair set out to make a fuller investigation.

His first steps were routine. He performed two divinations, searched the standard indexes, concordances, handbooks and formularies, evoked a demon whom he had previously found knowledgeable: all without success. He found no direct reference to cycles beyond the purple; the demon refused even to speculate.

Fair was by no means discouraged; if anything, the intensity of his interest increased. He re-read the journal, with particular care to the justification for purple magic, reasoning that McIntyre, groping for a lore beyond the purple, might well have used the methods which had yielded results before. Applying stains and ultraviolet light to the pages, Fair made legible a number of notes McIntyre had jotted down, then erased.

Fair was immensely stimulated. The notes assured him that he was on the right track, and further indicated a number of blind alleys which Fair profited by avoiding. He applied himself so successfully that before the week was out he had evoked a sprite of the green cycle.

It appeared in the semblance of a man with green glass eyes and a thatch of young eucalyptus leaves in the place of hair. It greeted Fair with cool courtesy, would not seat itself, and ignored Fair's proffer of coffee.

After wandering around the apartment inspecting Fair's books and curios with an air of negligent amusement, it agreed to respond to Fair's questions.

Fair asked permission to use his tape-recorder, which the sprite allowed, and Fair set the apparatus in motion. (When subsequently he replayed the interview, no sound could be heard.)

"What realms of magic lie beyond the green?" asked Fair.

"I can't give you an exact answer," replied the sprite, "because I don't know. There are at least two more, corresponding to the colors we call rawn and pallow, and very likely others."

Fair arranged the microphone where it would more directly intercept the voice of the sprite.

"What," he asked, "is the green cycle like? What is its physical semblance?"

The sprite paused to consider. Glistening mother-of-pearl films wandered across its face, reflecting the tinge of its thoughts. "I'm rather severely restricted by your use of the word 'physical.' And 'semblance' involves a subjective interpretation, which changes with the rise and fall of the seconds."

"By all means," Fair said hastily, "describe it in your own words."

"Well—we have four different regions, two of which floresce from the basic skeleton of the universe, and so subsede the others. The first of these is compressed and isthiated, but is notable for its wide pools of mottle which we use sometimes for deranging stations. We've transplanted clubmosses from Earth's Devonian and a few ice-fires from Perdition. They climb among the rods which we call devilhair—" he went on for several minutes but the meaning almost entirely escaped Fair. And it seemed as if the question by which he had hoped to break the ice might run away with the entire interview. He introduced another idea.

"Can we freely manipulate the physical extensions of Earth?" The sprite seemed amused. "You refer, so I assume, to the various aspects of space, time, mass, energy, life, thought and recollection."

"Exactly."

The sprite raised its green cornsilk eyebrows. "I might as sensibly ask, Can you break an egg by striking it with a club? The response is on a similar level of seriousness."

Fair had expected a certain amount of condescension and impatience, and was not abashed. "How may I learn these techniques?"

"In the usual manner: through diligent study."

"Ah, indeed—but where could I study? Who would teach me?"

The sprite made an easy gesture, and whorls of green smoke trailed from his fingers to spin through the air. "I could arrange the matter, but since I bear you no particular animosity, I'll do nothing of the sort. And now, I must be gone."

"Where do you go?" Fair asked in wonder and longing. "May I go with you?"

The sprite, swirling a drape of bright green dust over its shoulders, shook his head. "You would be less than comfortable."

"Other men have explored the worlds of magic!"

"True: your uncle Gerald McIntyre, for instance."

"My uncle Gerald learned green magic?"

"To the limit of his capabilities. He found no pleasure in his learning. You would do well to profit by his experience and modify your ambitions." The sprite turned and walked away.

Fair watched it depart. The sprite receded in space and dimension, but never reached the wall of Fair's room. At a distance which might have been fifty yards, the sprite glanced back, as if to make sure that Fair was not following, then stepped off at another angle and disappeared.

Fair's first impulse was to take heed and limit his explorations. He was an adept in white magic, and had mastered the black art—occasionally he evoked a demon to liven a social gathering which otherwise threatened to become dull—but he had by no means illuminated every mystery of purple magic, which is the realm of Incarnate Symbols.

Howard Fair might have turned away from the green cycle except for three factors.

First was his physical appearance. He stood rather under medium height, with a swarthy face, sparse black hair, a gnarled nose, a small heavy mouth. He felt no great sensitivity about his appearance, but realized that it might be improved. In his mind's eye he pictured the personified ideal of himself: he was taller by six inches, his nose thin and keen, his skin cleared of its muddy undertone. A striking figure, but still recognizable as Howard Fair. He wanted the love of women, but he wanted it without the interposition of his craft. Many times he had brought beautiful girls to his bed, lips wet and eyes shining; but purple magic had seduced them rather than Howard Fair, and he took limited satisfaction in such conquests.

Here was the first factor which drew Howard Fair back to the green lore; the second was his yearning for extended, perhaps eternal, life; the third was simple thirst for knowledge.

The fact of Gerald McIntyre's death, or dissolution, or disappearance—whatever had happened to him—was naturally a matter of concern. If he had won to a goal so precious, why had he died so quickly? Was the "infinite reward" so miraculous, so exquisite, that the mind failed under its possession? (If such were the case, the reward was hardly a reward.)

Fair could not restrain himself, and by degrees returned to a study of green magic. Rather than again invoke the sprite whose air of indulgent contempt he had found exasperating, he decided to seek knowledge by an indirect method, employing the most advanced concepts of technical and cabalistic science.

He obtained a portable television transmitter which he loaded into his panel truck along with a receiver. On a Monday night in early May, he drove to an abandoned graveyard far out in the wooded hills, and there, by the light of a waning moon, he buried the television camera in graveyard clay until only the lens protruded from the soil.

With a sharp alder twig he scratched on the ground a monstrous outline. The television lens served for one eye, a beer bottle pushed neck-first into the soil the other.

During the middle hours, while the moon died behind wisps of pale cloud, he carved a word on the dark forehead; then recited the activating incantation.

The ground rumbled and moaned, the golem heaved up to blot out the stars.

The glass eyes stared down at Fair, secure in his pentagon.

"Speak!" called out Fair. *"Enteresthes, Akmai Adonai Bidemgir! Elohim, pa rahulli! Enteresthes, HVOI!* Speak!"

"Return me to earth, return my clay to the quiet clay from whence you roused me."

"First you must serve."

The golem stumbled forward to crush Fair, but was halted by the pang of protective magic.

"Serve you I will, if serve you I must."

Fair stepped boldly forth from the pentagon, strung forty yards of green ribbon down the road in the shape of a narrow V. "Go forth into the realm of green magic," he told the monster. "The ribbons reach forty miles, walk to the end, turn about, return, and then fall back, return to the earth from which you rose."

The golem turned, shuffled into the V of green ribbon, shaking off clods of mold, jarring the ground with its ponderous tread.

Fair watched the squat shape dwindle, recede, yet never reach the angle of the magic V. He returned to his panel truck, tuned the television receiver to the golem's eye, and surveyed the fantastic vistas of the green realm.

Two elementals of the green realm met on a spun-silver landscape. They were Jaadian and Misthemar, and they fell to discussing the earthen monster which had stalked forty miles through the region known as Cil; which then, turning in its tracks, had retraced its steps, gradually increasing its pace until at the end it moved in a shambling rush, leaving a trail of clods on the fragile moth-wing mosaics.

"Events, events, events," Misthemar fretted, "they crowd the chute of time till the bounds bulge. Or then again, the course is as lean and spare as a stretched tendon . . . But in regard to this incursion . . ." He paused for a period of reflection, and silver clouds moved over his head and under his feet.

Jaadian remarked, "You are aware that I conversed with Howard Fair; he is so obsessed to escape the squalor of his world that he acts with recklessness."

"The man Gerald McIntyre was his uncle," mused Misthemar. "McIntyre besought, we yielded; as perhaps now we must yield to Howard Fair."

Jaadian uneasily opened his hand, shook off a spray of emerald fire. "Events press, both in and out. I find myself unable to act in this regard."

"I likewise do not care to be the agent of tragedy."

A Meaning came fluttering up from below: "A disturbance among the spiral towers! A caterpillar of glass and metal has come clanking; it has thrust electric eyes into the Portinone and broke open the Egg of Innocence. Howard Fair is the fault."

Jaadian and Misthemar consulted each other with wry disinclination. "Very well, both of us will go; such a duty needs two souls in support."

They impinged upon Earth and found Howard Fair in a wall booth at a cocktail bar. He looked up at the two strangers and one of them asked, "May we join you?"

Fair examined the two men. Both wore conservative suits and carried cashmere topcoats over their arms. Fair noticed that the left thumb-nail of each man glistened green.

Fair rose politely to his feet. "Will you sit down?"

The green sprites hung up their overcoats and slid into the booth. Fair looked from one to the other. He addressed Jaadian. "Aren't you he whom I interviewed several weeks ago?"

Jaadian assented. "You have not accepted my advice."

Fair shrugged. "You asked me to remain ignorant, to accept my stupidity and ineptitude."

"And why should you not?" asked Jaadian gently. "You are a primitive in a primitive realm; nevertheless not one man in a thousand can match your achievements."

Fair agreed, smiling faintly. "But knowledge creates a craving for further knowledge. Where is the harm in knowledge?"

Misthemar, the more mercurial of the sprites, spoke angrily. "Where is the harm? Consider your earthen monster! It befouled forty miles of delicacy, the record of ten million years. Consider your caterpillar! It trampled our pillars of carved milk, our dreaming towers, damaged the nerve-skeins which extrude and waft us our Meanings."

"I'm dreadfully sorry," said Fair. "I meant no destruction."

The sprites nodded. "But your apology conveys no guarantee of restraint."

Fair toyed with his glass. A waiter approached the table, addressed the two sprites. "Something for you two gentlemen?"

Jaadian ordered a glass of charged water, as did Misthemar. Fair called for another highball.

"What do you hope to gain from this activity?" inquired Misthemar. "Destructive forays teach you nothing!"

Fair agreed. "I have learned little. But I have seen miraculous sights. I am more than ever anxious to learn."

The green sprites glumly watched the bubbles rising in their glasses. Jaadian at last drew a deep sigh. "Perhaps we can obviate toil on your part and disturbance on ours. Explicitly, what gains or advantages do you hope to derive from green magic?"

Fair, smiling, leaned back into the red imitation-leather cushions. "I want many things. Extended life—mobility in time—comprehensive memory—augmented perception, with vision across the whole spectrum. I want physical charm and magnetism, the semblance of youth, muscular endurance . . . Then there are qualities more or less speculative, such as—"

Jaadian interrupted. "These qualities and characteristics we will confer upon you. In return you will undertake never again to disturb the green realm. You will evade centuries of toil; we will be spared the nuisance of your presence, and the inevitable tragedy."

"Tragedy?" inquired Fair in wonder. "Why tragedy?"

Jaadian spoke in a deep reverberating voice. "You are a man of Earth. Your goals are not our goals. Green magic makes you aware of our goals."

Fair thoughtfully sipped his highball. "I can't see that this is a disadvantage. I am willing to submit to the discipline of instruction. Surely a knowledge of green magic will not change me into a different entity?"

"No. And this is the basic tragedy!"

Misthemar spoke in exasperation. "We are forbidden to harm lesser creatures, and so you are fortunate; for to dissolve you into air would end all the annoyance."

Fair laughed. "I apologize again for making such a nuisance of myself. But surely you understand how important this is to me?"

Jaadian asked hopefully, "Then you agree to our offer?"

Fair shook his head. "How could I live, forever young, capable of extended learning, but limited to knowledge which I already see bounds to? I would be bored, restless, miserable."

"That well may be," said Jaadian. "But not so bored, restless and miserable as if you were learned in green magic."

Fair drew himself erect. "I must learn green magic. It is an opportunity which only a person both torpid and stupid could refuse."

Jaadian sighed. "In your place I would make the same response." The sprites rose to their feet. "Come then, we will teach you."

"Don't say we didn't warn you," said Misthemar.

Time passed. Sunset waned and twilight darkened. A man walked up the stairs, entered Howard Fair's apartment. He was tall, unobtrusively muscular. His face was sensitive, keen, humorous; his left thumb-nail glistened green.

Time is a function of vital processes. The people of Earth had perceived the motion of their clocks. On this understanding, two hours had elapsed since Howard Fair had followed the green sprites from the bar.

Howard Fair had perceived other criteria. For him the interval had been seven hundred years, during which he had lived in the green realm, learning to the utmost capacity of his brain.

He had occupied two years training his senses to the new conditions. Gradually he learned to walk in the six basic three-dimensional directions, and accustomed himself to the fourth-dimensional short-cuts. By easy stages the blinds over his eyes were removed, so that the dazzling over-human intricacy of the landscape never completely confounded him.

Another year was spent training him to the use of a code-language—an intermediate step between the vocalizations of Earth and the meaning-patterns of the green realm, where a hundred symbol-flakes (each a flitting spot of delicate iridescence) might be displayed in a single swirl of import. During this time Howard Fair's eyes and brain were altered, to allow him the use of the many new colors, without which the meaning-flakes could not be recognized.

These were preliminary steps. For forty years he studied the flakes, of which there were almost a million. Another forty years was given to elementary permutations and shifts, and another forty to parallels, attenuation, diminishments and extensions; and during this time he was introduced to flake patterns, and certain of the more obvious displays.

Now he was able to study without recourse to the code-language, and his progress became more marked. Another twenty years found him able to recognize more complicated Meanings, and he was introduced to a more varied program. He floated over the field of moth-wing mosaics, which still showed the footprints of the golem. He sweated in embarrassment, the extent of his wicked willfulness now clear to him.

So passed the years. Howard Fair learned as much green magic as his brain could encompass.

He explored much of the green realm, finding so much beauty that he feared his brain might burst. He tasted, he heard, he felt, he sensed, and each one of his senses was a hundred times more discriminating than before. Nourishment came in a thousand different forms: from pink eggs which burst into a hot sweet gas, suffusing his entire body; from passing through a rain of stinging metal crystals; from simple contemplation of the proper symbol.

Homesickness for Earth waxed and waned. Sometimes it was insupportable and he was ready to forsake all he had learned and abandon his hopes for the future. At other times the magnificence of the green realm permeated him, and the thought of departure seemed like the threat of death itself.

By stages so gradual he never realized them he learned green magic.

But the new faculty gave him no pride: between his crude ineptitudes and the poetic elegance of the sprites remained a tremendous gap—and he felt his innate inferiority much more keenly than he ever had in his old state. Worse, his most earnest efforts failed to improve his technique, and sometimes, observing the singing joy of an improvised manifestation by one of the sprites, and contrasting it to his own labored constructions, he felt futility and shame.

The longer he remained in the green realm, the stronger the easy environment of Earth, where each of his acts would not shout aloud of vulgarity and crassness. At times he would watch the sprites (in the gossamer forms natural to them) at play among the pearlpetals, or twining like quick flashes of music through the forest of pink spirals. The contrast between their verve and his brutish fumbling could not be borne and he would turn away. His self-respect dwindled with each passing hour, and instead of pride in his learning, he felt a sullen ache for what he was not and could never become. The first few hundred years he worked with the enthusiasm of ignorance, for the next few he was buoyed by hope. During the last part of his time, only dogged obstinacy kept him plodding through what now he knew for infantile exercises.

In one terrible bitter-sweet spasm, he gave up. He found Jaadian weaving tinkling fragments of various magics into a warp of shining long splines. With grave courtesy, Jaadian gave Fair his attention, and Fair laboriously set forth his meaning.

Jaadian returned a message. "I recognize your discomfort, and extend my sympathy. It is best that you now return to your native home."

He put aside his weaving and conveyed Fair down through the requisite vortices. Along the way they passed Misthemar. No flicker of meaning was expressed or exchanged, but Howard Fair thought to feel a tinge of faintly malicious amusement.

Howard Fair sat in his apartment. His perceptions, augmented and sharpened by his sojourn in the green realm, took note of the surroundings. Only two hours before, by the clocks of Earth, he had found them both restful and stimulating; now they were neither. His books: superstition, spuriousness, earnest nonsense. His private journals and workbooks: a pathetic scrawl of infantilisms. Gravity tugged at his feet, held him rigid. The shoddy construction of the house, which heretofore he never had noticed, oppressed him. Everywhere he looked he saw slipshod disorder, primitive filth. The thought of the food he must now eat revolted him.

He went out on his little balcony which overlooked the street. The air was impregnated with organic smells. Across the street he could look into windows where his fellow humans lived in stupid squalor.

Fair smiled sadly. He had tried to prepare himself for these reactions, but now was surprised by their intensity. He returned into his apartment. He must accustom himself to the old environment. And after all there were compensations. The most desirable commodities of the world were now his to enjoy.

Howard Fair plunged into the enjoyment of these pleasures. He forced himself to drink quantities of expensive wines, brandies, liqueurs, even though they offended his palate. Hunger overcame his nausea, he forced himself to the consumption of what he thought of as fried animal tissue, the hypertrophied sexual organs of plants. He experimented with erotic sensations, but found that beautiful women no longer seemed different from the plain ones, and that he could barely steel himself to the untidy contacts. He bought libraries of erudite books, glanced through them with contempt. He tried to amuse himself with his old magics; they seemed ridiculous.

He forced himself to enjoy these pleasures for a month; then he fled the city and established a crystal bubble on a crag in the Andes. To nourish himself, he contrived a thick liquid, which, while by no means as exhilarating as the substances of the green realm, was innocent of organic contamination.

After a certain degree of improvisation and make-shift, he arranged his life to its minimum discomfort. The view was one of austere grandeur; not even the condors came to disturb him. He sat back to ponder the chain of events which had started with his discovery of Gerald McIntyre's workbook. He frowned. Gerald McIntyre. He jumped to his feet, looked far off over the crags.

He found Gerald McIntyre at a wayside service station in the heart of the South Dakota prairie. McIntyre was sitting in an old wooden chair, tilted back against the peeling yellow paint of the service station, a straw hat shading his eyes from the sun.

He was a magnetically handsome man, blond of hair, brown of skin, with blue eyes whose gaze stung like the touch of icicle. His left thumb-nail glistened green.

Fair greeted him casually; the two men surveyed each other with wry curiosity.

"I see you have adapted yourself," said Howard Fair.

McIntyre shrugged. "As well as possible. I try to maintain a balance between solitude and the pressure of humanity." He looked into the bright blue sky where crows flapped and called. "For many years I lived in isolation. I began to detest the sound of my own breathing."

Along the highway came a glittering automobile, rococo as a hybrid goldfish. With the perceptions now available to them, Fair and McIntyre could see the driver to be red-faced and truculent, his companion a peevish woman in expensive clothes.

"There are other advantages to residence here," said McIntyre. "For instance, I am able to enrich the lives of passers-by with trifles of novel adventure." He made a small gesture; two dozen crows swooped down and flew beside the automobile. They settled on the fenders, strutted back and forth along the hood, fouled the windshield.

The automobile squealed to a halt, the driver jumped out, put the birds to flight. He threw an ineffectual rock, waved his arms in outrage, returned to his car, proceeded.

"A paltry affair," said McIntyre with a sigh. "The truth of the matter is that I am bored." He pursed his mouth and blew forth three bright puffs of smoke: first red, then yellow, then blazing blue. "I have arrived at the estate of foolishness, as you can see."

Fair surveyed his great-uncle with a trace of uneasiness. McIntyre laughed. "No more pranks. I predict, however, that you will presently share my malaise."

"I share it already," said Fair. "Sometimes I wish I could abandon all my magic and return to my former innocence."

"I have toyed with the idea," McIntyre replied thoughtfully. "In fact I have made all the necessary arrangements. It is really a simple matter." He led Fair to a small room behind the station. Although the door was open, the interior showed a thick darkness.

McIntyre, standing well back, surveyed the darkness with a quizzical curl to his lip. "You need only enter. All your magic, all your recollections of the green realm will depart. You will be no wiser than the next man you meet. And with your knowledge will go your boredom, your melancholy, your dissatisfaction."

Fair contemplated the dark doorway. A single step would resolve his discomfort.

He glanced at McIntyre; the two surveyed each other with sardonic amusement. They returned to the front of the building.

"Sometimes I stand by the door and look into the darkness," said McIntyre. "Then I am reminded how dearly I cherish my boredom, and what a precious commodity is so much misery."

Fair made himself ready for departure. "I thank you for

this new wisdom, which a hundred more years in the green realm would not have taught me. And now—for a time, at least—I go back to my crag in the Andes."

McIntyre tilted his chair against the wall of the service station. "And I—for a time, at least—will wait for the next passer-by."

"Goodby then, Uncle Gerald."

"Goodby, Howard."

Richard Wilson

DENY THE SLAKE

Tony Boucher and I met only half a dozen times; over the years I knew him better through his notes accepting or rejecting a story or asking for a revision. He never sent a mere rejection slip. His suggestions for rewrites were always clear and detailed—virtual blueprints from which I profited enormously. I'm proud of the fact that Tony chose my story "Love" to inaugurate Fantasy and Science Fiction's *switch from abstract cover designs to covers based on stories in the magazine. Ed Emshwiller's evocative cover painting for that June, 1952, issue now hangs in my study. I'm particularly proud because "Love" was the first story of mine that Tony bought.*

THE SKIPPER looked at what Ernest Hotaling had scribbled on the slip of paper.

The color of my true love's cheek
Will turn to gray within a week.

The skipper read it and exploded. "What kind of nonsense is this?"

"Of course it wouldn't rhyme in a literal translation," Ernest said mildly. "But that's the sense of it."

"Doggerel!" the skipper exclaimed. "Is this the message of the ages? Is this the secret of the lost civilization?"

"There are others, too," Ernest said. He was the psychologist-linguist of the crew. "You've got to expect them to be obscure at first. They didn't purposely leave any message for us."

Ernest sorted through his scraps of paper and picked one out:

They warn me once, they warn me twice.
Alas! my heedn't turns me spice.

"There seems to be something there," Ernest said.

The skipper snorted.

"No, really," Ernest insisted. "An air of pessimism—even doom—runs all through this stuff. Take this one, for instance:

"Music sings within my brain:
I think I may go mad again."

"Now that begins to make some sense," said Rosco, the communications chief. "It ties in with what Doc Braddon found."

The skipper looked searchingly at his technicians, as if he suspected a joke. But they were serious.

"All right," the skipper said. "It baffles me, but I'm just a simple spacefaring man. *You're* the experts. I'm going to my cabin and communicate with the liquor chest. When you think you've got something I can understand, let me know. 'I think I may go mad again.' Huh! I think I may get drunk, myself."

What the technicians of the research ship *Pringle* were trying to learn was why the people of Planetoid S743 had turned to dust.

They had thought at first they were coming to a living, if tiny, world. There had been lights on the nightside and movement along what seemed to be roads.

But when they landed and explored, they found only powder in the places where there should have been people. There were heaps of fine-grained gray powder in the streets, in the driving compartments of the small cars—themselves perfectly preserved—and scattered all through the larger vehicles that looked like buses.

There was powder in the homes. In one home they found a heap of the gray stuff in front of a cookstove which was still warm, and another heap on a chair and on the floor under the chair. It was as if a woman and the man for whom she'd been preparing a meal had gone *poof*, in an instant.

The crew member who'd been on watch and reported the lights said later they could have been atmospherics. The skipper himself had seen the movement along the roads; he maintained a dignified silence.

It had been a highly developed little world and the buildings were incredibly old. The weather had beaten at them, rounding their edges and softening their colors, but they were as sturdy as if they'd been built last week.

All the cities on the little world were similar. And all were dead. The *Pringle* flew over a dozen of them, then returned to the big one near the plain where the ship had come down originally.

The tallest building in each city was ornate out of all proportion to the rest. The researchers reasoned that this was the palace, or seat of government. Each of these buildings had a network of metal tubing at its peak. Where there were great distances between cities, tall towers rose from the plains or sat on tops of mountains, each with a similar metal network at the apex.

The communications chief guessed that they were radio-video towers but he was proved wrong. There were no radio or television sets anywhere, or anything resembling them.

Still, it was obvious that they were a kind of communications device.

Doc Braddon got part of the answer from some of the gray dust he'd performed an "autopsy" on.

The dust had been found in a neat mound at the bottom of a large metal container on the second-story of a medium-sized dwelling. Doc theorized that one of the people had been taking some sort of waterless bath in the container when the dust death came. The remains were thus complete, not scattered or intermingled as most of the others were.

Doc sorted the particles as best he could and found two types, one definitely inorganic. He conferred with Rosco on the inorganic residue. Rosco thought this might be the remains of a tiny pararadio transceiver. Possibly each of the people had carried one around with him, or built into him.

"We're only guessing that they were people," Doc said cautiously, though it would seem safe to assume it, since we've found dust everywhere people could be expected to be. What we need is a whole corpse."

While patrols were out looking for bodies, Rosco tested his theory by sending a radio signal from one of the towers and watching a feeble reaction in the dust.

"If we can assume that they were people," Rosco said, "they apparently communicated over distances by personalized radio. Maybe through a mechanism built into the skull. Would that mean there wouldn't be any written language, Ernest?"

Ernest Hotaling shrugged. "Not necessarily. I should think they'd have kept records of some kind. They could have been written, or taped—or chipped into stone, for that matter."

He asked the lieutenant to enlarge his search. "Bring me anything that looks like a book, or parchment, or microfilm, or tape. If it's chipped in stone," he added with a grin, "I'll come to it."

Meanwhile they ran off the film that had been grinding away automatically ever since the planetoid came within photoradar range of the ship. The film confirmed what the lookout reported—there had been lights on the nightside.

Furthermore, one of the sensitized strips at the side of the film showed that signals, which had been going out from the tower tops in a steady stream, increased furiously as the

Pringle approached. Then, as the ship came closer, they stopped altogether. At the same instant the lights on the nightside of the planetoid went out. The film showed that the road movement the skipper had seen stopped then, too.

Ernest tried to analyze the signals reproduced on the film. He had small success. If they represented a language, it would take years before he could even guess what they meant. The only thing he was sure of was that the signals, just before they died, had become a thousand times more powerful.

"Maybe that's what killed them," Rosco said.

"Possibly," Ernest said. "It begins to look as if the people were deliberately killed, or committed suicide, all at once, when we hove into sight. But why?"

"You tell me," Rosco said. "That sounds like your department."

But Ernest could tell him nothing until after the lieutenant came back with a long, slender cylinder enclosing a seemingly endless coil of fine wire. The lieutenant also brought a companion cylinder, apparently a means of playing back what was recorded on the coil.

Ernest experimented until he learned how to operate it, then shooed everybody out of his cabin and went to work.

Ernest Hotaling had joined the crew of the research ship *Pringle* on Ganymede as a replacement for Old Craddock, who'd decided on short notice that thirty years of spacefaring were enough. It would be another ten or twelve years before the *Pringle* returned to Earth and though Craddock was only seventy-eight his yearning to start a proper bee farm became overwhelming.

The others were not unhappy about his departure. The swarm he'd kept in his cabin was small but the bees were gregarious and were as likely to be found in the recreation room as in their hive. So when Craddock and the paraphernalia he'd collected over the decades had debarked, the rest of the crew sighed in collective relief and the skipper went looking for a replacement.

Ernest Hotaling, fresh out of Ganymede U., was the only man qualified, on the record, for the job. He had the necessary languages and his doctorate was in psychology, though his specialty was child therapy.

The skipper puzzled through the copy of Ernest's master's thesis. The lad—he was twenty-three then—had devoted it to children's folklore. The skipper, admittedly a simple man, wasn't sure it contributed profitably to the world's knowledge to spend a year in the study and explanation of *Winnie the Pooh,* or *Step on a crack/Break your mother's back,* or *The Wizard of Oz.*

The skipper had gone to Space Prep at the age of fourteen and later to the Academy itself and there were obviously wide areas of childhood that had passed him by. He'd never heard of *Struwwelpeter,* for instance, or *Ibbety bibbety gibbety goat,* and he wondered if a grown man who immersed himself in this sort of thing was the one for the job.

What was worse was that Hotaling, according to the University yearbook, was a poet.

But when the skipper interviewed Hotaling and found him to be a lean, muscular young man who'd obviously had a haircut in the past week and who laughed genuinely at one of the skipper's more purple stories, he signed him on immediately.

The skipper had one last thought. "You don't keep bees, do you?"

"Not even in my bonnet," Ernest said.

"Then we'll get along. Just keep your nursery rhymes to yourself."

"Aye, aye, sir," said Ernest.

"Look," Ernest told the skipper, "I've studied their literature, if that's what it is, until I'm saturated with it. Maybe it doesn't make sense to you but I've worked out a sort of pattern. It's an alien culture, sure, and there are gaps in it, but what there is fits together."

"All right," the skipper said. "I'm not questioning your

findings. I just want to know why it has to be in that ridiculous rhyme."

"Because they were a poetic people, that's why. And it doesn't *have* to be in rhyme. I could give you the literal translation, but it was rhymed originally and when I make it rhyme in English too you get a more exact idea of the kind of people they were."

"I suppose so," the skipper said. "As long as we don't have to report to the Flagship in the sonnet form I guess I can put up with it. I just don't want to become the laughing stock of the fleet."

"It's no laughing matter," Ernest said. "It's pretty tragic, in any number of ways. In the first place, as Rosco suspected, they communicated by radio. But they had no privacy and couldn't hide anything from anybody. They were always listened in on by the big boys in the palace."

"How do you know?"

"By the coil I worked from. It's a listening-storing device. These aren't official records I've transcribed; they're the everyday expressions of everyday people. And every one of them had been taken down and stored away, presumably so it could be used against the person who expressed it, if it ever became necessary.

"But they couldn't always get through to the person they wanted to reach, even though they got through to the coil. Here's a sad little lover's lament, for instance:

"My plea to her is lost, as though
The other three command the flow."

"Like a busy signal?" asked the skipper.

"Very much like one," Ernest said, pleased by the skipper's comprehension. "On the other hand, they always got the messages from the palace. These took priority over all other traffic and were apt to come at any time of the day or night. The people were just one big captive audience."

"What about the dust? That seems to be a recurring theme in those jingles of yours."

"It is." Ernest quoted:

"Dust is he and dust his brother;
They all follow one another."

"They're all dust now," the skipper said. "Did they have a revolution, finally, that killed everybody off?"

"Both sides—the rulers and the ruled, simultaneously? Maybe so." Ernest sorted through his pieces of paper. "There's this one, with its inference of the death of royalty along with that of the common man:

"Comes the King! O hear him rustle;
Falter, step, and wither, muscle."

The skipper was beginning to be exasperated again.

"I'll be in my cabin," he said. "You seem to accomplish more when I keep out of your way. But if you want to join me in a little whiskey to keep the falters and withers at bay, come along."

The lieutenant knocked at Ernest's door in the middle of the night. "Mister Hotaling!" he called urgently.

Ernest fumbled into a pair of pants and opened the door.

"One of the men found this thing," the lieutenant said. "We were going to keep it locked up till morning but it's driving me crazy. Figured you'd better have a look at it."

The thing was a blue-green puppet of a creature wearing—or made of—a kind of metallic sailcloth. It was about three feet tall, a caricature of a human being. It hung limp by one arm from the lieutenant's grasp, its head lolling on its shoulder.

"What is it?" Ernest asked sleepily, "a doll?"

"No; it's just playing dead now. It was doing a clog step in the cage before." He gave the thing a shake. "The worst of it is, it hummed all the time. And the humming seems to mean something."

"Bring it in here," Ernest said. He was fully awake now. "Put it in the armchair and stick around in case I can't handle it."

The creature sat awkwardly where it was put. But then the eyes, which a moment ago had seemed to be pained on the face, shifted and looked squarely at Ernest. It hummed at him.

"I see what you mean," he told the lieutenant. "It seems to be trying to communicate. It's the same language as on the coils." He stared at it. "I wish it didn't remind me of Raggedy Andy. Where did you find it?"

"In the throneroom of the palace. One of the men on guard there grabbed it as it came out of a panel in the wall. He grabbed it and it went limp, like a doll."

"Listen," said Ernest.

"Don't you cry, boys; don't you quiver,
Though all the sand is in your liver."

"What's that?" the lieutenant said. "Do you feel all right, Mister Hotaling?"

"Sure. That's what he said. Raggedy Andy here. I translated it—with a little poetic license."

"What does it mean?"

"I don't think it's a direct message to us. More likely it's something filed away inside his brain, or electronic storage chamber or whatever he's got. The verse is in the pattern of the ones I translated the other day. The question now is whether Andy has any original thoughts in his head or whether he's just a walking record library."

"How can you tell?"

"By continuing to listen to him, I suppose. A parrot might fool you into thinking it had intelligence of its own, if you didn't know anything about parrots, but after a while you'd realize it was just a mimic. Right, Andy?"

The puppet-like creature hummed again and Ernest listened, gesturing the lieutenant to be quiet.

Finally Ernest said:

"Down the valley, down the glen
Come the Mercials, ten by ten."

"That makes as much sense as the one about the liver," the lieutenant said.

"Takes it a bit further, I think. No, seriously. 'Mercials' is a set of syllables I made up, as short for 'commercials'—or the sand in their craw, the thumb in their soup—all the things they had to put up with as the most captive of all audiences."

"That wasn't an original thought, then?"

"Probably not. Andy may be trying me out with a few simple couplets before he throws a really hard one. I wonder if he knows he's got through to me." He laughed as the lieutenant looked at him oddly. "I don't mean *he*, personally. I know as well as you do he's some kind of robot."

"I see. You mean, is somebody controlling him now, or is he just reacting to a stimulus the way he was built to do?"

"Exactly." Ernest frowned at the doll-like creature. "I suppose the scientific way would be to dissect him—it. Take it apart, I mean. I've got to stop thinking of it as a him. We'd better get Doc Braddon in on this."

He punched the 'com button to Doc's cabin. The sleepy voice that answered became alert as Ernest explained. Doc arrived minutes later with an instrument kit, looking eager.

"So this is your new toy," he said. The creature, which had been slumped listlessly in the chair, seemed to look at Doc with distaste. It hummed something. Doc looked inquiringly at Ernest. "Have you two established communication?"

"It's a robot," Ernest said defensively. "The question is, could we learn more by leaving it intact and pumping it for whatever information is stored up inside it, or by taking it apart? For instance, it just said:

"Uninterred beyond the hills
Lie never weres and never wills."

Doc became excited. "It really said that?"

"Well, not in so many words. It said—"

"I know, I know your poetic license hasn't expired. I mean, that *is* the gist of it? That somewhere back of the hills there's a charnel heap—a dump of corpses, or miscarriages—something of the sort?"

"You could put that interpretation on it," Ernest said. "I got the impression of something abortive."

"That's the best lead yet," Doc said. "If we could find anything other than dust piles, no matter how embryonic—Lieutenant, your boys must have been looking in the wrong places. How soon can you get a detail out over the hills?"

The lieutenant looked at his watch. "If I've got this screwy rotation figured out, dawn's about half an hour off. That soon enough?"

"It'll have to do."

"What about Raggedy Andy here?" Ernest asked. "Do we keep him intact?"

"Don't touch a hair of his precious head," Doc said. "He's earned a stay of dissection."

The creature, still quiet in the chair, its eyes vacant now, hummed almost inaudibly. Ernest bent to listen.

"Well?" Doc said.

"Strictly a non-sequitur," Ernest told him:

"Here we go, lass, through the heather;
Naught to daunt us save the tether."

"It makes me sad," Doc said. He yawned. "Maybe it's just the hour."

Cook had accomplished his usual legerdemain with the space rations but the breakfast table was less appreciative than usual.

"The detail's been gone a long time," Doc Braddon said,

toying with an omelet. "Do you think it's a wild goose chase?"

"Reminds me of a time off Venus," the skipper said. "Before any of you were born, probably . . ."

His juniors listened politely until the familiar narrative was interrupted by the 'com on the bulkhead. They recognized the voice of Sergeant Maraffi, the non-com in charge of the crew in the scoutcraft.

"We found something. Looks like bodies. Well preserved but incomplete. Humanoid."

"Bring 'em back," the skipper said. "As many as you've got room for in the sling." He added as an afterthought: "Do they smell?"

"Who knows?" Maraffi said. "I sure don't aim to take off my helmet to find out. They're not decomposed, though."

The skipper grumbled to Doc: "I thought you checked the atmosphere."

"There isn't any," Doc said, annoyed. "Didn't you read my report?"

"All right," the skipper said, not looking at him. "I can't do everything. I naturally assumed these people breathed."

"If they did, it wasn't air," Doc said.

"Bring back all you can, Maraffi," the skipper said. "But leave them outside the ship. Everybody on the detail takes double decontamination. And we'll put you down for hazard pay."

"Aye, aye, sir. We're on our way."

"They're androids," Doc said. He'd gone out in a protective suit to the grisly pile. "These must be the false starts."

The other technicians watched him on a closed-circuit hookup from inside the ship.

"Are they like us?" Ernest asked. "They look it from here —what there is of them."

"Damn near," Doc said. "Smaller and darker, though. Rosco, you were right about the communication. There's a tiny transceiver built into their skulls. Those that have heads, that is."

"If that's the case," Rosco said, "then why weren't these—stillbirths, whatever you want to call them—turned to dust like the others?"

"Because they'd never been activated," Doc said. "You can't blow a fuse if it isn't screwed in. Skipper, I've seen about all my stomach can stand for now. I suppose I'm a hell of a queasy sawbones, but these—things—are too much like human beings for me to take much more of them at the moment."

"Come on back," the skipper said. "I don't feel too sturdy myself."

Ernest Hotaling was writing verse in his cabin when the lieutenant intercommed him. He had just written, in free translation:

> A girl is scarcely long for the road
> If passion'd arms make her corrode.

Ernest wasn't entirely satisfied with the rhyme, though he felt he'd captured the sense of it. The lieutenant's call interrupted his polishing. He touched the 'com and said: "Hotaling."

"Patrol's back, Mister Hotaling. You'll want to see what they found."

"Another heap of the false starts? No, thanks."

"Not this time. They found some people. Two live people."

"Alive! Be right there."

He raced down, then fretted as he waited for Doc to fumigate the people as they came through the airlock. Ernest saw them dimly through the thick glass. They were quite human-looking. But how had they survived whatever had turned thousands of their fellows to dust? Or were these—a man and a woman, elderly and fragile-looking—the rulers who had dusted the others?

"How much longer, Doc?" he asked.

Doc grinned. "In about two quatrains and a jingle, Ernest."

They brought the couple to the main lounge and set them down at a long table. The skipper took a seat at the far end. Apparently he planned to listen but not take part in the questioning. That would be up to Ernest Hotaling, if he could establish communication.

He'd mastered the language to the extent that he'd been able to transcribe the record-coils and understand the robot, but whether he could speak it intelligibly enough so that these living—he almost thought "breathing"—people would understand him was a question.

Doc Braddon took a seat next to the couple. Rosco was on the other side of them and Ernest opposite them, across the table.

Up close, it was obvious that they were androids. But they had been remarkably made. They had none of the jerkiness of movement or blankness of expression that had characterized Earth's attempts along the same lines.

Ernest explained his doubts about his ability to make himself understood and asked his shipmates to be patient with him. He smiled at the couple and said to them in English: "Welcome to our ship." Then he repeated it in their humming language.

They returned his smile and the old woman said something to the man. Rosco looked inquiringly at Ernest, who shook his head.

Ernest made a face. "I forgot to put it in verse. I'll try again."

This time the response was immediate. Both man and woman spoke at once. Then the woman smiled and nodded to the man to talk for both of them.

It was just a curious sing-song humming for the rest of them, but Ernest listened with rapt attention and apparent comprehension, though not without strain.

Finally the man stopped.

"What did he say?" Rosco demanded.

"Let me get the rest of it first," Ernest said. He spoke to the man briefly. His expression became grave as he listened to the reply.

"Well, come *on!*" Doc said impatiently. "Give us a translation."

"All right," Ernest said. He looked troubled. "These two are the only ones left of their race. The rest are dead—deactivated. The others—the other race—left the planetoid some time ago."

Ernest spoke again to the man. Listening to his reply, he found it difficult to think of him as non-human. There was a sadness, a fatalism, in his eyes, yet a dignity that came only with humanity. Only a hairline separated these two from mankind.

The impatience of the others made Ernest interrupt, so he could give them a resumé.

"As I said, they're the last. They survived only because they'd made a pilgrimage to a kind of underground shrine. The signals that killed the others didn't reach them through the layers of rock. Apparently the shrine had something to do with a planned revolt against the electronic law that governed them.

"It was an insidious law," Ernest went on, "with built-in enforcement. Any infraction could be punished instantly from central control in the palace. The infraction would trigger a shock wave, turned to the individual frequency of the offender. The intensity of the wave was geared to the seriousness of the offense. Treason meant death from the strongest wave of all—the one that turned them to dust."

"Absolute rule," Doc said. "Pretty hopeless."

"Yes, in one way. But paradoxically they had an infinite amount of freedom of speech. You see that in their verses. No one was punished for what he said—only for what he did. I suppose it had to be that way, otherwise there'd have been wholesale slaughter."

"Which there was, at the end," Doc pointed out. "Who do you think exercised the control that killed all the others?"

"We did," Ernest said. "We killed them."

"We killed them?" Doc said. "You're crazy!"

"You'd better explain yourself, Hotaling," the skipper said. "Stop talking in riddles."

"Aye, aye, sir. When I say we killed them, I don't mean directly or deliberately. And of course I don't mean killed, since they were all androids. But we de-activated them by triggering some mechanism when our ship came to the planetoid their masters had left."

"Hold on," the skipper said. "Now you're going too fast. Since they were androids, and were created, the important thing is to find out where these creators went—and whether it was last month or ten thousand years ago."

Ernest spoke to the couple.

"It was a long time before we came," he translated. "They don't know how long—their feeling of time is vague. They kept no records of their own and because there were no children they have no conception of generations. They were created adults, in various stages of maturity. As for who the others were—they were the Masters, with a capital M; gods, almost, in their view, with absolute power over them."

"Where did they go?" the skipper asked. "And why? Let's try to get more facts and less philosophy."

"They went looking for a better world, where conditions for life would be more favorable. Whether that means for the Masters or for their creations isn't clear. Nobody consulted them. They'd been given experimental life, only it was more a loan than a gift, to be foreclosed if they displeased the Masters or in any way threatened their experiment.

"The Masters were like themselves in appearance. Whether they were air breathers isn't clear because these two have no conception of what breathing is. The Masters did wear elaborate costumes but whether these were breathing suits or merely the trappings of their superiority is a question.

"I asked if the Masters were trying to create a new set of bodies for themselves, possibly because their own were breaking down or were diseased. The answer to that, like the answer to so many other questions, is that they simply don't know."

There was a commotion at the doorway. The soldier on guard there made a futile grab at something. The something was the puppet-like creature Ernest had named Andy, which evaded him and ran into the room. It jumped lightly to the table, faced the old couple and pointed both its arms at them.

Their expressions, as they regarded the puppet, were of sorrowful resignation. The man clasped the woman's hand.

The puppet spoke, in a brief piercing hum. There was an instant of quiet, then the dullest of popping sounds. The couple, who one second had seemed as alive as any of the Earthmen, the next second were little mounds of gray powder on the chairs and under the chairs.

The lieutenant burst in, followed by the sergeant. "The Andy doll got out of the cage!" he cried. "Did it come in here?"

"Did it come in here?" the skipper mimicked. "Get out, lieutenant, and take your comic-opera soldiers with you." To the technicians at the table he yelled: "Grab that obscene thing!"

The doll, grabbed from several directions, was torn apart, spilling out a reddish-brown spongelike substance.

Something else came out, too: a perforated disk the size of a fist. Rosco retrieved it as it rolled along the table, then quickly dropped it in an ash tray.

"The damn thing's hot," he said.

Doc Braddon, still looking stunned, asked Ernest: "What did the doll say to them before it destroyed them?"

"It was a sort of law-enforcing robot. They told me about it. A kind of custodian the Masters left behind to keep things in line." Ernest stared dully at the empty chairs.

"It said:

"You hid, and I
Now bid you die!"

Rosco toyed with the ash tray in which he'd put the disk.

"There's a clue to the Masters right in this gadget," he said. "Maybe it's simply a servo-mechanism that was set once and has been functioning automatically ever since. But on the other hand it may still be linked directly to the Masters."

"Good point," the skipper said. "Give it a run-through for what it's worth. If it does give us a line on where they got to, I'll ask the Flagship for permission to track them down."

Doc Braddon said to Ernest: "You said the Masters were godlike. You're not implying anything supernatural?"

"No. That was the androids' view, not mine. As a race of almost-people created in a laboratory they naturally held their creators in a certain awe. They hoped for liberation, and even tried to do something about it; but they knew it was futile. The Masters built them so they'd turn to dust if they misbehaved and when they left they fixed it so the vibrations of any spaceship other than their own would do the same thing—presumably so their creations wouldn't fall into other hands. The sad thing is that the almost-people knew it. One of their verses went:

"If comes the ship to make us free,
It killeth you, it killeth me."

"Do you mean we could have saved them if we'd come in with engines silent?" the skipper asked.

"I don't know," Ernest said. "They certainly didn't think much of their potential. There's a fatalism, a sense of thwarted destiny running all through their literature. Their hope died on the vine, so to speak. If you can stand one more of their verses, this one might sum up their philosophy:

"This they give to us they make:
They give us thirst, deny the slake."

The skipper was silent for a time, staring down at the little mounds of gray dust.

Then he said to his technicians:

"You've done a good job, all of you. We'll send a co-ordinated report to the Flagship tomorrow and stand by for orders. In the meantime, if there's anyone here with an honest physical thirst, I'd be glad to have him join me in slaking it in my cabin. No offense implied, Ernest."

"None taken, sir."